Praise for Att

BLUEBIRD, BLUEBIRD

Winner of the Edgar Award for Best Novel
Finalist for the *Los Angeles Times* Book Prize
One of the Best Mysteries of the Year
Washington Post • *New York Times Book Review* • *Boston Globe* • *Wall Street Journal* • *The Guardian* • *Financial Times* • *Vulture* • *Dallas Morning News* • *Texas Monthly Strand Magazine* • *Southern Living* • *Daily Beast South Florida Sun Sentinel* • *Milwaukee Journal Sentinel Book Riot* • *Lit Hub* • Minnesota Public Radio *Publishers Weekly* • *Kirkus Reviews*

"Attica Locke's fourth novel may be her best yet: a lyrical and suspenseful East Texas saga in which a black Texas Ranger investigates two possibly related small-town murders, both apparently racially motivated ... The award-winning Locke is a wonderful stylist, able to conjure vivid impressions with a single phrase."

—Tom Nolan, *Wall Street Journal*

"The plot has legs, and Locke's blues-infused idiom lends a strain of melancholy to her lyrical style."

—Marilyn Stasio, *New York Times Book Review*
(Best Crime Novels of the Year)

"Attica Locke is a brisk writer with a sharp eye for the racial tensions that continue to simmer in small Southern communities."

—*Washington Post* (Best Thrillers and Mysteries of the Year)

"In *Bluebird, Bluebird* Attica Locke has both mastered the thriller and exceeded it. Ranger Darren Mathews is tough, honor-bound, and profoundly alive in a corrupt world. I loved everything about this book."   —Ann Patchett

"Locke's writing is both sharp-edged and lyrical. This is thoughtful, piercing storytelling with the power to transport."
                                                —Diana Evans, *Financial Times*

"Few contemporary writers have portrayed black Southern life with as much wit and heart-pounding drama as Attica Locke... A dazzling work of rural noir that throws into question whether justice can be equally served on both sides of the race line."
                                                —Amy Brady, *Los Angeles Times*

"Locke's latest is steeped in the blood of history but alive with the racial tensions of today. It's a twisty, carefully plotted thriller."
                                                —Chris Vognar, *Dallas Morning News*

"*Bluebird, Bluebird* has the impeccable pacing, memorable characters, and deepening sense of mystery and dread we expect in the finest noir thrillers. But this novel is so much more. Darren Mathews, the black Texas Ranger at the story's center, is a man caught up in the complex and at times contradictory loyalties of geography, profession, race, and family. He is a brilliantly realized character, and in his refusal to settle for easy answers, he leads himself and the reader toward the most elemental of contradictions: the inextricable link between hate and love. Attica Locke has written a marvelous novel."
                                                —Ron Rash, author of *The Risen*

"A rich sense of place and relentless feeling of dread permeate Attica Locke's heartbreakingly resonant new novel about race and justice in America... An emotionally dense and intricately detailed thriller, roiling with conflicting emotions steeped in this nation's troubled past and present... *Bluebird, Bluebird* is no simple morality tale. Far from it. It rises above 'left and right' and 'black and white' and follows the threads that inevitably bind us together, even as we rip them apart."   —James Endrst, *USA Today*

"Locke's mesmerizing new novel bears all the hallmarks of modern crime fiction: the alcoholic protagonist with the damaged marriage, the townsfolk who close rank against outsiders, the small-town law enforcement agent with murky loyalties. But *Bluebird, Bluebird* is a true original in the way it twists these conventions into a narrative of exhilarating immediacy... Locke has a vivid sense of characterization, using everything from dialect to the fabric of one's clothes to make subtle class distinctions and depict mental states... Locke is building a compelling body of work. In this age of enduring and renewed racial tensions, we need her voice more than ever."
—Esi Edugyan, *The Guardian*

"Attica Locke's *Bluebird, Bluebird* reads like a blues song to East Texas, with all its troubles over property, race, and love. Taut where it has to be to keep a murder investigation on its toes, this novel is also languid when you need to understand just what would keep a black woman or man in a place where so much troubled history lies. This novel marks Love's (and Hatred's) comings and goings among black and white, and all the shades in between. Locke's small-town murder investigation reveals what lies at the heart of America's confusion over race."   —Walter Mosley, author of *Down the River unto the Sea*

"This tale of Darren Mathews, black Texas Ranger, tackling a murder mystery in a blink-and-you'll-miss-it town in East Texas, is lyrical and elemental, and it pulls no punches, exposing racial tensions past and present while a killer blues soundtrack plays perpetually in the background."   —Daneet Steffens, *Boston Globe*

"Attica Locke knows Texas, a place that has shaped both her characters and her life. Locke's new book, *Bluebird, Bluebird,* is evidence of her deep knowledge and love of her community and a deep talent for writing hype thrillers that also manage to be timely, relevant, and keenly insightful."   —Joe Ide, author of *IQ* and *Righteous*

"Powerful... Locke is a master of plot who's honed her craft... The deepest pleasures to be found in *Bluebird, Bluebird,* though, are in her renderings of those who've loved and lost but still want to believe in the world's benevolence."
          —Leigh Haber, *O, The Oprah Magazine*

"Attica Locke pens a poignant love letter to the lazy red-dirt roads and piney woods that serve as a backdrop to a noir thriller as murky as the bayous and bloodlines that thread through the region... Locke shows off her chops as a superb storyteller... She is adept at crafting characters who don't easily fit the archetypes of good and evil, but exist in the thick grayness of humanness, the knotty demands of loyalties, and the baseness of survival. Locke holds up the mirror of the racial debate in America and shows us how the light bends and fractures what is right and wrong, and what simply is the way it is—but perhaps not as it should be."
          —Jaundréa Clay, *Houston Chronicle*

"With *Bluebird, Bluebird,* Attica Locke brings freshness and vitality to a beloved form. Her storytelling touch is just so strong! From the first beautifully done scene until the finale, this is a very propulsive novel concerning old deeds that keep influencing the present, injustice, and courage—a powerful and dramatic look at contemporary black life in rural America." —Daniel Woodrell, author of *The Maid's Version*

"Gripping, suspenseful, and gut-wrenching...I've never bought the notion of the Great American Novel. I think when literary historians look back, they'll realize this time had many, but if Attica Locke's *Bluebird, Bluebird* isn't on the list, I'm coming back to haunt them...This is a layered portrait of a black man confronting his own racial ambivalence and ambition told with a pointed and poignant bluesy lyricism." —Carole Barrowman, *Milwaukee Journal Sentinel*

"Locke skillfully blends simmering noir atmosphere, police procedural, and small-town racial politics, and creates a hero engagingly caught between the world of his past and his future."
—Moira Macdonald, *Seattle Times*

"Attica Locke's stupendous fourth novel is suffused with the blues. Pushing her classic noir plot deep into history and culture, the Houston native sings her own unshakable, timeless lament. Streaked with wit and hard-earned wisdom, *Bluebird, Bluebird* soars."
—Lloyd Sachs, *Chicago Tribune*

"Brooding, timely, gripping." —*Family Circle*

"This page-turner combines heart and heat."
—Patrik Henry Bass, *Essence*

"This is Attica Locke's best work yet—and if you've read *Pleasantville* you know that's saying something. Just by her choice of protagonist (an African American Texas Ranger, tacking between two worlds as he solves a double homicide) you know Locke is a writer who makes bold choices, and whose fiction is powerfully connected to our troubled world."

—Ben Winters, author of *Underground Airlines*

"As poignant as this story is, it's Locke's elegiac writing and her characters that make this book unforgettable, even beautiful. Locke's feelings of being black are so fervent they make *Bluebird, Bluebird* a work of literature that will make you cry and read slowly to delay the ending."   —Jeffrey Mannix, *Durango Telegraph*

"Attica Locke is a must-read author who writes with power, grace, and heart, and *Bluebird, Bluebird* is a remarkable achievement. This is a rare novel that thrills, educates, and inspires all at once. Don't miss it."   —Michael Koryta, author of *How It Happened*

"A deftly plotted whodunit whose writing pulses throughout with a raw, blues-inflected lyricism."   —*Kirkus Reviews*

"Attica Locke knows how to tell a tale, her voice so direct and crisp that the dust from the side of Highway 59 will settle on your hands as you hold *Bluebird, Bluebird*. Nothing comes easy in Shelby County, where the lines between right and wrong blur a little more with each heartfelt page, and love and pain live together as one under the big Texas sun."

—Michael Farris Smith, author of *Desperation Road* and *Rivers*

BLUEBIRD, BLUEBIRD

ALSO BY ATTICA LOCKE

Pleasantville
The Cutting Season
Black Water Rising

BLUEBIRD, BLUEBIRD

A Novel

ATTICA LOCKE

MULHOLLAND BOOKS

Little, Brown and Company
New York Boston London

This book is a work of fiction. Any resemblance to persons, living or dead, is a coincidence and not intended by the author. There exists in Texas a town called Lark, but the one in Shelby County is purely my invention. —Attica Locke

Copyright © 2017 by Attica Locke

Hachette Book Group supports the right to free expression and the value of copyright. The purpose of copyright is to encourage writers and artists to produce the creative works that enrich our culture.

The scanning, uploading, and distribution of this book without permission is a theft of the author's intellectual property. If you would like permission to use material from the book (other than for review purposes), please contact permissions@hbgusa.com. Thank you for your support of the author's rights.

Mulholland Books / Little, Brown and Company
Hachette Book Group
1290 Avenue of the Americas, New York, NY 10104
mulhollandbooks.com

Originally published in hardcover by Mulholland Books, September 2017
First Mulholland Books paperback edition, August 2018

Mulholland Books is an imprint of Little, Brown and Company, a division of Hachette Book Group, Inc. The Mulholland Books name and logo are trademarks of Hachette Book Group, Inc.

The publisher is not responsible for websites (or their content) that are not owned by the publisher.

The Hachette Speakers Bureau provides a wide range of authors for speaking events. To find out more, go to hachettespeakersbureau.com or call (866) 376-6591.

ISBN 978-0-316-36329-7 (hc) / 978-0-316-36327-3 (pb)
LCCN 2017941350

Printing 9, 2024
LSC-C

Printed in the United States of America

To the
Hathorne
Jackson
Johnson
Jones
Locke
Mark
McClendon
McGowan
Perry
Sweats
Williams
men and women who said no

BLUEBIRD, BLUEBIRD

I told him, "No, Mr. Moore."

—Lightnin' Hopkins, "Tom Moore Blues"

Shelby County

Texas, 2016

Geneva Sweet ran an orange extension cord past Mayva Green-
wood, Beloved Wife and Mother, May She Rest with Her Heavenly
Father. Late morning sunlight pinpricked through the trees, dotting a constellation of light on the blanket of pine needles at
Geneva's feet as she snaked the cord between Mayva's sister and her
husband, Leland, Father and Brother in Christ. She gave the cord a
good tug, making her way up the modest hill, careful not to step
on the graves themselves, only the well-worn grooves between the
headstones, which were spaced at haphazard and odd angles, like
the teeth of a pauper.

She was lugging a paper shopping bag from the Brookshire
Brothers in Timpson along with a small radio from which a Muddy
Waters record, one of Joe's favorites, whistled through the speak-
ers—*Have you ever been walking, walking down that ol' lonesome road.*
When she arrived at the final resting place of Joe "Petey Pie" Sweet,
Husband and Father and, Forgive Him, Lord, a Devil on the Guitar,
she set the radio carefully on top of the polished chunk of granite,
snapping the power cord into its hiding place behind the head-

stone. The one next to it was identical in shape and size. It belonged to another Joe Sweet, younger by forty years and just as dead. Geneva opened the shopping bag and pulled out a paper plate covered in tinfoil, an offering for her only son. Two fried pies, perfect half-moons of hand-rolled dough filled with brown sugar and fruit and baptized in grease—Geneva's specialty and Lil' Joe's favorite. She could feel their warmth through the bottom of the plate, their buttery scent softening the sharp sting of pine in the air. She balanced the plate on the headstone, then bent down to brush fallen needles from the graves, keeping a hand on a slab of granite at all times, ever mindful of her arthritic knees. Below her, an eighteen-wheeler tore down Highway 59, sending up a gust of hot, gassy air through the trees. It was a warm one for October, but nowadays they all were. Near eighty today, she'd heard, and here she was thinking it was about time to pull the holiday decorations from the trailer out back of her place. *Climate change, they call it. This keep up and I'll live long enough to see hell on earth, I guess.* She told all this to two men in her life. Told them about the new fabric store in Timpson. The fact that Faith was bugging her for a car. The ugly shade of yellow Wally painted the icehouse. *Look like someone coughed up a big mess of phlegm and threw it on the walls.*

She didn't mention the killings, though, or the trouble bubbling in town.

She gave them that little bit of peace.

She kissed the tips of her fingers, laying them on the first headstone, then the second. She let her touch linger on her son's grave, giving out a weary sigh. Seemed like death had a mind to follow her around in this lifetime. It was a sly shadow at her back, as single-minded as a dog on a hunt; as faithful, too.

She heard a crunch of pine needles behind her, a rustling in the leaves blown from the nearby cottonwoods, and turned to see Mitty, the colored cemetery's unofficial groundskeeper. "They got batteries for them things," he said, nodding at the small radio while steadying himself by leaning on the concrete stone for Beth Anne Solomon, Daughter and Sister Gone Too Soon.

"You send me the propane bill time you get it," Geneva said.

Mitty was older than Geneva, nearing eighty, probably. He was a dark-skinned man and small, with two legs thin as twigs and ashy as chalk. He spent his afternoons in the small shed on the property, shooing off stray dogs and vermin. Five days a week he was out here with a racing magazine and a cheroot, watching over the gathering of souls, keeping an eye on his future home. He tolerated Geneva's particular way of caring for the dead—the quilts in the wintertime, the lights strung at Christmas, the pies, and the constant hum of the blues. He was eyeing the sweets, reaching a finger to lift the foil for a better look. "They peach," Geneva said, "and they ain't got your name nowhere on 'em."

The walk down the hill was always harder on her knees than the way up, and today was no different. She winced as she started toward her car, peeling off her husband's cardigan, one of the last ones in good-enough shape to wear daily. Her '98 Grand Am was parked on a flat of patchy grass and red dirt abutting the four-lane highway. She didn't even get her keys out of her purse before she could see Mitty eating one of the pies. Geneva rolled her eyes. The man couldn't even show her the common courtesy of waiting till she was gone.

She climbed into her Pontiac and eased slowly out of the makeshift parking lot, keeping an eye out for semis and speeding cars before pulling onto 59 and heading north to Lark. She rode the three-quarters of a mile to her place in silence, running through inventory in her head. She was down two twenty-ounce cans of fruit cocktail, eight heads of lettuce, syrup for the soda machine, the Dr Pepper she could never keep in stock, plus a bottle or two of Ezra Brooks whiskey, which she kept under the register for her regulars. She wondered if the sheriff had arrived yet, if the mess that had washed up in her backyard this morning was still there, that girl lying out there all alone. She had a vague worry about what all this might do to her business, but mostly she tried to comprehend what in God's name was happening to the town in which she'd spent all her sixty-nine years.

Two bodies inside a week.

What in the devil was going on?

She eased off the highway, pulling in front of Geneva Sweet's Sweets, a low-slung flat-roofed cafe painted red and white. It had cinched curtains in the windows and a sign out front with a lit-up arrow pointing to the front door. Black-and-red letters advertised BBQ PORK SANDWICH $4.99 and BEST FRIED PIES IN SHELBY COUNTY. She parked in her usual spot, a Pontiac-size groove in the dirt along the side of the cafe, between the building's wooden siding and the weeds in the open lot on the other side. She'd been in this location for decades, back when it was just Geneva's, a one-room shack that had been built by hand. The paved parking spots by the gas pump were for paying customers. And Wendy, of course, Geneva's sometime business associate. Her ancient green Mercury was stationed right in front of the door. The rusting twenty-year-old car looked like a piñata beaten past its breaking point, overflowing with old license plates, iron skillets, two wig stands, old clothes, and a small TV whose antenna was sticking out the left rear window.

The tiny brass bell on the cafe's door rang softly as Geneva let herself in.

Two of her regulars looked up from their seats at the counter: Huxley, a local retiree, and Tim, a long-haul trucker who stayed on a Houston–Chicago route week in and week out. "Sheriff's here," Huxley said as Geneva passed behind him. At the end of the counter, she opened the gate that led to her "main office," the space between the kitchen and her customers. "Rolled in 'bout thirty minutes after you left," he said, both he and Tim craning their necks to gauge her reaction.

"Must have made ninety miles an hour the whole way," Tim said.

Geneva kept her lips pressed together, swallowing a pill of rage.

She lifted an apron from a hook by the door that led to the kitchen. It was an old one, yellow, with two faded roses for pockets.

"It was a whole day with the other one—ain't that what you said?" Tim was halfway through a ham sandwich and talking with his mouth full. He swallowed and washed it down with a swig of Coke. "Van Horn took his sweet time then."

"Sheriff?" Wendy said from her perch at the other end of the counter. She was sitting in front of a collection of mason jars, each filled with the very best of her garden. Plump red peppers, chopped green tomatoes threaded with cabbage and onion, whole stalks of okra soaked in vinegar. Geneva lifted each jar one by one, holding it up to the light and double-checking the seal.

"I got some other stuff outside," Wendy said as Geneva pulled a marker from the pocket of her apron and started writing a price on the lid of each jar.

"You can leave the chow chow and the pickled okra," Geneva said, "but I got to draw the line on all that other junk you trying to sell." She nodded out the front window to Wendy's car. Wendy and

Geneva were the same age, though Wendy had a tendency to adjust her age from year to year depending on her audience or mood. She was a short woman, with mannish shoulders and an affected disregard for her appearance. Her hair was gray and pomaded into a tight bun. At least it *had* been tight last she combed it, which could have been anywhere from three to seven days ago. She was wearing the bottom half of a yellow pantsuit, a faded Houston Rockets T-shirt, and men's brogues on her feet.

"Geneva, people like to buy old shit off the highway. Makes them feel good about how well they living now. They call it antiques."

"I call it rust," Geneva said. "And the answer is no."

Wendy looked around the cafe—from Geneva to Tim and Huxley to the two other customers sitting in one of the vinyl booths—all the way to the other end of the shop, where food service ended and Isaac Snow rented fifty square feet that housed a mirror and a pea-green barber's chair. Isaac was a slender man in his late fifties, light-skinned, with coppery freckles. He spoke as little as he had to to get by, but for a ten-spot he'd cut the hair of anyone who asked. Otherwise Geneva let him sweep up a bit to earn the three meals a day he ate out of her kitchen.

The Lord hadn't made a soul Geneva wouldn't feed.

Her place had been born of an idea that colored folks who couldn't stop anywhere else in this county, well, they could stop here. Get a good meal, a little bite off a bottle of whiskey, if you could keep quiet about it; get your hair cleaned up before you made it to family up north or to the job you hoped would still be there by the time you got on the other side of Arkansas, 'cause there was no point in going if you didn't get way the hell past Arkansas. Forty-some-odd years after the death of Jim Crow, not much had changed;

Geneva's was as preserved in time as the yellowing calendars on the cafe's walls. She was a constant along a highway that was forever carrying people past her.

Wendy looked at the black faces in the room, trying to figure some reason for the grim mood, the tension running plain. Behind her, the jukebox flipped to another of the fifty tunes it played around the clock, this one a Charley Pride ballad with a gospel hurt on it, a plaintive plea for grace.

For a moment, no one spoke.

To Geneva, Wendy said, "What in hell's got you so testy this morning?"

"Sheriff Van Horn is out back," Huxley said, nodding toward the cafe's rear wall, papered with curling wall calendars—advertising everything from malt liquor to a local funeral home to Jimmie Clark's failed bid for county commissioner—going back fifteen years. Behind the rear wall was the kitchen, where Dennis was working on a pot of oxtails. Geneva could smell bay leaves soaking in beef fat and garlic, onion and liquid smoke. Beyond the kitchen's screen door lay a wide plot of land, red dirt dotted with buttercup weeds and crabgrass, rolling a hundred yards or so to the banks of a rust-colored bayou that was Shelby County's western border. "Brought three deputies, too."

"What's going on?"

Geneva sighed. "They pulled a body out the bayou this morning."

Wendy looked dumbfounded. "Another one?"

"A *white* one."

"Aw, shit."

Huxley nodded, pushing his coffee away. "Y'all remember when that white girl got killed down to Corrigan, they hauled in nearly every black man within thirty miles. In and out of every church and juke joint, every black-owned business, hunting for the killer or anybody who fit the bill they had in mind."

Geneva felt something dislodge in her breast, felt the fear she'd been trying to staunch give way, rising till it liked to choke her from the inside out.

"And ain't nobody done a damn thing about that black man got killed up the road just last week," Huxley said.

"They ain't thinking about that man," Tim said, tossing a grease-stained napkin on his plate. "Not when a white girl come up dead."

"Mark my words," Huxley said, looking gravely at each and every black face in the cafe. "Somebody is going down for this."

Part One

1.

DARREN MATHEWS set his Stetson on the edge of the witness stand, brim down, the way his uncles had taught him. For court today, the Rangers let him wear the official uniform—a button-down starched within an inch of its life and a pair of pressed dark slacks. The silver badge was pinned above his left breast pocket. He hadn't worn it in weeks, not since the Ronnie Malvo investigation, which had led to his suspension; hadn't worn his wedding ring in as long, either. It, too, was a part of the day's costume. He resisted the urge to fiddle with it, turning the metal around the ring finger of his inexplicably swollen hand.

He again circled the drain of his single memory past eight o'clock last night: a Styrofoam plate of smoked chicken, a TV tray, a bottle of Jim Beam, and blues on his uncles' hi-fi. The clink of ice, that first pour, these were the last things he remembered. And the relief, of course, that comes with surrender. Yes, he was powerless over his marriage, step one. Step two, pour three fingers and repeat. Step three, let Johnnie Taylor's raw vocals take over—his plainspoken masculinity, his claim on the things a man ought to have in this lifetime, including the love of a good woman, her loyalty and willingness to wade through shit creek with him, if that's what it took to get to the other side. The blue guitar, the amber warmth of bourbon, they floated through the edge of his memory. And then there was nothing but the sudden hardness of the wood on the back porch at his family homestead, where Darren had awakened at dawn.

He'd had a splinter in his cheek and no idea what had happened to his hand. There was no blood, just bruising above the knuckles and a gnawing pain that wouldn't let up without four Motrin, but he had clearly made contact with something on the property, something that had hit back *hard*. The familiar morning-after fog of shame he'd been living in since he and Lisa split had dulled his curiosity, and he'd made no attempt to piece together what had happened. The facts as he knew them: He drank alone and woke up alone. His car keys were still in the freezer, where he'd left them in a moment of spectacular prescience. It appeared he'd hurt no one but himself, and he could live with that. He was damn tired, though, tired of sleeping alone, eating alone, nothing to do but wait: on the results of this grand jury and his wife to tell him he could come home.

"And how do you know the defendant?" Frank Vaughn, the district attorney of San Jacinto County, asked from his stand at the podium.

"Mack has worked with—"

"Pardon?"

"Rutherford McMillan...Mack," Darren said, explaining. "He's worked with my family for over twenty years."

Which is why the night Mack pulled a gun on Ronnie Malvo, Darren made it from Houston to Mack's house in San Jacinto

County in less than an hour. Lisa had begged him not to go. He was off duty, she said. But they both knew there was no such thing. He'd just come off a month on the road, and she was furious that he would so easily leave her again. *Darren, don't.* But he left her anyway, flying to Mack's aid, and now he was a witness in a homicide investigation. He'd been paying for Lisa's *I told you so* ever since.

Vaughn nodded and glanced at the grand jurors, local men and women pulled off farms and out of post offices and barbershops, for whom a day at the courthouse counted as genuine excitement— entertainment, even—no matter that a man's life was at stake. The DA had a storyteller's instinct for pacing and plot twists, the leisurely parceling out of key information. There was no judge here, only a bailiff, the prosecutor, a court reporter, and the twelve members of the grand jury, who had the solemn task of deciding whether or not to indict Rutherford McMillan for first-degree homicide. Because all grand jury proceedings are private, the honey-colored benches in the gallery were empty. The deck was stacked squarely in the state's favor. Neither the defendant nor his counsel was allowed to weigh in on the state's presentation of evidence. Darren was ostensibly here on behalf of the prosecution. But he planned to do what he could to sow a seed of doubt in the grand jurors' minds. The trick was to do that *and* keep his job, a risk he was willing to take. He didn't want to believe that Mack had killed someone in cold blood.

"In what capacity does he work for your family?" Vaughn asked.

"He looks after our property in the county, fifteen acres in Camilla. It's the house where I was raised, but no one lives there anymore, not full-time, not for years," he said. "Well, I guess I technically live there now. See, my wife and I are going through a little something, and she asked for space to—"

Objection: nonresponsive.

It's what he would have said if he were Vaughn, if this were a real trial.

But there was no judge here. And Darren, the former law student, knew he could use that to *his* advantage, too. He wanted the jurors to get to know him, to be more inclined than not to believe he was telling the truth. He didn't trust that the badge would be enough, not looking the way he did now. The pits of his dress shirt were damp, and there was a rank funk seeping from his pores. He felt the first roil of a hangover that had been hiding behind the pain in his hand. His stomach lurched, and he belched up something moist and sour.

He'd broken one of his uncles' cardinal rules: never go to town looking sorry or second-rate or like a man who felt like explaining himself fifteen times a day. Even his uncle Clayton, a onetime defense lawyer and professor of constitutional law, was known to say that for *men like us,* a pair of baggy pants or a shirttail hanging out was "walking probable cause." His identical twin and ideological foil, William, a lawman and Ranger himself, was quick to agree. *Don't give them a reason to stop you, son.* The men rarely stood on common ground—belying the trope of twins who think with one mind—but for the fact that they were Mathews men, a tribe going back generations in rural East Texas, black men for whom self-regard was both a natural state of being and a survival technique. His uncles adhered to those ancient rules of southern living, for they understood how easily a colored man's general comportment could turn into a matter of life and death. Darren had always wanted to believe that theirs was the last generation to have to live that way, that change might trickle down from the White House.

When in fact the opposite had proved to be true.

In the wake of Obama, America had told on itself.

Still, they were giants to him, his uncles, men of stature and purpose, who each believed he'd found in his respective profession a way to make the country fundamentally hospitable to black life. For William, the Ranger, the law would save us by *protecting* us— by prosecuting crimes against us as zealously as it prosecutes crimes against whites. No, Clayton, the defense lawyer, said: the law is a lie black folks need protection *from*—a set of rules that were written against us from the time ink was first set to parchment. It was a sacred debate that held black life as holy, worthy of continuance, and in need of safekeeping, a debate that Darren had been following since he was toddling between their long legs under the kitchen table, when the brothers still lived together, before they'd had a falling-out over a woman. They'd raised Darren since he was only a few days old, and he'd spent his life straddling the family's ideological divide.

Vaughn cut him off, moving to his next question. "So when Mr. McMillan called you that night, was it as a friend or as a member of the Texas Rangers?"

Objection: calls for speculation, Darren thought.

"Both, I imagine," he said.

"And do you know why Mr. McMillan called you instead of calling nine one one?"

Lisa had asked the same thing. Sitting on their bed, in a faded SMU T-shirt, she asked why Mack hadn't called local authorities, why Darren was getting involved at all. Darren had assured her that Mack had called the local sheriff. He was wrong, which he found out too late. But he wouldn't tell the grand jury that. "I think he felt more comfortable dealing with someone he knew," he said.

Vaughn's sandy eyebrows drew together. He was a white man in his midforties, a few years older than Darren, with chestnut-colored hair that was two shades darker than his eyebrows. Darren guessed he dyed it, and he got a sudden and terrible image of Vaughn wandering the aisles of the Brookshire Brothers grocery in town, hunting for Miss Clairol. Vaughn was a government man through and through, dressed plainly in a blue suit and polished tan ropers. He'd been told that Darren didn't want this indictment, that he thought the Rangers and the state of Texas were making a mistake. And he'd been sniffing out a trick on Darren's part since they'd first met to prepare his testimony.

"Someone he knew, yes," Vaughn said, glancing at the jurors. "An officer of the law. But still a friend, wouldn't you say?"

Darren was careful with this one. "Friendly, yes."

"Well, you drove up from Houston to help him. Don't think you'd do that for just anyone."

"The man had a known criminal on his property."

"A peckerwood, didn't Mack call him?"

"After Malvo called him a nigger," Darren said.

The word, laid plain in court, shot a jolt of alarm through the room. Several of the white jurors visibly tensed, as if they believed that merely saying the word aloud in mixed company might incite violence, or summon Al Sharpton.

But Darren wanted it made clear: Ronnie "Redrum" Malvo was a tatted-up cracker with ties to the Aryan Brotherhood of Texas, a criminal organization that made money off meth production and the sale of illegal guns—a gang whose only initiation rite was to kill a nigger. Ronnie had been harassing Mack's granddaughter, Breanna, a part-time student at Sam Houston State, for weeks—following her in his car as she walked to and from town, calling out words she didn't want to repeat, driving back and forth in front of her house when he knew she was home, cussing her color, her body, the way she wore her "nappy" hair. The girl was understandably terrified. Ronnie was known to shoot a dog for shitting in his yard, to threaten that and more to any black person who came within fifteen feet of the tilting shack he called home. He used to beat up kids in high school, vandalize black-owned farms, yanking up crops and tearing down fencing, and he got arrested once for setting fire to an AME church in nearby Camilla, Darren's hometown. Ronnie was built like a fireplug, short and barrel-chested, with a pointy head and thinning hair he hid beneath bandannas. Mack was a seventy-year-old black man who remembered the Klan, remembered huddling behind his daddy and a shotgun, fears of nighttime raids and tales of Klansmen riding up from towns like Goodrich and Shepherd. But this was 2016, and Rutherford McMillan wasn't having that shit.

"That's right," Vaughn said. "A known criminal and, as you say, known white supremacist was threatening the defendant—"

"I don't know for a fact that Ronnie threatened him." He looked at the first row of jurors, four men and two women, all white. "But Mark had every right to protect his property," Darren said. Two of the white jurors nodded.

There were grade-schoolers in Texas who could recite the Castle Doctrine, the state's "stand your ground" law, as easily as the pledge of allegiance.

Mack's was a textbook case.

Ronnie Malvo had breached Mack's property line by cover of darkness, pulling up in a late-model Dodge Charger, hopped up on twenty-inch wheels, likely paid for with drug money. He'd left the engine idling with the lights off, warm air curling up from the twin tailpipes and disappearing like smoke among the steeple-topped pines lining Mack's little plot of land at the edge of San Jacinto County, the nearest neighbor at least a fourth of a mile down the single-lane road that ran in front of Mack's house.

Breanna, who was home alone, stepped on the porch of the clapboard cottage she shared with Mack, trying to see who was sitting out there in the dark, watching the house. When she saw the Dodge and Ronnie Malvo's silhouette in the front seat, she screamed and dropped her cell phone, cracking it in two places. She ran inside and bolted the door, then called her granddaddy from the kitchen phone. From the cab of his ancient Ford pickup, Mack then called Darren as he sped home from a job in nearby Wolf Creek. When Mack pulled into his driveway, his truck blocked Ronnie Malvo's only way out.

Mack hollered for Breanna to grab his pistol from the house. She came out a few seconds later with a snub-nosed .38 revolver. Mack didn't know if Ronnie was armed. But pulling a gun on a man was certainly the fastest way to find out.

By the time Darren arrived, the two men were in a standoff.

He'd rolled up to Mack's place with his headlamps dark, parking his truck under the branches of an old oak tree. Toeing his way up the dirt-and-gravel drive, Darren came upon the following scene: Mack, standing among the junk in his yard, .38 to Ronnie's head, and Ronnie swearing he was just trying to talk to the girl, saying, "But I ain't gon' stand here and let this nigger shoot me cold." He had a .357 aimed at Mack's chest, a gun with more firing power than the Colt .45 Darren pulled from his holster. Ronnie seemed exasperated by the foolishness on display. He needed the "old cotton-head nigger" to move his goddamned truck if he wanted him off his property so goddamned bad. Mack told Ronnie to get his "peckerwood ass" in the Dodge first. Spit was flying, foreheads slick with rage.

"Put down the gun, Malvo," Darren said. "Let's all get out of this clean."

"Tell that to the nigger," Ronnie said, nodding his head toward Mack.

"Which nigger you talking to, Ronnie?" Darren said. "And before you answer, remember one of these niggers is a Texas Ranger who got out of bed for this. I'm not exactly in a patient frame of mind." The Colt caught light off the front-porch lamp. For a moment, Ronnie looked cornered and scared, but Darren knew that wasn't necessarily a good thing. Ronnie was starting to twitch. Two guns at his head, he was shaking in his biker boots, late to the realization that he'd carried a prank too far, had been called out and made a fool of. Pride was a hell of a thing, and Darren knew men had been shot over far less.

He made a quick tactical shift.

"Mack, drop the gun," Darren said. Of the two, Mack was the one he figured he could talk some sense into. But he was wrong.

"The hell I will," the older man said.

"I got this, Mack."

"I don't want no trouble, man," Ronnie said.

Darren could hear Breanna crying on the porch.

"I want this motherfucker off my property," Mack said.

"Put the gun down, Mack. It's not worth it."

"I got every right to protect my property."

"Yeah, but every minute you holding that pistol brings us closer to a situation I can't get you out of. Listen to me, Mack. Don't let him goad you into prison. I'll get him on trespassing, okay, if you just put down the gun."

"Don't care about that," Mack said, his rheumy eyes glistening. "I want him dead or gone, nothing in between."

"Just move the truck, and I'll go," Ronnie said. "Was just messing with the girl. Ought to be happy anybody wants to look at her monkey ass."

"Toss Bre your keys, Mack," Darren said. The old man did as he was told, but he didn't lower his pistol—what looked like a toy pop gun in his large hand. Darren told Breanna to get in Mack's Ford and ease it out onto the road, giving Ronnie Malvo a way to get out of the driveway and off the property.

By now, Mack was damn near crying himself, mumbling so that strings of spit gathered in the corners of his mouth. "Got no right coming onto my land, sniffing around my girl. Don't have to take no shit off a cracker like him."

Darren felt a shift in Mack's breathing, which was bullish and on the march. He thought they had but a few seconds before the old man gave in to the rage that was pulling at every muscle in his lean body. "Move the truck now!"

As Breanna ran off the porch to Mack's Ford, Darren used the distraction to move in on Mack. He reached for his right arm at the wrist, yanking it down in one motion while keeping his Colt trained on Ronnie. Mack cursed but then let go, collapsing onto the patchy grass. Ronnie immediately lowered his weapon. He tossed it through the open driver's-side window of his Dodge, then jumped into the front seat behind it, moving like his ass was on fire.

Darren capped this testimony by reciting the Castle Doctrine verbatim.

Vaughn bristled. "I'll handle the law in here, Mr. Mathews."

"That's *Ranger* Mathews."

"The fact of the matter, Ranger Mathews, is that instead of calling nine one one, the defendant made sure to call a Ranger he knew, a fellow African American who would certainly understand the anger this incident stirred—"

"Objection." This one Darren said out loud.

Vaughn glared at him from the podium, his right hand grasping its edge so tightly that his knuckles blanched. "Mr. Mathews—"

"I'm a Texas Ranger, counselor."

"Then act like one."

Vaughn knew he'd gone too far as soon as he said it. The women in the front row of the jury box shook their heads at the way he'd spoken to a member of the most revered law enforcement agency in the state. One of the two black men in the second row crossed his arms sternly, rocking a toothpick from one side of his mouth to the other, a little dagger pointed right at the DA.

"Ask another question," Darren said, pressing his advantage.

"Mr. Malvo left of his own accord that night, didn't he?"

"Yes. Malvo threw his weapon into his vehicle and fled the scene."

Two days later, when Ronnie was found dead in a ditch alongside his property, two .38 slugs in his chest, it was Darren's incident report that put Mack on the suspect list. He felt responsible for this whole ordeal. A hundred times a day Darren wished he'd never shown up that night, that he'd never filed that report. He'd actually paused after typing it up, staring warily at the pages as he pulled them from the printer, knowing that just putting Mack's name on an incident report, victim or not, was opening a door through which Mack might never return. Criminality, once it touched black life, was a stain hard to remove. But Darren was a cop, so he did his job. He'd followed the rules, and it had landed them all here—a grand jury deciding whether to charge the old man with murder. If indicted, he'd go to trial, a man in his seventies who'd done nothing but work and love his family his whole life. If convicted, he'd be put on death row.

The truth was that Ronnie Malvo was affiliated with one of the most violent gangs in American history, men who ate their own, especially the ones they suspected of betraying them. Darren knew of an Aryan Brotherhood of Texas captain who once ordered a particularly vicious hit on an underling suspected of talking to the cops. They found the nineteen-year-old rumored snitch, strung up by what little flesh was still on his bones, hanging from a fence on a wheat farm in Liberty County. Anybody could have killed Ronnie Malvo, who actually *was* a criminal informant for the federal government. Darren was the only person in the courtroom, including the DA, who knew this. He was based out of the Rangers office in Houston, and a few months before the Malvo homicide, he'd begged his way onto a multiagency task force that was investigating the ABT with the feds. Of course he wasn't allowed to utter a word about it, but he knew the Brotherhood had reason to put Ronnie in a bag—if someone had found out he was talking.

"Mr. McMillan was pretty angry that night, wouldn't you say?"

Darren downgraded it to "concerned," adding, "He didn't seem bent on revenge, if that's what you mean."

"We don't want you to speculate."

"All I can tell you is what I saw, and Mack didn't shoot anybody."

Vaughn pursed his lips together. This was off the script, and Darren knew it.

"Ronnie Malvo was shot with a thirty-eight revolver, correct?"

"I did not work the investigation."

"And why is that?"

"Didn't get assigned," he said casually.

"Lieutenant Fred Wilson said you were too close to this, did he not?"

"Yes, Ronnie Malvo was shot with a thirty-eight." Darren conceded the point.

"And the night you were on his property, you saw Mr. McMillan brandish a thirty-eight revolver at the deceased, correct?"

"Which he didn't fire." Darren shifted in his seat. "He just wanted to be left alone, to feel safe in his home. That's why he had me stay."

The moment Ronnie fled Mack's property, revving his engine and churning up a cloud of dirt and gravel, Darren had knelt beside Mack, a man he'd never seen sniffle in twenty years, let alone cry openly the way he did that night, undone by how close he'd come to killing a man. Darren made it clear he could go after Ronnie or he could stay with the man and his granddaughter.

Quietly, Mack asked him to stay.

Darren ended up spending all night on Mack's front porch, pistol in hand, on the lookout for any pair of headlights that might come creeping by the house. He kept watch till morning clouds rolled in, low and laced rust-red, East Texas dirt reflected in the sky. He kept watch on that tiny corner of the state so Rutherford McMillan could get the night of peace he'd been owed for a lifetime.

Two days later, Ronnie Malvo was found dead behind his own house.

"Which leads to my last question," Vaughn said, his hands clasped behind his back. Darren saw the teeny-tiniest lift at the corners of his mouth. "You weren't with the defendant for the next forty-eight hours, were you?"

"I went back home. I went back to work."

And to Lisa telling him to go back to law school. *Just think about it, Darren.*

It would be that easy, he knew.

Choose a life she understood and go home.

"That's a no?"

"No, I wasn't with him."

"So you would have no way of knowing if, in that forty-eight-hour time frame, Mr. McMillan left his home with that same gun and went and shot and killed Mr. Malvo, would you?"

"No," Darren said. A line of sweat was sliding down his right side now. He worried it showed through his shirt, just as he worried that he'd sunk Mack.

2.

"THE GUN is still missing."

"Which is why they don't have a case," Greg said over the phone.

"You think the good people of San Jacinto County care one whit about the limits of a circumstantial case?" Darren said, pouring out the last of the Big Red soda he'd ordered at Kay's Kountry Kitchen, across from the courthouse, ignoring for today its indiscriminate use of the letter *K*—a flagrant act of microaggression, Texas-style— because the cafe was open and close and his hand needed help. As he poured, he made sure to save the ice, dumping pink melting globs of it into a handkerchief he'd found in his glove box. He wrapped the edges of the handkerchief together, then pressed the homemade ice pack across the sore knuckles of his left hand. "Hell, half of 'em probably wished they'd shot him themselves. Ronnie Malvo is what they call grade A white trash, and hatred of them is the last kind still allowed in polite company."

"Maybe they'll treat McMillan like a hero, then—spare him an indictment."

"No good can come from folks out here thinking Mack is a

killer," Darren said, his back leaned against the driver's-side door of his Chevy truck. "The rules ain't the same for him, and you know it, Greg," he said, looking around the tiny town square of Coldspring. It was one flashing light at a single intersection, surrounded on all sides by antiques stores and consignment shops, selling everything from old guns to used cribs and rusted iron Lone Stars set out on wooden porches. Nothing new came or went through San Jacinto County. It was an economy that ran on its own waste.

"This is just the feds trying to protect their investigation," Darren said.

Greg Heglund faked a wounded sigh.

He was Agent Heglund, actually, with the Criminal Investigative Division of the Houston field office of the FBI. They'd met in that very city years ago, when Darren's uncle Clayton had gotten him into a private high school in Houston, as nothing in San Jacinto County would ever be good enough for his nephew. Lisa and Greg were the first friends Darren made at the school, from which he later graduated. All three had gone into some aspect of the law, and he and Greg had kept in touch all these years.

Greg was a white guy who ran with black dudes most of his life—played ball, dated black girls, eschewed two-stepping for step shows, the whole bit. All that stopped, of course, the second he joined the Bureau, trading his Jordans for Johnston & Murphys. But Darren didn't hold it against him. He'd practically taught Greg the art of code-switching, if only by osmosis. To Darren it was balletic sport in which every black man should be schooled. Besides basketball, it was their one true come-up. At Rangers social events, Darren had once or twice professed a love for Vince Gill or Kenny Chesney that he didn't really feel, had made Lisa twirl along the dance floor with him. He could tolerate Johnny Cash and Hank Williams, the classic country he grew up around—had an uncontrollable affection for Charley Pride on principle—but blues was a black Texan's true legacy. He had Greg listening to Clarence "Gatemouth" Brown and Freddie King long before either of them had heard of Jay Z or Sean Combs. The point was Darren knew he could keep it real with Greg, always. They had it like that.

Greg was not part of the task force that had been tracking the Aryan Brotherhood of Texas, detailing their activities in and out of the state's correctional facilities—including the sale of metham-phetamine and automatic handguns, multiple homicides, and conspiracy—but he knew a good deal about the investigation's ins and outs. Ronnie Malvo had turned state's evidence a few months back, skirting his own conspiracy charges by agreeing to testify when the time came. He held in his tattooed hands enough testi-mony to take down several captains of the ABT. If anyone inside the Brotherhood had gotten wind of his plans, Ronnie Malvo was bound to end up dead, one way or another. Darren offered the same assessment he'd been repeating for weeks. "This has the ABT's name all over it."

Greg argued the other side. "Two bullet wounds and no carnage? That's not really their calling card." He was cautioning Darren not to get too attached to his way of thinking, to remember what stand-ing up for Mack could cost him.

"That's as circumstantial as the idea that Mack did it just because he owns a thirty-eight."

"A thirty-eight that's missing."

"He reported that gun stolen." Darren knew it sounded bad.

"He reported it the day before Malvo's body was found. You know we don't truck in coincidence down in these parts," Greg said, playfully drawing out every vowel within reach. "They still think you had something to do with it?"

"Nobody has the balls to say that to my face," Darren said. "For the record, they're merely claiming I never should have gone out there that night in an official capacity, given my relationship to Mack. Or they're saying that I should have abandoned Mack and gone after Malvo in pursuit. But the suspension is also a convenient way to bump me off the task force without admitting that my blackness causes a problem in the field. It gets me away from the ABT."

"You can't be the first Ranger to ever have a hit out on him."

"That supposed to make me feel better?"

The whispers had started shortly after Darren joined the task force. His lieutenant, Ranger Fred Wilson, was reluctant to let him join the task force at first, for reasons he wouldn't, or *couldn't,* put into words without acknowledging the one thing a Ranger never mentions: race. They were Rangers first—and men, women, white, brown, or black second. But Darren didn't understand how the feds, with the help of the Texas Rangers, could investigate an organization called the Aryan Brotherhood of Texas and *not* mention race. The feds wanted the ABT on drug charges and conspiracy, and Lieutenant Wilson wanted to make sure Darren understood that when he agreed to let him join the Rangers unit assisting the feds out of Houston. "This ain't some *In the Heat of the Night*–type deal here, Mathews," he'd said. "These men are running a serious and sophisticated criminal enterprise, making millions in illegal activity across this state." All true. But trying to take down the Brotherhood without dealing with the racial hatred at its core was like trying to take a dip in a swimming hole without getting wet.

It was a few weeks after he'd conducted his first interviews on behalf of the task force when Mack called to say that the family house in Camilla—the farmhouse where Darren was raised—had been broken into. Dog feces—and human, Mack suspected—had been thrown at the walls inside and out, and two pistols had been stolen, one a thirty-year-old pearl-handled revolver that had belonged to his uncle William. That in particular ate at Darren. There were so few things of his uncle's he had left. Most of his effects, including his Rangers badge and the Stetson he'd retired in, went to William's son, Aaron, a state trooper who resented the hell out of Darren for using up all the Mathewses' nepotism with the Texas Rangers before he could. Darren wanted to believe that his degree from Princeton and two years of law school might have made him a star in his own right, but he knew Aaron had a point. If Darren weren't William Mathews's nephew, he'd have probably been fired over this business with Mack weeks ago. In a way, his uncle was still looking out for him.

The incident was reported and recorded, but on its face it didn't fit the profile of Brotherhood violence, which leaned heavily on the element of surprise, shed a great deal more blood, and didn't fool around with warnings and empty theatrics. But Darren's name had come up on a few ABT websites and in the social-media swamp where white nationalism grew like fungus, a fact Greg now downplayed. "Reports of your imminent death are greatly exaggerated," he said, reaching for some lightness in the situation and coming up short. "It's just chatter—rumors, really, nothing concrete. I promise if there was more to it, we'd get involved on our end. You're perfectly safe."

"Tell that to my wife."

Lisa had never gotten over his career choice, the fact that she lay down on her wedding night with a would-be lawyer and woke up years later with a cop. His well-bred wife, who wore St. John every day and pulled her Lexus sedan into the private parking garage of the law firm where she worked, did not understand the compulsion to confront madness or the allure of the Texas Rangers and the five-point star he wore. *What is it about that damn badge?* It won't protect you, she said, because it was never intended to. *It was never intended for you.* She would never forgive him, she said, if he got himself killed.

"Indicting Mack sells their story of a race crime, just some small-time shit as old as time itself," Darren said. "If rumors get going that Ronnie Malvo was taken out in what looks like a hit, the Brotherhood'll get itchy, maybe change up routines or shut down operations altogether, which would decimate the feds' investigation. I don't think Mack should pay with his life to save their case."

"Did you?" Greg finally asked. "Help Mack with the gun?"

"Jesus, not you, too."

"It's just I know how you feel about Mack...and a guy like Malvo."

"I'm a cop first." But even as he said it, he wasn't sure it was true. This morning he'd already come as close to committing perjury as he could without being escorted out of the building in handcuffs. He just didn't think a black man should go to prison for pointing a weapon at a guy like Malvo. And maybe deep down he didn't think anyone should go to prison for shooting a guy like Malvo, either.

"'Cause they'll come for you, Darren. And I'm not just talking about the job. They'll indict your ass if they think you covered up evidence."

"You don't think I know that?" he said. "I didn't *do* anything. And neither did Mack."

"You so sure? Man messing with his granddaughter like that. If it was the other way around, that alone would have gotten Mack strung up in the old days. Maybe the old man played out a little rough justice of his own."

"Now you sound like Lisa."

"I'm not wading into that," Greg said. "And that's not why I called."

Darren shook out the pale blue handkerchief, watching as ice chips fell to the graveled concrete. On the sidewalk in front of his truck, a kid, maybe five years old, was staring open-mouthed at Darren as his mother yanked him and said, "Come on." Darren, remembering the awe that a real honest-to-God Texas Ranger could inspire in a child, tipped his hat with a smile.

Greg said, "You heard about the trouble up in Lark?"

"I've never heard of Lark."

"Shelby County, just past the western border, tiny little place. I don't think it counts more than two hundred people total."

"Yeah," Darren said, remembering a small cafe along the highway up there, stopping once for a Coke. "I've driven through, sure."

"Well, they got two bodies in the past six days. One a black guy from Chicago, a little younger than us, thirty-five, I think. Seems he was just passing through. Two days later someone pulled his body out of the Attoyac Bayou."

"Jesus."

"And just this morning another one washed up," Greg said. "A local white girl, twenty years old." Through the phone, Darren heard the shuffle of papers on the desk in Greg's cubicle. He'd only been with the Bureau a few years and had yet to land a big case, nothing that would make a career. "Melissa Dale."

"They connected?"

"That's what I'd like to know. Lark ain't had a homicide in years, and now they get two in one week."

"No coincidences, huh?" Darren said.

"Something's up."

Darren felt a familiar kick in his bloodstream at the mention of a race killing in the state, a quickening he couldn't help. "How do you know?"

"I have my spies," Greg said.

"What's her name?"

Greg chuckled, enjoying his reputation as a man with a talent for collecting women, especially ones who didn't mind being collected, which Darren wasn't sure was a talent at all. "Let's just say I got a call from someone in the Dallas County Medical Examiner's office. Shelby County had them do the autopsy on the man." More shuffling of papers, then Greg said his name. "Michael Wright. Soon as they unzipped the body bag and took a good look, they had a lot of questions for the sheriff."

"Why's that?"

"Something to do with the condition of the body. That's all I could get on the phone."

"What's the cause of death?"

"Drowning," Greg said. "But that just means he was still breathing when he went in. The drowning thing, the sheriff is no doubt going to cling to that, shutting down any other possibility. Nobody wants another Jasper."

The mention of Jasper, Texas, churned up Darren's insides, as Greg knew it would. Darren had been a twenty-three-year-old second-year law student in 1998, still grieving the sudden death of his uncle William that same year. He was in a student lounge getting a sandwich between summer classes when the reports of the dragging death of James Byrd Jr. came over every TV screen. Darren never made it to his next class. He stayed there and watched hour after hour of cable news coverage. It was hard to put into words the fury he felt at the fact that someone had literally dragged a black man through a town not a hundred miles from the place where Darren grew up, dragged him till his head came off. He felt ashamed of his country and ashamed of his home state.

But he also felt a hot rage at the students and professors around him, most of them white northerners, clucking their tongues and whispering *Texas* in a way that suggested both pity and disdain for a land that Darren loved, a state that had made him a gentleman and a fighter in equal measure. It was hard to put any of it into words. So he didn't try. He simply walked out. By the end of that summer, he'd applied to the Texas Department of Public Safety to be a state trooper, the first step in a nearly decade-long quest to become a member of the venerable law enforcement agency known as the Texas Rangers, the ones who rolled in when local agencies couldn't or *wouldn't* solve a crime. Darren had decided on the immediacy of the only law that mattered to him then: boots on the ground—hand-stitched, preferably, gator or cowhide—a badge, and a Colt .45. The internal scales that forever weighed on his heart tipped in favor of his uncle William. Clayton, the lawyer, when he heard that his nephew had quit law school, said only, "I'm profoundly disappointed in you, son."

"He was killed first?" Darren asked Greg.

"Pulled out the bayou on Friday, three days ago. Then the girl, washed up a quarter of a mile downstream just this morning."

Odd, Darren thought.

Southern fables usually went the other way around: a white woman killed or harmed in some way, real or imagined, and then, like the moon follows the sun, a black man ends up dead. "What's her cause of death?" he asked.

"No autopsy on her yet. Just the fact that she was found much the same way as the first body. Though there's some holler about a sexual assault maybe."

"Why not send an agent up there?"

"Sheriff ain't asking for one, or any outside help, for that matter, and I don't have the authority to make that kind of a call."

"So what do you want me to do?"

"Go up there and poke around a bit, see if there's more to this than the sheriff wants to admit. The Klan or worse. What'd you call it...some race shit as old as time? I just think it deserves a real investigation. I know this is the kind of case that made you go for the badge."

"I'm on suspension, Greg. I don't have a badge."

But when he looked down, he saw he was still wearing the five-point star from court, was in his full uniform, in fact. "And what do you get out of it?"

"You mean besides justice?"

"I mean be straight with me."

"If it's something real, a bigger mess than the sheriff is saying, some Sandra Bland shit, shit they're hiding out there, and I get to be the one to call it in, I don't have to tell you that it could bump me out of this little cubicle."

"Come on, Greg," Darren said, frowning at the naked ambition even while he understood it. He'd been miserable stationed at his desk in Houston, offering assists on mostly corruption and corporate crimes. He'd only truly come alive as a lawman when he was living in the true spirit of his title as a Texas Ranger, a man *on the range* across this great state. Joining the task force had changed his life, but it had put a terrible strain on his marriage. The time on the road is the thing Lisa resented most about the job.

"Something stinks out there, D, and you know it."

He didn't know shit, not really.

Except that black men's bodies don't come up in rivers like weeds.

"Just give it a day or two," Greg said. "You don't get an instinct on something by then, turn around and go home."

But Darren wasn't sure where home was these days.

"I'll do it," he said.

He already knew he was going, knew it the minute Greg had laid out the scene in Lark. It was his anger about the grand jury and Mack that got him going as well as his resentment of the Rangers for hemming him in.

"And D, keep your head up out there. They got ABT in Shelby County, too." As if he needed Greg to tell him that. He nodded grimly as he climbed into the cab of his truck and wrapped his sore hand around the steering wheel.

3.

HE WENT by his mother's first, 'cause he'd been promising her he would. She knew he was staying in Camilla, only a few minutes' drive from her place, and she knew he was staying scarce. Bell Callis lived on the eastern edge of San Jacinto County, down a red-dirt road lined with loblolly pines and Carolina basswood, their branches licking the sides of Darren's truck. Through the trees, he could make out the black tar roofs of his mother's neighbors, the small lean-tos and shotgun shacks in the weeds. Nearby, somebody was burning trash, the sour smoke from which wafted across the front end of Darren's truck, a familiar scent of hard living. Past a bend in the road, Darren nodded at his mother's landlord, a white man in his eighties named Puck, who let Bell rent a snatch of land around back of his place. He gave Darren a wave from his front porch, then went back to staring at the trees, which is how he spent most of his days. Darren made a left turn onto the property, then followed the twin tire tracks in the dirt and wild grass that led to his mother's trailer.

She was sitting on the concrete steps in front of the mobile home, smoking a Newport and picking nail polish off her big toe. She had a beer at her feet, but Darren knew better. The real shit was in the house. She looked up and saw the silver truck carrying her only son, but there was nothing in her drably indifferent expression to suggest that she'd been calling him nonstop for the past four days.

"You look skinny," she said when he climbed out of the truck.

"Right back at you," he said.

She was only sixteen years older than he was, and they shared the same length of bone in their arms and legs—they were lanky, whippet-thin but for the muscle Darren had built up in his torso and legs and the pad of fat around her hips Bell had managed to hold on to when every other inch of her seemed to have shriveled in retreat, bested by time. He'd never met his father. But his dad's older brothers, William and Clayton, were barely five feet eight inches tall.

In flesh, at least, Darren was all Callis.

"When was the last time you went to the store, Mama?"

Mama never failed to soften her.

They hadn't met until Darren was eight years old, before which his curiosity about his birth parents had been limited to stories about his father, the more swashbuckling the better—even though Darren "Duke" Mathews hadn't done much in his nineteen years besides knock up a country girl he'd fooled around with once or twice and then die in a helicopter accident in the last doleful days of Vietnam. His mother had been a curiosity that felt as removed from his real life as the distant Caddo Indian in the Mathews bloodline. She was *Miss Callis* for the first few years, then *Bell* when he got to high school and college. But sometime after he hit forty, the word *Mama* shot out as if it were a stubborn seed lodged in his teeth all these years that had finally popped free.

"I got some sausage and beans on the stove in there right now," she said, picking up the can of Pearl lager; you could still buy single cans of it at the bait-and-tackle shop next to the resort cabins on Lake Livingston, where Bell worked as a cleaning lady three days a week. "You hungry? Want me to fix you a plate?"

"I can't stay, Mama."

"Course you can't."

She stood on her bare feet then, waving off the chivalrous reach of his hand. She downed the beer and turned for the screen door to her trailer. "But you'll stay for a drink, I know that much." She wobbled a little on the top step before opening the screen door and disappearing inside. Darren followed, entering the two-room trailer, the floors of which were covered in matted putty-brown wall-to-wall carpeting.

"How many you in for today?" Darren said, glancing at his watch.

If it was more than eight drinks before noon, he'd have to take her car keys and walk them down to Puck's place for safekeeping, a move that both mother and son would resent, albeit for different reasons. "I'm enjoying myself" was all she said, sinking into the thin cushion resting on top of the L-shaped banquette that lined part of the living room and kitchenette. She was a fifty-seven-year-old woman who'd been an alcoholic most of her adult life, a fact that had confused Darren as a teenager and scared the shit out of him as an adult. Bell lifted a little bullet-shaped bottle of Cutty Sark and sucked on it like a nipple. They sold the little airplane-size bottles for fifty cents at the bait-and-tackle shop, and Bell had them lined up on the window ledge like a loaded clip of rifle shells.

"It's my day off."

"What do you want, Mama?"

"You too good to have a drink with your mama?" she said, patting the paisley seat cushion next to her. Her hair was braided into a bun, and there was a bottle of nail polish on the table. She's going somewhere tonight, he thought.

"I'm on duty."

"No, you ain't. Lisa told me so."

"No, she didn't."

It would be unprecedented, Lisa and his mother talking. Bell had not even come to the wedding, was left off the guest list at the insistence of both Lisa and Clayton, who held a particularly rigid dislike for Bell Callis. His uncle William used to give her a little something every month to keep her going, never asking where the money went. But that stopped the day he died. Clayton kept her at arm's length, forever stiffening at the mention of her name, as if he thought she might yet try to claim Darren one day, come along and try to redo his entire childhood, taking the only son Clayton had ever known. Every year, Christmas was with the Mathewses—Clayton; Naomi, William's widow; and their two kids, Rebecca and Aaron. Easter was with Lisa's parents at their second home, in New Mexico. Thanksgiving was with friends, usually Greg and Darren's extended Ranger family. Darren didn't think his mother and his wife had ever been in the same room together. The idea that Lisa disclosed his professional trouble to his mother meant either Bell was lying or his wife was a hell of a lot angrier than he thought.

"Won't be called a liar in my own house, Darren," Bell said. "I called down to Houston couple of times when you ain't answer at the Mathews place." She always called his family homestead by that rather formal title, making clear the line past which she was sure she didn't belong. His parents had never dated, not in any proper sense of the word, and Duke never brought Bell home. Theirs was a romance of stolen kisses in the woods, her back up against the rough bark of a live oak, Duke dropping her home by nightfall. When Duke died and Darren was born a few months later, Clayton had scooped in within days to take possession of his nephew. "She said you was in a little trouble at work, something about a shooting and Rutherford McMillan, and she didn't know where you were staying these days, but I seen your truck in Camilla, Darren."

"We're just taking a little space, that's all."

"Could have told you that one was gon' be hard to please," she said, leaning forward to slide her fingers into an open pack of Newports. She lit a fresh one and blew out a burst of smoke. "But you ain't asked me, did you?"

He hadn't stepped more than a foot over the door's threshold. He kept his hat tucked under his arm, the top of his head nearly touching the ceiling. "You were looking for me, and now you got me. So what do you want, Mama?"

"I need you to talk to Fisher."

"I don't want to get involved in any of that."

"But he ain't been paying me regular. I'm like to starve, Darren."

"You said you had food." He glanced at the kitchenette's two-burner stove and saw the crust of something that had been prepared at least a week ago. The sausage and beans had been a wish, a gesture of the mother she wanted to be.

"Why hasn't he paid you?" Darren asked, 'cause he knew there was more to the story, always was. Fisher was Bell's employer at the Starfish Resort Cabins and RV Hook-Up near Lake Livingston. He was also her boyfriend and married to the other maid on the payroll. It was a sad soap opera that Darren didn't want to deal with.

"He claims I took a hundred dollars out of his wallet."

"Jesus, Mama, you're lucky he didn't fire you or call the sheriff."

She clucked her teeth, smiling a little as she reached for another bottle on the window ledge. "He ain't gon' do that, knowing I got a Ranger for a son."

"Not a Ranger—not right now, at least," he said, looking for a way out.

"He don't know that," she said slyly. "How much longer they gon' let you wear that?" She nodded toward the silver badge pinned to his breast.

"They'll be looking for me if I don't show up with it by tomorrow."

"Plenty of time."

"How much do you need?" he said, because it was easier that way. To do nothing was to invite her petulance, the pout of a grown woman who felt perpetually undervalued and angry about it. She felt the men in her life, especially her son, owed her more than they'd made good on. And despite the fact that his mother hadn't raised him, couldn't for years be bothered to send a Christmas card, he, too, felt like he owed her something for his life. He just wasn't sure what. Today it was two hundred dollars in cash, most of what he had on him.

She took it with little fanfare, tucking it into the pocket of her shirt. "And get something to eat," he said. "Spend at least fifty of that on groceries." She might and she might not, she said, reaching for another bottle on the window ledge.

4.

US Highway 59 is a line that runs through the heart of East Texas, a thread on the map that ties together small towns like knots on a string, from Laredo to Texarkana, on the northern border. For black folks born and bred in the rural communities along the highway's north-south route, Highway 59 has always represented an arc of possibility, hope paved and pointing north.

Not Darren's people, though.

He was Texas-bred on both sides, going all the way back to slavery. Since Reconstruction, no one had ever left the piney woods of the eastern edge of the state save for a few uncles and cousins fleeing the law on his mother's side. Her people stayed because they were poor; the Mathewses stayed because they were not. From early on, they owned farm-rich land, bequeathed by the same man who gave his favored slaves the surname Mathews, or so the legend went, and black folks didn't just up and leave that kind of wealth to start over someplace foreign and cold. No, the Mathewses dug deeper into the soil, planting cotton and corn and the roots of a family that would be theirs alone—and not a pecuniary unit, convertible to cash at will. They farmed hard and made enough to raise generations of men and women and send dozens of them to college and graduate school; they made a life that could rival what was possible in Chicago or Detroit or Gary, Indiana. They were not willing to cede an entire state to the hatred of a bunch of nut-scratching, tobacco-spitting crackers. Money allowed for that choice, sure it did. But money also demanded something of them, and the Mathewses were willing to give it. They built a colored school in Camilla, offered small-business loans to colored folks when they could, and dedicated their lives to public service, becoming teachers and country doctors and lawyers and agitators when the times called for it.

What they were *not* going to be was run off.

The belief that they were special, that they had the stones to endure what others couldn't, was the most quintessentially Texas thing about them. It was an arrogance born of genuine fortitude and a streak of hardheadedness six generations deep, a Homeric shield against the petty jealousies and lethal injustices that so occupied white folks' free time, their oppressive and intrusive gaze into every aspect of black life—from what you eat to who you marry to the clothes you wear to the music you play to the way you wear your hair to how you address them on the street. The Mathews family recognized it for what it was: a fevered obsession that didn't really have anything to do with them, a preoccupation that weakened a man looking anywhere but at himself.

No, we weren't going anywhere.

Darren had heard it his entire life.

You could run, wouldn't nobody judge you if you did. But you could also stay and fight. Sunsets on the back porch at the old home place in Camilla, William, hat brim down on the porch railing, used to look out over the family's land and say to Darren, "The no-bility is in the fight, son, in all things."

It was the fight that had called Darren home all those years ago, that put Darren's four wheels on Highway 59 now, pointed north toward Shelby County.

He shared Greg's hunch that the murders there were connected, that race was tangled up in it somehow, that it was worthy of asking the question, at least. He admitted an affinity for working homi-cides with a racial element—murders with a particularly ugly taint on them, something in the method of killing or the motive that shamed our better selves, crimes that had to be condemned in or-der for a nation to hold its head up. Darren was careful not to call these hate crimes, though, as he had learned all too quickly that Texas cops were squeamish on the issue of marking any one crime as more heinous than another. He'd gotten shit his first year on the job when he'd proposed establishing a hate crimes unit on par with the Rangers' Public Corruption Department and their investiga-tion team for unsolved crimes. He envisioned a unit bound not by company or region but by the similarities among the cases them-selves. He wrote up a report on the nature of hate crimes—citing case law and successful court convictions from other states—and presented it to both his lieutenant and captain in Company A, in Houston, and to Rangers headquarters, in Austin. The report had done little more than mark him as overly interested in something for which he was imagined to have an outsize personal stake, which brought little respect from his higher-ups and courted the resent-ment of more than a few white Rangers. The idea had been roundly dismissed. That, and now this thing with Mack maybe being in-dicted, had him questioning his allegiance to the Rangers.

It was a two-hour drive to Shelby County, shaded by the wealth of pines along the highway and the waterlogged cypress trees dotting the creeks and bayous shooting off the San Jacinto River. He crossed a rusted iron bridge outside of Leggett, then pulled over a few miles up when he saw a hand-painted strip of cardboard nailed to the trunk of a Spanish oak. The sign advertised boiled peanuts, but the gal who'd set up a stand on the bed of her pickup truck was also peddling pears and pepper jelly, homemade, and when she saw the five-point star pinned to his shirt, she offered him a free pumpkin. She had a box of the lumpy gourds at her feet. He declined politely, instead paying a few dollars for a bag of peanuts and two pears. He ate his makeshift lunch in the cab of his truck, rolling up his sleeves to let the pear juice run down his forearms. Across the front seat, his phone beeped at him. It was a text from Mack: *How did it go?*

Darren wasn't technically allowed to speak about the secret grand jury proceedings, nor would he chance more professional trouble by leaving a digital trail of contact with the defendant. Instead he rang his uncle, hoping to leave a simple voice-mail message—words to be relayed to Mack—but he actually caught Clayton between classes. He heard the chatter of passing students and the faint huff and puff of a man in his late sixties crossing the sprawling campus. Naomi, his brother's widow, had gotten Clayton a Fitbit for Christmas last year. He now paced during his constitutional law lectures instead of holding court from the podium, and he walked on any day that didn't see rain. *Naomi has given me a new lease on life,* he said at least once a month, with no regard for the discomfort it caused Darren or Naomi's children from her marriage to William, Clayton's niece and nephew. "I was hoping I'd have heard from you by now," Clayton said.

His voice sounded so much like his brother's—dulcet, with a faint rasp—that every time he talked to Clayton, Darren experienced a wretched moment of dislocation that gave him hope that William was somehow still alive. Their striking similarity made all the more plain the loss of the one he really wanted, a pining for something he could no longer have. He guessed it half explained Clayton's present romance with Naomi, who was clinging to matching DNA, a perfect science that made for what had to be a second-rate romance.

"I went by Mama's," Darren said.

This Clayton ignored. "Well, let's have it, then. How did Vaughn do? Like shooting fish in a barrel with any Texas grand jury, I know, but tell me the son of a bitch made some misstep, anything that might save Mack's behind."

Darren told the truth, that it didn't look good—the stolen .38 and all that—and he wasn't sure he'd done enough, not with the DA getting him to admit the words that were flying that night, coming from Ronnie Malvo *and* from Mack. "I might have got at a couple of 'em," he said, thinking of the two black jurors.

"You did what you could, son, and I'm proud of you for that. Now it's time to turn in that badge and walk away. You talk to the dean in Chicago? Is it still the same guy?"

"Actually it's a woman now," Darren said. He'd gotten as far as the website, which, when Darren applied to law school, was one sad little page listing a bunch of phone numbers you had to call in order to get more information. Now you were required to do the entire application online, but Darren had never clicked on any links past the home page—not while he was sober, at least.

"Either way, son, you know I can get you a spot as a third-year here in Austin. You just need to fill out the application. You could start as early as the new year. And anyway," he said softly, "Texas may be better for you and Lisa."

So they've been talking, Darren thought.

"They're starting a new Innocence Project at the law school, dealing specifically with suspected police brutality in the interrogation process, and with your knowledge of the culture of law enforcement, this is something you could be running in a few years. You have the talent, son, the heart. Everything you've been trying to do, everything they won't let you do, you can do that here, son, protecting folks. This thing with Mack ought to show you—"

"I've made some good arrests, Pop. I've done good work."

"In service to whom, Darren?"

It was an argument they'd had dozens of times, more if you count the years when William, a fellow Ranger, was able to weigh in. Clayton strategically avoided taking it any further now. "Come by the house after you finish up with everything in Houston," he said. "Naomi and I will make a nice dinner. I'll show you around the law school, introduce you to folks making a difference for people like us," he said, ignoring, as he often did, the class dynamics that made his *us* quite complicated. "Lisa's talking about a potential transfer to her firm's Austin office. She would do that for you, Darren. You can start over, son."

His mother called three times before he made it even fifty miles, and at a certain point he turned the phone facedown on the truck cab's front seat, which is how he missed Greg's first text. The second popped up on his phone as he was gassing up a few miles outside of Nacogdoches. Three words: *check ur e-mail*. From his personal Yahoo account, Greg had sent Darren an e-mail outlining the little he knew about *Wright, Michael*, and *Dale, Melissa*—"Missy," as it turned out. After a few Google searches and liberal use of the Bureau's many databases, Greg had found out the following:

Michael Wright was thirty-five years old and actually a Texas native. Darren sat in his idling truck, reading. Michael Wright had been born in Tyler and gone through elementary school there before moving with his mother and father, both deceased, to Chicago. Married, he'd been traveling alone, at least according to the few eyewitness statements Greg had access to. He had no criminal record and was a graduate of both Purdue and the University of Chicago Law School and had stayed close to his adopted home up north. Here Greg had made a note in brackets: *Did you know him at U of C?* But of course Greg's math was way off, since Michael Wright would have still been in high school when Darren started law school. But the similarity in their backgrounds was not lost on him. There was a rush of recognition, a kinship that felt instant. In the attached photo—a head shot from Wright's law firm—Michael was fairer-skinned than Darren, whose color deepened to a rich hickory after just a few hours in the sun, and more sharply dressed. Still, he felt he knew Michael Wright. But for a few years' difference in age, they might have known each other at U of C, swapped stories about growing up as black boys in East Texas—drunk beer together and talked about girls, basketball, and constitutional law.

The wife has been notified.

It was Greg's final note on Michael Wright, along with the wife's name, Randie Winston, and the fact that her whereabouts at the time of the murder were still unclear. There was no picture of her. But Darren thought of Lisa—the buttery brown skin, the astral spray of moles across her cheeks, the lank curls that cost a hundred dollars a week to maintain. She had worried for years about getting a call like the one Michael Wright's wife had just received.

The rest of Greg's e-mail was a much lighter dossier on Missy

Dale. A graduate of Timpson High School; enrolled for a semester and a half in cosmetology studies at Panola College; a waitress at Jeff's Juice House, an icehouse right off 59 in Lark. The details of her life could fit on a postcard. The one thing of interest Darren almost missed at first glance. It was the mention of her marriage to Keith Avery Dale, of Lark, presently employed at Timpson Timber Holdings and fresh from a two-year stint at the Walls, in Huntsville, on drug charges—possession and intent to sell.

Greg had added a note: *ABT?*

The Aryan Brotherhood of Texas had been born in a Texas prison, and more than half their members were incarcerated at any given time—not that it stopped them from running their criminal organization. In fact prison was their breeding ground: recruits caught religion on the inside and came out desperate to kill their way into the gang. Initiation into the ABT required a black body, didn't matter which one, long as you skinned it yourself. Greg's point—that a few months after doing a deuce in a Texas correctional facility Keith Dale returned to a town that saw the death of a black man *and* Dale's wife in less than a month—was not lost on Darren. It irritated him that Greg probably knew about the potential Brotherhood connection when he'd called earlier but had waited until he imagined Darren was halfway to Shelby County before adding this bit of information. Darren could still turn around, if only for spite. But the mention of the Brotherhood put a little lead in his boot. He was back on the highway, doing eighty-five, before he knew it. He would have done well to slow down, to consider how his displeasure with the Rangers was racing him headlong into something he didn't know the half of. But he didn't—not then, at least.

When he crossed the line into Shelby County, he removed his badge, tossing the five-point star inside the glove box. It slid against a half-empty pint of Wild Turkey he'd forgotten was in there, clinking softly, a siren call he left unanswered for the moment. He felt naked without his beloved badge but also strangely protected by the anonymity of its absence. Without the star, he would draw no undue attention, make no advertisement of his presence to any rank-and-file Brotherhood in the county, rabid dogs always on the hunt. And no word would get back to Houston, where he was stationed, that he was poking around something, unauthorized by his superiors, something he guessed he *did* hold an outsize interest in as a cop, as a Texan, and as a man. In fact as long as he wasn't wearing the Rangers star, they couldn't stop him from doing any damn thing. Without the badge, he was just a black man traveling the highway alone.

Part Two

5.

THE BRASS bell on the front door of Geneva Sweet's Sweets trilled gently when Darren first walked into the cafe. It was an aged sleigh bell tied to the push-bar handle by an old piece of ribbon, plaid run through with red and Kelly green, the edges frayed like a puff of Christmas cotton, something someone had tied up one particularly festive December at least a decade back. Christmas was apparently a favored holiday at Geneva's. There was a string of colorful bulbs haloed over the door that led to the kitchen, a few feet behind a countertop that was also festooned with colored lights, the cord twisted and sticky with dried ketchup and barbecue sauce where it had been stapled to the warped plywood underneath. The calendars on the back wall by the kitchen were all turned to the final month of the year, pictures of poinsettias and pinecone wreaths and baby Jesus aglow, all yellowing in the afternoon sun pouring through the wide windows at the front of the cafe. Twice Darren had heard Mahalia Jackson singing "Silent Night" on the jukebox next to the booth where he'd been sitting for the past hour. The whole place was barely eight hundred square feet, doing good business for a one-room cafe in the middle of nowhere. The sign for Lark Darren had passed just over the county line read POPULATION 178. Part of Geneva's had been made over for a barbershop, an oddity in a room full of oddities and knickknacks. Texas license plates going back fifty years, an old electric guitar on display, plus rows of crocheted baby dolls on a high shelf. There was a middle-aged freckled black man sitting in a green barber's chair, reading a comic book.

Darren had been around places like this as a kid. Mary's Market & Eats, in Camilla, where he bought snow cones as a kid and brought home plates of fried catfish when his uncles didn't feel like cooking. Rochelle's, in Coldspring, sold lemonade so sweet it made your teeth ache, and on a summer day there'd be a line almost to the courthouse. For generations, black women in Texas had put up four walls, whipped up a favorite recipe, and counted the money as colored folks came from all over just to have a place where they were welcome. Geneva's was a throwback, and Darren wondered if twenty years from now places like this would even exist anymore. Maybe they would, he thought, if the food was this good.

He hadn't eaten anything besides the roadside snack.

He was halfway through a plate of black-eyed peas and oxtails, eating as slowly as he could in order to buy a seat at the window, through which he kept an eye on the town. This was about it, far as Darren could tell. There was Geneva's cafe, and at an angle across Highway 59, there was a large dome-topped house that was fenced on all sides, the wood whitewashed and pristine. A quarter mile north, on the same side of the highway as Geneva's, he'd passed an old-school icehouse, a drinking hole half out of doors, with a porch that wrapped around three sides of the flat-roofed box of a building, the wood a weathered gray, black and rotted in some spots. The bar's walls were covered in aluminum siding that was painted a dull ocher, and the neon sign across the building read JEFF'S JUICE HOUSE. He remembered the place from Greg's e-mail.

Whatever the town's other gems, they were tucked deep in the countryside or along the narrow farm roads that ran like rutted creek beds off the main highway, their red-dirt paths snaking between pine trees and leading to houses and trailers tucked into the piney woods. You could cover the whole of Lark, Texas, in the time it took to sneeze. Darren had driven through it and doubled back twice before he realized this was all there was. There had been two squad cars parked in front of Geneva's when he'd rolled into town, so he made the cafe his first stop. He knew the Attoyac Bayou, which made up the western border of the county, ran through the woods behind Geneva's restaurant.

A white trucker wandered in off the highway. Through the window Darren could see his bug-crusted plates: OHIO, THE HEART OF IT ALL. The man hovered in the doorway, lifting a ball cap off his sweaty hair and looking around, struck by the half dozen or so black faces that were staring back at him.

"What can I get you?" Geneva said.

"This the only truck stop around here?"

"There's one up to Timpson if you can make it that far."

The trucker glanced back at his rig, which was blocking half the parking lot, Geneva's lone gas pump dwarfed beside it. He was hesitating.

"But looks like you could stand to eat something, so come on. Don't worry, we'll let you sit at the counter." She smiled and caught Darren's eye, winking. He smiled back, despite himself. They'd exchanged only a few words when he'd ordered his meal, but he'd liked her at once. The trucker ordered a pork sandwich to go. And Darren took the opportunity to move in for conversation. He took the last open stool at the counter, sitting beside a black man in his sixties and a younger black guy who was wearing a nylon shirt that said TRANSWEST ALLIED TRUCKING.

"Don't mind my saying," Darren said to Geneva. "Couldn't help noticing you got a lot of men in uniform around your place. Everything all right?"

The man in his sixties whistled under his breath, snapping the edges of the newspaper in front of him, but said nothing. Geneva looked up from the paper bag she was stuffing with squares of prepackaged wet wipes. She, too, declined comment. It was the young black guy who spoke up. "Girl died back there," he said, looking up from his cell phone to give Darren a once-over. Then, deciding Darren was worthy of the whole story, he added, "A white girl."

The trucker from Ohio looked up. "How much longer on that sandwich?"

"She got a baby at home, don't she, Geneva?" the younger black guy said.

"Who? Missy?" said Geneva's cook, a man in a white apron coming out of the kitchen, holding a sandwich wrapped in white paper, thin streaks of barbecue sauce staining the sides. He set the sandwich inside the paper bag.

"Four-ninety-nine," Geneva said to the trucker, ignoring everyone else.

Ohio left a five in front of the register and booked it. A few seconds later, Darren heard the roar of the rig's engine as the trucker revved his way back onto the highway. Geneva ignored Darren, instead busying herself with a stack of mail on an open secretary's hutch pressed against the back wall.

"Huxley, you got some mail need to get out?"

"Not today," the older man said.

The younger man piped up. "Yeah, she got a baby, that's what you said."

"That's enough, Tim," Geneva said. She stacked her outgoing mail neatly and wrapped an orange hair band around it. She seemed to pointedly refuse to meet Darren's eyes. He wasn't one of them and therefore not entitled to any town secrets.

Fair enough.

Darren paid for his meal in cash, leaving a ridiculously large tip.

The bell dinged behind him as he stepped outside, heading for his truck. Behind the front seat, he kept a navy-blue duffel bag. Inside were a change of clothes, a couple hundred dollars in cash, extra clips for the Colt, deer jerky a friend at work had smoked himself, a hairbrush, and a pack of cigarettes. Darren didn't smoke, but he'd learned that people were less likely to ask questions of a man loitering long as he had a cigarette in his hand. He fingered a Camel from its pack and walked around to the back of the cafe. Behind Geneva's was a lumpy lot of dirt and crabgrass about a hundred yards long that ran right up to the weedy bank of the Attoyac Bayou, a flat stretch of water ten feet wide, moss-green in some places and rusted brown as an old penny in others, depending on which way the trees bent in the sun. Not a ripple winked across its surface, the water as still as tinted glass. There was no telling how deep the bayou was or what wildlife might live beneath its surface. He wondered again about the words *condition of the body* and what they meant, if some creature had made a meal of Michael Wright.

The thought made Darren's stomach lurch, the oxtails and peas swimming upstream. He turned his head and spit in the grass, willing himself not to retch. Between the fishy bayou and the fetid, sickly sweet odor of human decomposition, Darren felt like he might faint. He covered his mouth and nose. It wouldn't do a damn thing, never did, but it was an instinct not to be argued with. The corpse was already covered, but he knew it was her. It had to be. Michael Wright was on a medical examiner's table in Dallas. This was Missy Dale's final resting place. Darren noted the distance from the edge of the water to the cafe's back door—where Geneva's cook, the man in the apron, was leaning against the doorjamb, keeping an eye on the whole scene. There was also a rather sizable mobile home parked back here. White with green trim, it was a lot bigger than his mother's trailer—three bedrooms, maybe.

Whoever lived there was probably the one who'd found her.

"Tell Geneva she gon' have to keep her people from outta here," said a man in a pair of tight trousers, a sheriff's badge pinned to his white shirt.

He was speaking to Darren, who had wandered a little too close to the crime scene. On instinct, Darren opened his mouth to explain himself, but then thought better of it, remembered he was just a man out here. He'd been around small-town sheriffs his whole career. More than half the Rangers' work was in service to local law enforcement agencies that lacked the resources to do the kind of in-depth investigations the Texas Rangers could. Some welcomed the Rangers, Darren in particular, because he was perceived to have a special touch with suspects and witnesses of a dark hue; and some, like this five-foot-six barrel of a man before him now, were suspicious of any outsiders. They resented everything about the Rangers, from their sizable state funding to their intercounty jurisdiction and freedom to roam to the rapt awe they inspired.

Darren was fine playing the disinterested onlooker. The day had cooled, and so had his ill temper. He'd grown tired, he realized, the heavy food playing tricks on his nervous system. He actually allowed himself a thought of home.

The place in Camilla. Or Houston, if Lisa would have him.

He knew it was his thirst talking.

It had run out ahead of the wagon he'd pledged to ride, a wild stallion that had somehow gotten hold of the reins and was pulling Darren by the neck. He wanted a fucking drink. Maybe more than he wanted to solve a mystery. He could stick around till sundown, gather what he could for Greg, then drive back to Houston, as he'd told Lieutenant Wilson he would. Maybe there *was* something to his uncle's offer of dinner and a university tour in Austin. Maybe law school was something Darren couldn't afford to dismiss out of hand. He could already taste the bourbon that was waiting for him when this long-ass day was done. It would be his reward for being open-minded about his future, something even Lisa couldn't begrudge him. He felt the pull of surrender.

He backed past an invisible line in the dirt, just a few feet from the cafe's back door, and the sheriff nodded his approval.

"You got another one of those?" he heard.

Darren turned to see an aging black woman standing next to him. She was no taller than a middle schooler, but she was dressed like an elderly man who'd just discovered the concept of gender fluidity. She'd been watching the deputies working when Darren wandered back here. Now she had her hand out, pointing to his cigarette. He hadn't yet lit his prop, so he gallantly handed it to her. She made a face, and Darren reached into his pocket for the pack, lifting out a fresh one for her. "That's right," she said. She didn't ask for a light but pulled one out of her pocket. A little plastic thing with a dancing crocodile printed on the side. She lit her cigarette, then motioned for Darren to lean down so she could light his, too. She eyed him over the flame. "Who you?" she said.

"I'm sorry?"

"I ain't seen you around here before."

"Just passing through."

"You picked a day for it," she said, nodding at the grim scene.

"I see that," he said. "What happened?"

The woman spit an errant tobacco leaf onto the ground, then pulled at the sides of her jacket, gathering herself with great care, as if she were about to deliver the ten o'clock news. "A mess, that's what's happened. See, first it was the one who come through here last week, Wednesday, I believe Geneva said, and then he come up dead on Friday, and they trying to say drowning. And now this little girl, now somebody did whatever in God's name they done to her," she said, pointing to the body, the five-foot shape covered by a white nylon tarp. There were clumped strands of her blond hair peeking out on one end.

"Michael Wright was here?" he said.

It hadn't occurred to him that he'd been walking in the man's footsteps. If the woman found it odd that Darren knew the dead man's full name, she didn't say a word about it. "They found him farther up north. Behind the icehouse."

"But he was here, I mean. You said something about Geneva's."

"Where else a black man in this town gon' go?"

Darren nodded toward the mobile home. "Who lives there?"

"Geneva," the woman said, taking a pull on the tobacco. "She rents out a room in there sometimes, since it's six miles to the nearest motel, and she keeps some supplies in there, and some of Joe's things from when he was on the road."

"Joe?"

"Better not tell nobody around here you ain't heard of Joe Sweet."

A shadow fell across her face at the same time Darren felt a presence at his back, a smell of Aqua Velva and Vitalis that came wafting over his shoulders. He turned to see that a large white man had joined them. He was six two in boots and had a wide head and black hair he'd tamed into a thin pompadour, streaks of gray taking over at the temples. He had a cigarette in hand and a faint smile on his face, an inability to conceal his perverse excitement about the awful deeds afoot in this little town. "Looks like we got us a serial killer on our hands," he said, flicking ash off the end of a Marlboro red. He wore a wedding band studded with a diamond bigger than Lisa's. He gave a sidelong glance in Darren's direction, saw nothing of interest there, and went back to staring at the deputies.

"Who ever heard of a black serial killer?" the woman said.

"So you think the killer's black?"

"Ain't that what you think?" She sucked her cigarette down to the head.

"A white girl washes up a hundred yards behind the blackest spot in Shelby County. Now, what do *you* think?"

"I think it explains why the sheriff got here so lickety-split."

"This a local girl, Wendy. It's different."

"It's a white girl. That's why it's different."

Geneva was watching them all from her back door, standing beside her cook, who had his arms folded across the front of his stained apron, a line of irritation set in his tightly closed lips as he watched the sheriff and his men. The deputies were taking notes: glancing every so often toward Geneva's and jotting things down. Darren had seen the look on the cook's face on other black men before: a weary impatience to get it over with—the frisking, the talking-to, the interrogation, the inevitable moment in the spotlight. What you always knew was coming.

And sure enough, the sheriff came walking up then, nodding first to the white man standing by Wendy. "Wally, y'all gon' have to let us do our deal out here."

"Sure thing, Parker," Wally said.

The men were on a first-name basis, and the deference seemed to be going wholly in the wrong direction. Darren found it unseemly the way the sheriff tilted his head up to Wally, looking like a nervous schoolboy checking to see that he hadn't stepped on any toes. The sheriff then nodded toward the back of the cafe.

"Geneva," he said.

She gave a terse nod. "Sheriff Van Horn."

"You get that list to me soon as you can, while your mind is still fresh. Those you remember was in your place last night, and those you don't know by name you can just write a description. But we need that list right away."

Wendy spoke up. "Aw, hell, everybody know Missy was coming out of Wally's icehouse last night."

"We don't know anything at this point."

"Wendy, go on and let them do what they got to do back there," Geneva said. "The sooner they get her out of here, the better this gon' be for everybody. You call her parents, Sheriff?" she said softly. "She has a son, you know."

"I know it." Sheriff Van Horn sighed and ran a hand through his thinning hair. He was in his fifties or thereabouts, squat and built like an aging ballplayer, thick through the neck and broad across his back. "Her people stay in Timpson, but I got my men working on making contact. Keith left the mill soon as he heard. We gon' need a proper identification on the body, so—"

Geneva shuddered a little, but her voice came firm. "It's *her*."

"From family, ma'am. We'll need an identification from the family."

"Of course." Geneva nodded, her head as heavy as if she were carrying driftwood across her neck, and Darren knew at once that she'd been the one to find her. Van Horn went back to the work at hand, including attending to a coroner's van that had just arrived, pulling around from the front of the cafe, tooting its horn to warn deputies out of the way as it bumped over the uneven ground. Wally took in the macabre scene playing out before them, then turned and started for the cafe. "I'm sorry as hell about this, Geneva, I am. You ain't need this kind of trouble," he said, suggesting that trouble was for sure coming, by rules none of them had written. "You know I'll try to protect you if I can."

He started for the cafe's back door.

Geneva held up a hand to stop him. "No, you not going through the back door like you own the damn place," she said. "You go around to the front like everybody else. Don't care who your daddy was."

6.

DARREN PASSED through the cafe's front door a few steps behind Wally, who took the only open seat at the counter. Only he didn't sit, just hovered, like a bear over found food in the woods. There was a proprietary quality in his wide stance, his ostrich boots planted on the linoleum floor about two feet apart, his thick liver-spotted hands gripping the edge of the countertop. Tim, the young trucker, got as far away from him as he could, sliding off his stool and into an open booth near the window, leaving Huxley, the older man, eyeing Wally over the lenses of his reading glasses. Geneva, without so much as a nod from Wally, slid an empty coffee cup in front of him and poured from an orange-topped carafe that sat next to the domed glass display of pastries, square tea cakes, and turnovers that Darren took for fried pies, like the ones he scrounged up nickels for as a kid. Wally thanked her for the coffee, and Geneva gave him a slight but not unfriendly nod. Darren was struck by the peculiar rhythm between the two. As Wally reached for his wallet to pay, Geneva had already counted out change for the twenty she seemed to know would materialize from

Wally's sterling money clip. There was a familiarity there that was well worn yet reserved.

Wallace Jefferson III, as Darren would come to find out, owned that odd redbrick house across the highway and had a view of Geneva Sweet's Sweets from his front parlor. "Damn shame, all of this," Wally said, his voice coated in nicotine. "This highway is starting to pull in all kinds of trash. I can tell you right now, it don't look good to Van Horn and his men that that gal washed up in your backyard. You keep all kinds of company in here, truckers from as far north as Chicago, Detroit, and down to Laredo. Any one of them could have had their hands up in this. They talking Missy mighta been raped."

"You have a phone I can use?" Darren asked.

"What's wrong with the one in your hand?" Geneva said, nodding at his cell phone. Her earlier affection, so freely given when dinner was being served, had faded. She looked at him now as if she couldn't figure why he was still there. He'd eaten and paid and was not kin to her or a friend. She was busy filling salt and pepper shakers and in a bitter mood that had snuck up like a flash flood.

"Out of battery," he said.

"All our brains gon' be out of battery one day, fooling with them things," Wendy said as she entered from the kitchen. She'd followed Geneva in through the back door and now took a seat in the vinyl straight-backed chair parked in a corner behind the counter, lowering herself with a sigh. Geneva pointed with a pepper shaker toward a pay phone tucked in a corner of the cafe, behind a polyester curtain with pictures of ducks on it. Darren thanked her and crossed the room, having to say "Excuse me" twice to get Tim to move his work boots, which were sticking out of the booth, so he could pass. Tim had picked up on Geneva's cooling reception of

Darren and decided to back her play, whatever it was. He took his sweet time clearing a path so Darren could pass.

Behind the curtain, on a small wooden shelf, was a phone book for Timpson and environs—as thin as an elementary school yearbook—just as Darren had guessed there would be. Better to happen upon a ready directory than alert the town that he was looking for somebody. He thumbed through, searching for Keith Dale, Missy Dale's husband and a former resident of the Texas State Penitentiary at Huntsville, as hot a bed for the Aryan Brotherhood of Texas as they come. It was the thinnest lead on a double homicide, more speculation than would justify a search warrant. Wasn't much he could do here without the badge, and he found himself missing its power.

He remembered the first time he'd seen one up close.

Darren was twelve when William Mathews became one of the first black Texas Rangers in the department's nearly two-hundred-year history. He had been shooting water pistols with the Gatney boys next door when his uncle rolled up in his blue GMC pickup truck one day and waved him over. He had a couple of case files he needed to pick up from the sheriff's station in nearby Shepherd.

Come and take a ride with me, son.

Darren's damp legs were sticky on the vinyl seat in the cab. He kept staring at the gun at Pop's side, a .357 with a grip made of real walnut, polished so that it caught a wink of sun coming through the passenger-side window as they rolled through the southern part of the county. Newly married, William was stationed in Huntsville while he and Naomi were raising a family in Houston. Clayton, who'd been in love with Naomi since the three of them were in grade school, had courted her hard for years, only to lose that romantic contest to his identical twin while he was away at law school. *I'm sorry, Clay,* Naomi had said when she and William announced their engagement. Clayton had stopped speaking to his brother and even banned William from the house in Camilla, where both men had been born. William missed his firstborn, as he called Darren, who hadn't been allowed to attend his swearing-in with the Rangers.

They listened to one side of a John Lee Hooker album on his tape deck, and William promised him an ice-cold Coke from the store in town. Darren took pride in waving to people as they passed, the kids who didn't have a Ranger for an uncle. But he visibly tensed as they passed the highway sign for Shepherd: POPULATION 1,674. His whole life he'd been told to avoid the place, which for as long as his uncles could remember had been a Klan stronghold in the county. Darren had been warned never to ride his bike on any road that led to Shepherd.

But the badge changed things.

The white deputies in town did a double take when William walked into the station. And they showed him a level of deference Darren had never seen from white men. They had no choice: William outranked every last one of them. To this day Darren believed his uncle took him on that ride to show him the power of the Rangers badge. William assumed even then that he would win the battle with Clayton over law school for Darren, just as he had won the battle for Naomi.

Darren heard Tim say, "We not gon' let them put this on us."

"Who's *us*, son?" Wally said. "You a Houston boy, ain't you?"

"Watch that *boy* shit."

"Y'all too touchy," Wally said, looking around at the half dozen black folks in the cafe. "That's exactly what Van Horn is afraid of, one of your people in here got it in they mind something's hinky about that other fella, the one who drowned—"

"You mean the one who was *killed*," Geneva said.

"Ain't a single damned piece of evidence on that, and you know it."

"We don't know anything. They ain't telling us nothing."

Darren found an address for Keith Dale, but absent a warrant, there was no legal way to get inside the man's house. A black man snooping without a badge was a straight B and E. He felt another stab of uncertainty about coming here. What in hell did he really think he was going to accomplish? He was on suspension, for God's sake. Without the badge, he was no one. *Go home.*

But the thirst was whispering at him, too. It was coming on five o'clock, and he wasn't sure he could make it all the way to Houston without a little something to take the edge off. One drink, two at the most.

"We ain't had nothing like this around here since Joe died," Huxley said.

"Which one?"

"That's enough, Tim," Geneva said quickly.

"This kind of crime," Wally said, "lot of people gon' be looking at this as a way to push you out. You let me know when you're ready to talk. My offer still stands. I'll make sure there's a way for you to stay a part of things."

"If I was gonna sell you this place, I'd have done it a long time ago."

Darren interrupted, leaning into the space between Huxley and Wally, elbows on the Formica countertop. He tried to make eye contact with Geneva before leaving; his home training demanded no less for her time and food. Plus, if she was writing lists of customers in and out of her place the last few days, he wanted to be remembered as utterly harmless. For a man traveling without his superiors' knowledge, he'd already drawn more attention to himself than he'd intended.

"Thank you, ma'am."

Geneva gave him nothing in return.

Wally said, "Told Laura I'd bring her something."

"We got peach and apple butter." Geneva motioned to the fried pies on display. "How many you want?"

"Four of the peach and two apple butter."

She lifted the heavy glass lid on the pastry case. "The apple butter's an experiment. I won't charge you for those."

Again Geneva had the change counted and ready before Wally could produce another twenty—his currency of choice, apparently, no matter the size of the check. Darren wondered if he kept a mountain of unused fives and tens in the cab of his seventy-thousand-dollar truck, dealer's tags still on the windshield, which he'd driven the twenty or so yards from his front door to Geneva's cafe. Outside, Darren walked past Wally's black Ford F-250, so polished he could see his own reflection, the haggard expression he wore at the end of a day that had started with such righteous fervor. He climbed into his nine-year-old Chevy, gunned the engine, and pulled out onto Highway 59, heading for the icehouse. The girl, Missy Dale, had worked there, so Darren could still convince himself he was trying to do some good out here, that he was still turning over stones.

7.

HE MADE sure to call Lisa before the first drink.

He was in his truck, in the parking lot of the icehouse, the setting sun warming the back window of the Chevy's cab. Tomorrow he would start over. These were the words he planned to tell his wife. He practiced as he counted the rings trilling in his ear, not knowing if she would even pick up. She was at work still, a good enough excuse to ignore him. But Darren knew Clayton had probably called Lisa the second he'd gotten off the phone with him this morning, his uncle spinning the talk with Darren to Lisa. *He's ready*. Darren only had to say it out loud. Their relationship had been this way from the beginning—a straight line between two people that often shape-shifted into a triangle where his uncle Clayton was concerned. He'd approved of Lisa almost from the second Darren had brought her home, driving her in his used Toyota Tercel to dinner all the way up to the house in Camilla, holding her hand once he got the car into fifth gear. Darren wanted Lisa to see who he was at his core: a country boy raised in the shade of pines who had never owned a horse but could ride any you put in front of him; a boy who had made red mud pies on the back porch with his cousin Rebecca every Christmas; a boy who'd shot a twelve-gauge years before his voice changed. Lisa's parents had a second home in Santa Fe; Darren's people had the old home place in Camilla, and he was as proud as the wild peacocks that roamed the edges of the property to share it with his girlfriend. Lisa smiled and ate parts of a hog previously unknown to her, brushing dirt off the green metal porch seat before sitting down to eat, and he loved her for the effort she made, mistaking it for a seedling, a passion for country living that would sprout under his care. Years later she laughed when he suggested they live there one day. Clayton, who'd driven from Austin, where he stayed during the fall and spring semesters, thought Lisa was perfect for Darren. And if there were any doubts during Lisa and Darren's bumpy road to matrimony—the years spent at different universities—Clayton was always there to tell Darren to push through the hard times. *You won't find another girl like this.* Which Darren heard as a compliment to Lisa but also as a soft doubt about Darren's potential as a husband. He, too, believed he'd never find someone who would love him as Lisa did.

"Darren," she said when she answered.

She said his name as a sigh, but it was a sound nearer to relief than exasperation. He heard something click against the phone, then a kiss of quiet, and he knew she'd removed her earring. She was settling in for him, a fact that cracked him wide open. "I miss you," he said, the words tumbling out of their own accord, like beads that had slipped through his clumsy fingers, scattering everywhere. In the silence that followed, they both seemed to hold their breath.

"Come home," she said.

It came with such ease that he wasn't sure what to say, if he could trust it.

"I was out of line to ask you to do any less for Mack than you'd sworn to do for anybody else who needed you. It's the job," she said. It came out sounding more like an accusation than a concession. "I was just scared. I *am* scared. I don't want to lose you." Which wasn't true, he'd decided during these past weeks apart. What Lisa didn't want was to *share* him—with duty, with midnight calls, with the whole state of Texas, strangers he'd pledged his allegiance to.

He knew he shouldn't love her more for this—the knot of stinginess in his wife's heart, the parts of him she wanted for herself—but he did. "If something happened to you," Lisa said, unable to bear the end of that sentence.

"It's the job," he said, repeating her words.

"I've been too rigid. I know I have."

Some part of him knew she was only saying this because she thought he was through with the Rangers, but he didn't care. He'd been waiting for weeks to hear those words, might even trade his badge for them. "I love you, Lisa."

She was not the only woman he'd been with—he'd been a sex-starved college student for many years, with a girlfriend more than a thousand miles away; things had happened that they'd both agreed not to talk about—but she was the only woman he'd ever loved. It didn't hurt that Clayton adored her.

He was embarrassed by how much that mattered to him.

"I don't like the drinking," she said, offering up a condition.

"It's under control," he said, sitting in the parking lot of a bar.

He was just going to have a look around, for his own peace of mind, before he left this little town. And you couldn't very well walk into a bar and not drink anything. He'd need a prop, after all.

A bourbon before him was just like the cigarette in Geneva's backyard, only this time he planned to inhale.

"I've got something I have to finish up here."

"Where are you?"

"Doing a little job for Greg."

"Greg," she said, the single syllable hard as a stone.

Darren didn't bothering digging around behind the icy tone. He was too close to home base. He laid out his plans: he'd turn in his badge tomorrow, as Lieutenant Wilson expected, and they'd all see what happened next, whether Mack was indicted or not and what that meant for Darren. Lisa never said a word about law school, no mention of anything beyond tomorrow, and he loved her for that.

"I love you, too," she said.

He felt so good he almost considered skipping the bar altogether and heading out now. Highway 59 was a straight shot down to Houston. He could be there in time for one of the shows Lisa liked to watch—*Scandal* or *Real Housewives of Somewhere* or whatever it was. But no: he had a drink waiting.

He'd been in and out of honky-tonks many times in his life, had a crush on a drill-team captain his sophomore year—before he and Lisa got serious—and he'd spent nearly every weekend that fall semester burning up gasoline driving to a stomphouse in Victoria, almost two hours outside the city, where kids from his high school could drink without anyone asking questions. He never did learn to two-step or get more than a peck on the cheek from the girl, who said he was cute, but her daddy would kill her if she brought home a black guy. The white kids from his high school were cool with him, though. They let him sit at their tables, even bought him a beer or two. It was everybody else that was the problem. The

women who rolled their eyes if he got too close on the dance floor;
the men who made sure to give him a little shove every time they
passed, muttering *nigger* or *coon* loud enough so he could hear; the
stares he got, menacing eyes peering at him from beneath the brim
of ball caps and cowboy hats. He felt the same eyes on him now as
he entered Jeff's Juice House.

There was a pool game going.

At least there had been before Darren walked in.

To a man, the players around the felt table, dressed in grass-
stained Wranglers—one of them was wearing a Cruz 2016
T-shirt—stood stiff as stone, cues in hand, eyeing the black man
who'd just stepped over the bar's threshold. The interior of the icehouse was like an oversize playroom, with a station for pool, two
pinball machines, a dartboard, and a jukebox that, unlike the ancient one in Geneva's, played CDs. And country music, of course.
George Strait was singing, "Easy come, girl, easy go." The Dixie
flag was on display all over, pinned to the walls beside highway
signs and posters for Luke Bryan and Lady Antebellum shows in
Dallas. It was a mostly male clientele, and there was one buxom
bartender on duty. She was a woman on the wrong side of forty,
with thin bark-brown hair and a decent face marred by what looked
like late-stage acne or a telltale sign of meth. East Texas had a saying for white women like this: *rode hard and put up wet.*

He approached the bar and ordered bourbon, neat, and she took
no time putting into words the animus he felt coming from every
corner of the icehouse.

"You lost?" she said.

"Not even a little bit," he said, hiking up his left hip as he
climbed onto a bar stool, making sure the leather holster holding
his .45 showed. The bartender relented with a scowl. Darren

watched her pour, making sure nothing extra found its way past the lip of his glass. When she slid the drink across to him, he lifted the glass and said, "To open carry." He left a twenty on the bar to show he meant to stay awhile, then turned and found a seat near the back of the room.

There was another girl on duty, a waitress dressed in cutoff jeans and a tight Jeff's Juice House T-shirt, the same uniform Missy must have been wearing when she was working last night. He glanced at the men around the bar, ages nineteen to fifty, and considered the bullish energy in the room, the smell of cigarettes and sweat, the tits and ass on display everywhere. Boobs on bikes, on the hood of a Corvette. There were pictures of nearly naked girls everywhere. Maybe no woman was safe leaving here alone. It had to be considered, he would tell Greg, who, if he could get a copy of the autopsies, could do a lot more for Michael Wright and Missy Dale than Darren could kicking dust around this town. He sat back and let the bourbon settle in, like hot butter through his veins, everything coming loose. A bathroom door opened behind him, and, not liking his back exposed, he turned and was shocked to see not only that the icehouse *had* a women's restroom but also that the woman coming out of it was black.

She was wiping stray beads of water from her face. Drops of it darkened to caramel on the winter-white coat she was wearing— not an item that, if you knew any better, you would ever wear in a place like this. Her pallor was almost gray, and she clutched a black Furla handbag against her side as she wove through the sticky tables, making eye contact with no one, including Darren, who did not for an instant take his gaze off her. Only a few times in a cop's career does he feel the kind of certainty that came over Darren in that moment.

The wife has been notified.

At a table across the room, she sat alone, spoke to no one, only stared at her surroundings—the Confederate flags, the white men nudging each other in her presence, the plates piled with pork and beans and toast the size of textbooks—as if she were trying to read street signs in a foreign country, as if she didn't know where she was or how she'd gotten here. Darren rose at once, almost without thinking. Until he arrived at her table, and she looked up at him not with relief but confusion, he'd forgotten he wasn't wearing a badge, forgot his limited role in this. "Are you okay?" he asked. Her response was lost in the music and electronic games and the two televisions set to *Monday Night Football*. He sat down across from her and watched her flinch. He said his name—naked, without a title. She nodded and said something he still couldn't make out, so he leaned in, close enough to see the slack skin under her eyes, which were red-rimmed and moist. She shook her head and said, "I don't know why I'm here," then stood hastily, knocking over a water glass with the edge of her purse. The water rolled in shallow waves across the tabletop and landed in Darren's lap. "I shouldn't have come," she said, moving toward the door that led to the porch and the parking lot. Darren grabbed her hand and stood to follow her out. "Don't touch me," she said, yanking herself free of him.

They'd created a scene by now.

The bartender nodded to a guy in a black shirt and a Steelers cap at the far end of the bar. He uncrossed his beefy, tattooed arms and started toward them. Michael Wright's wife pushed past Darren and marched toward the front door. He followed a few steps behind, chasing her through a room full of men who were all staring. Outside, the music faded, and a rig heading south roared past the icehouse, blanketing the parking lot in a cloud of exhaust. The sun was gone, and the bar's neon sign painted the ground amber and a bluish white, the name of the icehouse reflected in the windshields of the pickup trucks in the lot.

Darren was at the bottom of the porch steps when he heard the sound of boots behind him. He turned to see the big guy in the Steelers cap now guarding the front door. "Go on and get," he said, pronouncing it *git* and shooing them as if they were stray dogs. "Both of you, go on and get the hell out of here."

Darren scanned the parking lot, searching for her.

"Not looking for any trouble," he said to the man in the black T-shirt.

"Well, you in the wrong place, then."

The man stepped forward, just enough to catch light coming off the neon sign, enough for Darren to see the ink on his arms. He counted at least three marks that meant trouble. Matching crests on both biceps, outlined in black and topped with the letters *A* and *B* and shot through with a T-shaped dagger, dripping a tiny dot of blood. And a pair of SS lightning bolts on his left wrist.

The door behind the big dude opened, and four other men stepped out onto the porch. Darren recognized at least one of them from the halted pool game. Two of them were strapped. So was Darren, of course, but he was grossly outnumbered. He knew even a gesture in the general direction of his holster would get him—and maybe Michael Wright's wife, too—killed in a matter of seconds. She'd come up from behind him then. "I want to know what happened," she said, her voice rougher than it was before. She was speaking to the men standing sentry in front of the icehouse. There was an accusation in there somewhere. Darren heard it, and he knew the mob on the porch did, too. He held out an arm to stop her from coming any closer to the men, who would cut her in two as soon as look at her.

"Someone here knows something," she said.

Chicago, Darren remembered suddenly.

She has no idea where she is.

She was dressed in clothes that, as Darren knew from living with Lisa, cost a lot of money, including that white cashmere coat. It was October cool, by Texas standards, but the coat was too much, and she was starting to sweat, that gray pallor spreading across her face from her hairline down. She wore it loose, waves of it in a bob that fluffed in the humid air. He looked directly into her eyes, which were round and wide and the same shade of amber he met in a glass most nights.

"Don't do this," Darren whispered.

"Someone must have seen something," she said. There were actual tears now, twin streams running down the sides of her face. "What did you all do to him?" She marched past Darren to the foot of the stairs, where she was met by one of the men from the pool game. He was in his early thirties, his icy blue eyes red-rimmed and desperate, shooting his own tear-streaked rage from beneath the bill of his ball cap. He wasn't going to let her talk anymore, if he had to lay hands on her to stop it. He reached out as if to grab her.

"Keith!"

The beefed-up man in black stomped down the steps, coming up behind him, putting a suppressing hand on the smaller man's shoulder. *Keith.* The name tickled the hairs at the back of Darren's neck. Was this Keith Dale?

"Lady, you need to quit all that hollering and listen to your man here," the tattooed man in black said, making cheap assumptions about the two black people in front of him. Behind him, one of the armed men lifted the flap on his holster as he, too, came down the steps. By Darren's calculation, the night was about sixty seconds from taking a very bad turn. This woman did not seem to understand in the least what those tattoos meant. But she saw and understood the guns, and for the first time he felt her backing up behind him. He needed to get her out of here right now, away from these men, hopped up on hate and suddenly gifted with a physical target for their rage: a black woman talking too much. Darren's truck was close enough for him to say, "Get in."

He grabbed her by the elbow, guiding her to the Chevy.

"I have a rental car."

"Where?"

"I parked . . ."

She scanned the lot as if she couldn't remember which American-made sedan was hers. Ford, Chevy, Chrysler—they all looked the same to her. She was panicked and confused about which way to go, the tears blurring everything.

"Leave it."

As he opened the passenger-side door to his truck, she said, "I'm not getting in a car with you." Her hands were shaking as she fished for her rental-car keys.

He leaned into the Chevy's cab and opened his glove box so that in the light from the icehouse his badge shone. The familiar words rolled out, and he felt the same swell of purpose as he had the very first time he'd said them. "My name is Darren Mathews, ma'am," he said. "And I'm a Texas Ranger."

8.

HER NAME was Randie Winston, and she'd gotten the call three days ago—from her agent, actually, who'd reached her in Saint Albans, outside London, where she'd been on assignment, photographing a spread for British *Vogue*. She'd been traveling nonstop ever since—a train ride into London, then an eight-hour flight to New York, where she had to change planes to get to Dallas, because she'd been told it was closer to the Shelby County sheriff's office where she was to meet Sheriff Parker Van Horn. Except it wasn't the sheriff who'd greeted her at the tiny station in Center, Texas—another three-hour drive on top of the twelve hours she'd been traveling—but a deputy who couldn't have been a day over nineteen, the class ring on his right hand cutting into the extra pounds he'd put on since graduation. He'd been sucking down a gas-station chili dog when she walked in, and he nearly choked when she gave her name. "Michael Wright's wife," she said, the last word nearly swallowed by a sob that rose in her throat.

She and Michael had been separated for more than a year, but she was his wife until the end, dropping everything and arriving with only the clothes she'd been working in. She was a fashion photographer, rather sought after around the world, and the cashmere and fine jewelry that suited her world marked her as an outsider here. Her camera equipment was still in the rental car, and Darren told her repeatedly that he would get it, walk the six miles back to the icehouse if he had to. He'd gotten them rooms for the night at a motel up the highway a piece from Lark. She was shaking by the time the truck hit the highway, leaving the icehouse in Darren's rearview. In the front seat of the truck, exhaustion and grief collapsed her limbs. She was going on fumes by then.

The motel was a ten-room horseshoe-shaped building with a neon sign atop a twenty-foot tower made of old tires. The Lucky Ten, it was called. The desk clerk in the lobby offered them two rooms without Darren having to ask, her eyes sliding between the wedding band on his left hand and the one that was clearly missing from Randie's. The clerk had what could only be a home permanent, the curls tight and dry and the color of tarnished silver. She was in her sixties and wore a gold cross around her mottled neck, and she made sure they each had only one key. Darren had given Randie the room with the bigger bed. She was sitting on the edge of it now, facing the thick yellow curtains.

Darren was in a straight-backed chair cushioned in dark green vinyl. He kept both boots dug into the thick pile carpeting, kept his hands where she could see them, and took no notes. He wanted her to know she was safe.

"So the sheriff never talked to you?"

"He was out of the office," she said.

She'd peeled off the coat and was sitting in jeans and a gray T-shirt, and Darren saw how thin she was. Her shoulders were hunched, and she'd pulled her hair back so that he saw more of her face now. Darren knew Van Horn had been in Lark this afternoon, but he said nothing. He hadn't mentioned the other death or the name Missy Dale, and he wouldn't now—not yet, at least.

He could hear semis passing every few minutes on 59, late-night hollers down the highway followed by pockets of quiet when nothing moved out there, when there was no sound but the whir of tree frogs in the surrounding woods.

"I met with one of his deputies," she said. "He laid out a plastic bag containing my husband's things, saying 'I'm sorry' and 'The body is in Dallas' and a lot of other stuff I can't really remember. And then he asked me to ID him from a photo."

"What things?"

She turned and felt along the bedcover for her purse. From inside she pulled a small plastic bag, cloudy with condensation, packed more sloppily than a cop ought to wrap his lunch let alone potential evidence. *Drowning,* the official autopsy report had said. But according to Greg, the medical examiner had stumbled over the *manner* of death, whether what happened to Michael Wright was a homicide. Darren felt the question in the air. It was in the foul odor coming through the plastic bag, the stink of the bayou wafting over this case. He had latex gloves in his truck, a whole box of them. But he wouldn't leave her right now. Instead he inspected what he could through the plastic. Inside there was a wallet, black leather, waterlogged and swollen; a gold band, not unlike the one on Darren's hand, the one he'd worn as a gesture of hope to the courthouse this morning; and a BMW key chain, a leaf, black and torn, stuck in the grooves of the silver ring, which held half a dozen keys. All of it weighed less than a pound, what was left of Michael Wright. "This is what they found on his body," she said. "He'd been in the bayou for a few days before being discovered, and he was swollen almost beyond recognition." Her voice caught. She swallowed and tried to go on. "It was the wallet—that's how I knew it was Michael," she said. "I bought it for him our last Christmas together." She started to cry again, softly and with a sense of deflation, oxygen leaking out slowly as she sank into herself, salty tears falling.

Darren walked to the bathroom, where a box of pulpy, hard tissues sat inside a plastic holder covered in an array of rose decals, pink and red. He brought over the whole thing and sat it beside her on the bed before resuming his seat a few feet away from her. Boots back on the ground, his hands visible, sitting beneath a framed ranch landscape, steers painted black and brown.

Randie blew her nose. "It's just that what he said made no sense."

"The deputy told you something other than drowning?"

"He said the sheriff thinks Michael was robbed."

This was the first Darren had heard this. "Robbed?"

"That he was coming out of the icehouse that night. The sheriff's deputy said he might have been drunk."

Based on what? Darren thought, remembering that, by Greg's telling, there hadn't been a word about an unusual blood alcohol level in the autopsy report, which Darren now suddenly wanted to get his hands on.

She grabbed another tissue. "But his credit cards are still in his wallet."

"You touched it?" he said, even though one glance at the bag told him it didn't matter. Any evidence on these items had already been destroyed.

"I opened it right in front of the deputy. Credit cards and more than a hundred dollars in cash. Maybe someone took his watch, or maybe it fell off in the water. But how could he have been robbed if his wallet wasn't touched?"

"The car," he said, not because he believed it, necessarily, but any cop would have to consider it. Randie looked at him, surprised that he guessed.

She nodded. "Michael was in a 'real nice car,' as the deputy put it, like that itself was a crime, and he said that somebody might have jumped Michael for it."

"But his car key is here," Darren said.

"He kept a spare in the glove box. Anybody could have gotten hold of it," Randie explained. "Michael wasn't from around here, so they think he got lost—on foot, probably, walking in the woods—then fell into the bayou. The car will turn up eventually, they said." She shook her head. "But you saw that place. Michael would never even walk into a place like that."

The same place where Missy Dale worked, Darren thought.

"How was your marriage?" he asked, offhand.

"How's yours?" she said.

It was the first time he saw the woman behind the tears, the way her eyes, though wide, could narrow to twin points of outrage, the way her jaw squared in the lamplight. She resented the question. He didn't particularly like it being lobbed in his direction, either. "You said 'separated,' that's all," he said.

"He cheated on me."

She said it matter-of-factly, then left the awkward silence for him to fill.

"I'm sorry," he said quickly, realizing too late that this was the first condolence he'd offered, and it was for the fact that her husband was fucking another woman.

"I'm sorry," he said again, this time for the social fumble. But she waved it off, then grew quiet, looking down at her naked ring finger. "So you left him?"

"No," she said. She wasn't crying anymore, but her voice was strangled with regret. "I didn't *do* anything. I didn't divorce him, but I didn't forgive him, either. I didn't leave, but I didn't stay, either. I went to work for months on end, took every assignment I could get my hands on, kept as far away as I could."

"Did you love him?"

"Does it matter?"

She was, he saw more clearly now, a beautiful woman, and he couldn't understand a universe in which a man who had the love of a woman like that would fuck around. But he had to broach the question. He still didn't know why Michael had come to Texas on his own. "Was he still seeing other women?"

"Michael and I haven't spoken in months," she said with a formality that hadn't been there before, a cold shoulder in Darren's direction.

"Do you know why he drove here? A thousand miles from Chicago?"

She glanced at the edge of the bed, where the plastic bag of her husband's possessions was still resting. The answer wasn't there.

"What was in Lark?"

"I have no idea," she said. In the seven years they'd been together, Randie said, Michael had never once taken her to his hometown, which she mistakenly believed was a few towns over, confusing Timpson and Tyler.

Darren thanked her, told her he had some deer jerky and crackers in his truck and that she was welcome to them, since the clerk had said the motel's vending machines were locked after midnight. Randie said she was starving and not picky. "Thank you." She managed a wan smile, a reflexive expression of gratitude that women can muster even when they're in pain. But when Darren rose from his chair and started for the door, she leaped off the bed and grabbed his arm, a look of wild panic on her face, as if she thought he might not come back. Her fingers dug into the muscle above his elbow. "You're going to find out what happened to him? Because I did love him—I did," she said, pleading for him to believe her, as if he might not help if she didn't love him. "You're going to find out who did this, right? I mean, that's why they sent you, right?"

Darren couldn't bring himself to tell her that no one had actually sent or asked for him, that she was the only one in the world who wanted him there.

Because right then, that was enough.

"Get some rest," he said, patting her on the arm. "I'm not leaving you."

He texted Lisa only after he knew she'd be asleep. Any conversation about his not coming home would have to wait until tomorrow. Randie had passed out after tearing through a package of saltines, and he'd closed her hotel room door softly, her rental-car keys in his other hand. Then he waited. Outside room 9, he stood watch, leaning against the slim patch of stucco between their two rooms, his gaze traveling between the parking lot, which was empty save for his truck, and the four-lane highway beyond until he was satisfied that no one was on the hunt—the thugs from the bar or anyone else who by then knew the wife was in town. It was as safe as it would get before sunrise, he knew, but he waited another hour to be sure, figuring, correctly, that no bar in East Texas stayed open past the devil's hour of 2:00 a.m. Then he took off for the highway.

He went out on foot, Maglite in hand, .45 on his hip, and the half-full pint of Wild Turkey tucked in his back pocket. It was only enough bourbon to leave him wanting more, but it was better than nothing. It made the night sky feel low, stars dusting the top of the pines like snow. The air had a cool bite to it now, and he regretted not wearing his jacket, but he needed the white shirt to keep him alive, a torso-size reflector for any headlights passing at seventy miles an hour. He stayed to the shoulder, mostly, crunching on gravel and dirt underfoot, his ear open for the sound of any restless wildlife in the woods flanking the highway. This time of night, the semis were few and far between, and in the hush of the country, his mind cleared. He took a swig or two of the bourbon—for warmth and, he could admit, courage. Staying in Lark would cost him something; he knew that going in. He just didn't know *what*. Nor could he figure what it was about these murders that bothered him so much. Something about their supposed simplicity— homicide theories that rolled out effortlessly, buoyed by the waves of hundreds of years of history—made Darren suspicious.

It started with the order of the killings: black man dies, *then* the white girl. It didn't fit any agreed-upon American script, didn't match the warnings he'd gotten from his uncles about fooling around with white girls or even making an off-color remark in their direction, and it suggested a level of vengeance for the murder of Michael—a stranger in Lark—on the part of black folks in town that didn't make much sense. At Geneva's, he'd felt no vitriol from her customers toward anyone but the law enforcement lurking behind the cafe, and he heard not one bad word about Missy Dale. In fact Geneva had spoken kindly about the young woman's child. Tim, the trucker, had seemed equally concerned. It was Wally, frankly, who was positing that Missy had died as a result of some bad feelings on the part of black folks in Lark, that her murder followed that of Michael Wright as a matter of causation and not happenstance. Well, Wally *and* Sheriff Van Horn—who had asked

Geneva for a list of the men and women who'd been inside her cafe last night—were thinking along those lines. He heard Greg's voice in his head, was reminded of his tribe's reluctance to give in to the idle power of *coincidence*—the tribe of law enforcement, that is. But cops digging where nothing was buried could lead to its own set of problems. And the more he thought about it, the more he thought it was entirely possible that someone had seen a late-model BMW and jacked Michael for it, leaving him alone and dazed on a dark night like this one. It was possible he *had* gotten lost. At least it had to be considered. And the issue of Missy, and the awful manner in which she was found, might have nothing to do with Michael Wright and everything to do with the clientele at the icehouse, the rough characters she worked around, any of whom might have a jacket full of rape charges. *It had to be considered,* he told himself again, even as his doubt lingered.

It was near six miles to the icehouse, and his feet ached inside the soles of his boots, a pecan-colored pair of cowhide ropers that would split if he asked them to make this walk again. He was glad to see the rental car, a blue two-door Ford, sitting alone in the darkened parking lot. The neon sign had been put to bed, and the lights inside were likewise dark for the night. He'd been prepared to find the car vandalized, but it looked in order, and through the windows his flashlight lit up Randie's bags in the backseat, including a black camera case. He'd grown damp with sweat on the walk, and as soon as he turned the engine over, he rolled down the windows and let a little air hit him in the face as he drove.

He didn't go back to the motel, though, not yet.

He left the parking lot heading in the opposite direction, his knees practically pressed to his chest in the tiny car as he crept along 59. He found the turnoff for FM 19, a farm road that led through the woods from the highway to the Attoyac Bayou, which ran behind both Geneva's cafe and Wally's icehouse—with only a distance of about a quarter mile between the two establishments and their two different worlds. Down the farm road, Darren bumped along the sliver of pavement, which had no dividing line, small-town folks being accustomed to yielding to courtesy. Through the floorboard he felt every bump in the road and every crack in the asphalt, his head nearly touching the car's ceiling every few seconds. He got about fifty yards down the road before rolling the car to a stop. The driver's-side door creaked as he opened it, the only sound in the dark save for crickets and tree frogs chirruping together in song. He was walled in on two sides by sky-scraping pines, dwarfing him and the tiny Ford, gnats and night beetles dancing in the light of the car's high beams. As an experiment, he reached through the car window and shut off the headlights. The dark was extraordinary, thick enough to touch, a velvet quilt of black stitched through with stars, tiny knots of light barely bright enough to let you see your hand in front of your face. Darren knew Michael had been found back here, a stone's throw from the ice-house, but what was Michael doing on this road in the first place?

If the sheriff's theory held any water, there was no way Michael's car was stolen from the icehouse parking lot. Michael was a smart man, graduated law school, for God's sake. Surely he would have just walked the relatively well-lit highway back to Geneva's. No, something had gotten Michael on this farm road, and this is where he got jacked for the car. *Had to be.* At this hour, without a passing car on the highway—headlights showing the way out of these woods—it was possible to lose your bearings in the dark, to get twisted and turned around, especially after a few drinks. Darren would put himself at a .09 right now, just fuzzy enough for a man of his habits to have a sense that he ought to stop but not at all drunk enough by his standards to miss the problem with the sheriff's theory. If he stood still enough, he could actually hear the water.

The bayou was in front of him, he realized, maybe fifty yards from where he was standing. If Michael was left without a vehicle and stranded out here alone, why would he walk toward a body of water he couldn't see? No one in his right mind would do what Darren was doing now: walk through a thick of dark woods he didn't know his way around. But walking toward the unknown was what he'd signed up for, and he hadn't turned in his badge yet.

He walked straight ahead, past where the farm road curved to the south, and continued straight ahead into raw woodland; he was following the tinkling sound of the bayou. He ducked beneath low-hanging branches, pushing the larger ones out of his way, one hand still on his pocket-size flashlight, its weak beam no match for the thickening woods. He had the thought to turn around and turn the Ford's headlights back on for guidance, what a man at a .05 would have known made a hell of a lot more sense than walking blindly in the dark. It was as he turned back to the car, the sloppy pivot of his left foot, that he slipped. The drop wasn't deep, but the shock of it made it impossible to stop the fall. He twisted his body as he went down, turning to claw at the earth to stop the slide into the water, but he couldn't gain enough purchase and lost his flashlight in the process. He went into the bayou boots first, shooting in horizontally and feeling the water seep across the front of his body.

He closed his eyes just in time, but still the water burned.

He clamped his mouth shut and felt so starved for air that he had to beat back panic through sheer force of will. *I'm not dying here tonight.* He moved his arms in some approximation of a breaststroke, keeping his body afloat. One kick of his legs was all it took for his right foot to hit the bed of the bayou. Darren felt his toe jam up against the inside of his boot. With the pain came a bolt of realization. *Just stand, man. Just stand.* Within seconds, Darren was on his feet, the bayou water coming no higher than the tops of his thighs, and he knew there was no way Michael Wright had walked into the bayou on his own and drowned.

Part Three

9.

HE WOKE up cotton-mouthed, his eyes still burning. His cell phone was shrieking at him from the bedside table, where it sat beside the gun he'd disassembled last night and left on a motel towel to dry. *Lisa,* he thought.

But it was worse, much worse.

Wilson, his lieutenant, was calling from Company A headquarters in Houston, and he was in his ear before Darren could even clear his throat to say, *Morning, sir.* "What in hell is this I'm hearing about a double homicide in Lark?" Darren sat up, mumbled, "Sir," and was immediately cut off. "First of all, no one from Shelby County called for an assist. Two, that's Tom Randall's beat. And three, and most goddamned important here, you're on suspension, Ranger."

Darren glanced at the clock. It was past seven. He'd meant to be up hours ago. He thought about the wife in the other room—ransacked his brain for a minute trying to remember her name—and wondered if she was okay, if she'd woken up frightened and alone. *Randie.* He nearly whispered it.

"Tell me you're not in Shelby County right now," Wilson said. "Please tell me I don't have to call the captain and tell him not to bother weighing your fate, to just go ahead and fire your ass for insubordination."

Wilson had hired him eight years ago, championing his promotion from state trooper to Texas Ranger, even going to bat for him against members of the top brass who didn't think Darren had the soul of a Ranger, that Princeton and law school would burden him with a level of intellect and self-consciousness that wouldn't serve him in the field, where instinct often ruled and the simplest conclusion was nearly always the right one, especially when it came to murders in rural Texas, which are nearly always preceded by someone proclaiming to anyone within earshot of the local watering hole that *Some things just need killing.*

Wilson had served in Company A with Darren's uncle when William became one of the first black Texas Rangers in the department. He thought the world of William and the Mathews name and pushed for Darren's ascendancy, suggesting that the company keep him at headquarters, in Houston, where he could work in the department's Public Corruption Unit, investigating crimes for which paperwork was everything. Darren had been bored and restless, and he'd begged to get on the ABT task force and always felt like Wilson treated him differently after that, that he'd somehow let down his biggest booster by so nakedly proclaiming his interest in black life, his feeling that some crimes mattered more than others. The meth and the guns were one thing, but in his heart he knew he wanted to destroy the Aryan Brotherhood of Texas for different reasons. And Wilson knew it, too.

"We had a deal, Mathews," Wilson said, his voice strained to the point of near breathlessness. It occurred to Darren that Wilson was trying to keep his voice down in the office, that news hadn't yet spread and Darren might still be able to save himself. "I was expecting you to walk into my office this morning."

"How did you know?" Darren said.

He had a sudden, panicked thought that Greg had said something. It was paranoid, disloyal thinking, the hangover talking. He stood and walked to the room's sink, which sat outside the actual bathroom. He cupped water in his right hand and sucked it down, drops of it wetting the front of his undershirt.

"The wife," Wilson said. "She has some media contacts."

"She's a photographer."

"Right. Well, she called somebody at the *Chicago Tribune*, and I get a call this morning, not ten minutes ago, from a reporter asking about a suspicious death, and I don't know what in hell he's talking about, except he mentions your name and asks if the Rangers are investigating a hate crime, something the local sheriff out there is trying to cover up. What in hell have you started, Mathews?"

"It's a drowning that ain't a drowning, I can tell you that much."

"I know the sheriff out there. Parker's a good cop."

"Then let me talk to him," Darren said. "Let me do my job." He was asking for something more than a ten-minute talk with Van Horn, and they both knew it. It was the thing that hadn't been discussed on the phone with his wife yesterday—the fact that his conscience might not let him quit, that the badge was who he'd become, the only way he knew to navigate his life as a Texan. "It's not just the one," he said. "The black man. There's another body, a girl, white and local. She washed up out of the same bayou just a few days later. Michael Wright was at the icehouse where the girl worked on the night he disappeared."

It was quiet on Wilson's end of the line, and Darren knew he was taking that in—no one in law enforcement would hear those details and not know there was more to this story. Darren slid in for a home run. "And listen, if you got the *Tribune* already thinking there's a black Ranger out here investigating the unexplained death of one of his own, it'll sure as shit look bad if I up and leave now that folks' imaginations have been stirred. Let me dig around, see what I can put together about both murders. I'll report to you daily, I promise."

"Daily?" Wilson balked. "How long you planning to be out there?"

"As long as it takes."

"I want you out of there inside a week. You check in with me every day, Mathews. I don't hear from you, I'm taking this whole thing up to the captain and let him deal with your ass."

"What about the grand jury? You hear anything?"

Wilson sighed at what he considered Darren's inappropriate level of interest in the Rutherford McMillan case, what he believed had gotten Darren into trouble in the first place. *Never should have gone out there, son.* He'd said it more than once. Unlike others, he did not believe that Darren had actually hidden evidence to protect Mack, or if he did believe it, he wasn't saying so. Darren was William Mathews's boy, and that was worth the benefit of the doubt every time.

"No bill of indictment...yet," Wilson said. "No word either way."

Darren felt relief and dread in equal measure. He wondered how Mack and Breanna were holding up. Even before Darren testified, Mack was already talking about selling his place, asking Darren to look after his granddaughter if he got sent away. *Make sure she finishes school.* The money from the house and his truck should get her through senior year, he'd said. *Promise me, Darren.*

"I'll give Sheriff Van Horn in Shelby County a call," Wilson said. "Let him know you're only there to help."

"I'll need a copy of that autopsy."

"Put in a request through the sheriff," Wilson said. "Follow protocol and keep his defenses down. Don't go in there shaking your fist and making a lot of noise about hate crimes and the like until we know for sure what this is. I'm serious, Darren," he said before adding, "And get that wife under control."

He'd have to find her first.

The rental car was gone from the parking lot, and there was absolute silence when he knocked on the door to her room. The front-desk clerk would answer none of his questions, including the most basic one: how did Randie get the keys to the rental car from his room when the only other person with access to Darren's room was the desk clerk herself? "I don't get in people's business, but if a lady says a man's got her car keys, and she can't leave, well, I don't believe in standing idly by. I watch *Dateline*." She'd apparently let herself in, with Randie waiting just outside the room, and had gone through Darren's pants while he was passed out. "I want your things out of that room right now. I don't want your kind around here," she said, the gold cross on her neck catching the morning sun through the front window. He had a thought to flash the badge, to make a stink, but he'd just promised his boss he wouldn't. He paid for one night, tried to cover the cost of Randie's room, too, but the clerk wouldn't let him.

"Did she check out?" he asked, alarmed by the idea of her roaming the town alone.

"Wouldn't tell you if she did," the woman said. "You got ten minutes."

Darren took a hot and fast shower to rid himself of the lingering bayou stink, then he dressed and reassembled the Colt .45, got in his truck, and went looking for her.

The icehouse parking lot was already half full at eight thirty in the morning, but the blue Ford was not in the parking lot, nor did he find the car down the road apiece in the lot out front of Geneva's cafe. When he pulled in near the gas pump to turn his truck around, he saw a familiar tableau through the cafe's front windows—Geneva behind the counter, Wendy dressed colorfully atop one of the red vinyl stools, and Huxley with his newspaper. The glint off the chrome trim on Darren's Chevy caught Geneva's attention. She looked up, saw Darren behind the wheel of the truck, and frowned. Darren reversed gears and started back on the highway. He'd covered what little constituted Lark's main drag. Only place left were the back roads. As soon as he had the thought, he knew where the widow had gone. The unmarked grave of her husband.

He turned off Highway 59 and onto FM 19, the farm-to-market road that led to the water. He came upon the Ford so fast he had to slam on his brakes to keep from hitting the hatchback's rear end. He threw the truck into Park and hopped out, the soles of his boots still damp from last night's slip and fall. There was no one in the driver's seat, and he didn't find her until he left the paved farm road on foot, walking through the same stand of trees he'd nosed through last night. By daylight, he saw clearly the line where the bank dropped steeply and the bayou water licked and softened the shoreline a few feet below. Randie was standing too close to the edge for Darren's comfort. She had a black camera in hand, with a lens, both literal and figurative, pointed toward the water, as if the camera were the only way she could understand what she was seeing.

Darren crunched twigs under his boot heels, making sure she

would hear him coming. "You scared me," he said, "taking off like that."

Randie turned to face him, red-eyed with rage. She was wearing the same ridiculous white coat, now dotted with leaves and dirt from her trek through the thicket. She was wearing the same black jeans and gray T-shirt, the same high-heeled ankle boots, which were now mud-caked and damp. "You lied to me," she said.

"Listen, Randie—"

"You're not even a cop."

"That's not true."

"I have a contact at the *Tribune* who said that no one from the Rangers was assigned to investigate what happened to Michael. I called the Rangers officer myself and was told that Darren Mathews is 'currently on suspension.'"

"Not anymore," he said, feeling a guilty gratitude for this woman whose loss had put his life back on course. "I spoke to my lieutenant this morning, and I'm in this now. I'm investigating your husband's death."

She shoved past him, walking back to her rental car, her heels sinking in the soft earth. "And what did you do to my car? The seat was wet this morning. I found a bottle on the floor, and it smells fucking terrible." Darren reached for her hand to steady her on the uneven ground. "Get away from me," she said.

"He didn't drown, Randie."

She stopped and turned back toward him, the distance between them less than a foot, the land studded with pinecones in the dirt. The wind around them lifted, but Randie stood perfectly still, hardened in places that were weak with hurt the night before. He guessed she needed a place for her anger to land, and he was as good a target as any. She continued on to her car as if she hadn't heard him. He followed closely behind, wanting her to trust and believe him, to know that he was more than the man she saw before her, more than the wrinkled, stained pants and the empty pint in her car. "Michael didn't drown."

"You're saying he was killed."

She knew it, but saying the words aloud seemed to cut her in new places.

Darren nodded grimly. "There was a woman, too."

"What are you talking about?"

"Another murder," he said.

She looked astonished but also terrified, shivering as she pulled the sides of her coat more tightly around her. The morning was still stiff and cool, the sky a slate gray, the low light making the world over in black and white.

"She was pulled out of the bayou behind Geneva's yesterday—"

"Where?" she asked, confused.

"A white girl was killed, too." He needed to make that part clear.

"You knew this and didn't tell me?"

"I had just gotten here myself, wasn't sure what I was dealing with."

"Did Michael..." She lost her words for a second. "Did he know her?"

"I don't know," Darren said. "But she worked at the icehouse where the sheriff said your husband was drinking on Wednesday night. I don't know that those two things are related, but I've been doing this long enough to guess that the answer is yes."

Randie fell silent. Darren could hear the faint ripple of wind across the bayou, the kiss of tree leaves falling and skimming the surface of the water.

"How do I know you're telling the truth?" she said. "About the Rangers letting you investigate this?"

"You can call if you want. Lieutenant Fred Wilson, Company A in Houston. He's already set up a meeting between me and the sheriff."

Her spine stiffened at once. "I want to be there."

Darren started to object, but Randie held firm. "I'm going," she said.

Get the wife under control.

But Darren had a different idea. *Get the wife some protection. Get the wife some help. Get the wife the answer she deserves.* If he were Michael Wright, Darren would have wanted someone to do the same for his wife. "I'll drive," he said.

10.

SHERIFF PARKER Van Horn had temporarily set up a satellite office right in Wally Jefferson's living room, where Darren had been told he was expecting them. But when they rolled up to the sprawling home, Darren didn't see a squad car in the circular driveway among the line of luxury cars parked there, which included two Lincolns, a Cadillac, and a Chrysler. The land on which Wally's house stood stretched over many acres and was manicured on its face—with a crisp green lawn and puffs of red hydrangeas planted along the house's facade—but was backed by raw countryside creeping up behind the property.

Darren parked next to Wally's truck and heard Randie beside him let out a little puff of air. Not quite a laugh, but close. "You've got to be kidding me," she said, staring at the house. Darren took a second look through his gnat-spattered windshield, craning his neck to see each red brick and white column in context. The house, he now saw, was a nearly perfect replica of Thomas Jefferson's Monticello. Randie opened the passenger-side door, grabbing her camera on instinct. Unfazed, Darren climbed out of the truck. He'd seen weirder on Texas roads: lighthouses in fields of corn, life-size gingerbread houses, a barn with Donald Trump's face on it, country folks offering a show for the cars trucking down long stretches of highway, anything to break up the miles and miles of pines and cedar-choked backwoods.

He was less interested in the house than he was in the view. From the front of Wally's home, which was just a few yards from the fence line, he could see Geneva's cafe, could damn near read what was on the menu through her windows. It struck him as odd that with all the land on either side of their respective properties that these two had wound up being the worst kind of neighbors, those you don't like but have to spend every damn day looking at. Maybe that explained Wally's efforts to buy her out, if only to improve his view. Darren wondered which had come first, Wally's house or Geneva's cafe.

"You're seeing this, right?" Randie said.

Darren turned to see her staring at a smaller property behind the house. To the rear of Monticello was a twenty-foot-tall doghouse that was a perfect scaled-down model of the White House. A black Labrador lazed in the doorway, but when he saw Randie and the camera, he came up on all fours, growling. Darren stepped in front of her just as the dog charged. The Lab came for his leg, and Darren gave a little kick in the dirt with the toe of his boot, just to scare him. The Lab trotted back a few steps, but when he realized he hadn't actually been hit, he came back harder. He'd just gotten hold of Darren's right pants leg when the door to the house opened. "Butch!" Wally yelled, marching down his front steps. The dog released Darren's pants leg and trotted amiably to his master's side, licking at the tips of Wally's thick fingers.

"You're late."

If Wally remembered Darren from Geneva's yesterday, he didn't let on, nor did he react in any visible way to the badge that was once again pinned to Darren's chest. Wally was wearing a polo shirt tucked into his Wranglers, which were pressed to a knife-sharp crease. The skin around his neck was slack, but his color was ruddy and strong. Darren couldn't place the man's age—or his line of work, for that matter. There wasn't a cow or a bale of hay anywhere on the property that he could see, no fields of wheat or cotton, not a single sign of industry. The cop in Darren noted the presence of extreme wealth absent a stitch of evidence of the hard work that made it possible.

"I'm Darren Mathews."

"Oh, I know," Wally said, taking pleasure in being two steps ahead.

Turning to Randie, he added, "I'm sorry about your husband, ma'am. But you ought to know that no one from around here had anything to do with that."

"Well, that remains to be seen," Darren said.

Wally looked vaguely amused as he shooed Butch back to the White House, then turned and opened his front door. "Sheriff'll be back any minute."

Inside, the walls were washed white, and the thick carpet was the color of churned butter. Wally nodded toward what he called the davenport and told Randie and Darren to have a seat. "Laura," he called to the back of the house. Randie lowered herself onto the sofa, upholstered in a rose-printed fabric, but Darren, by his training as a Ranger and man, remained standing. Randie's eyes scanned the living room, taking in the brass knickknacks and porcelain figurines of angels and quarter horses, as well as the photographic portraits of Wally and a fiftysomething white woman with reddish-brown hair who favored turquoise and sweater sets. She appeared in the flesh a few seconds later, holding a squirming toddler on her hip. She looked as surprised to see Darren as he was to see a child in her arms. There wasn't a single photo of children or grandchildren in the front parlor. She straightened her shirt where it had ridden up her torso from the weight of the baby, a towheaded little thing who'd probably barely been walking a year. "Ranger," the woman said politely. She glanced at Randie but did not let her gaze linger, as if sudden widowhood might be contagious. She started to inch back out of the living room, but Wally stopped her. "Laura, get these good people a glass of water, a Coke or something."

"Can I get you something, Ranger?" Laura said. "Miss?"

"I'm fine," Randie said.

Darren wished she'd put a *ma'am* on it or a *thank you,* wished she understood you'd do well down here to meet white folks with a hefty benefit of the doubt. You'd know their real colors soon enough, so it didn't hurt to be civil up top, insurance against pissing off the ones who were on your side.

"No, thank you, ma'am," he said to Wally's wife.

As Laura left the living room, Darren heard the child's squeals fade.

"Yours?" he said to Wally.

"That's Missy's boy, Keith Junior," the older man said. "Laura's watching him while Missy's people are putting together services. Don't know if she'll be buried here or up to Timpson, but Keith ain't able to handle much of nothing right now, his child least of all. He's plumb tore up is what they're saying."

"Where's the sheriff?" Randie asked impatiently.

Darren shot her a look before stepping in.

To Wally, he said, "You own the icehouse up the highway?"

"Michael was there," Randie said, the words sounding like a question wrapped around an accusation. Darren wished she'd let him handle this.

"Did you see anything?" he said.

"I wasn't at the bar on Wednesday."

"How'd you know it was Wednesday?"

"Parker's kept me apprised," Wally said. "I'm a well-regarded man in this community, a property owner and businessman, been on this land for four generations. There's no police force in Lark, so I like to keep an eye on things in my town, be on the lookout for outsiders and such. Parker keeps me in the know."

Just then Van Horn let himself through the front door, pausing long enough to wipe his boots on the mud rug just inside the threshold before he plodded across the carpet on his squat legs. "Ranger Mathews," he said, coming toward Darren but stopping just short of shaking his hand. "I'm gon' be clear about this from the top. I don't want you here, and I didn't ask for you to be here. But I've been backed into this thing by the wife and what all making noise about this being something more than it is—"

"Parker," Wally said.

Van Horn halted his tirade long enough to see Randie on the sofa, to understand his blunder, but he ran right over it and kept talking. He was on day two of his uniform, and his pits were damp. He looked both exasperated and utterly bemused by his circumstances. "We gon' do this real nice like. I'm gon' be cordial and accepting of your presence in my county. But let's be real clear: this is my deal down here. Lieutenant Wilson practically said as much. You're here so when Chicago or New York or whoever in the hell comes crawling down to see the rednecks out of their cages, they'll see your face and know everything is on the up-and-up in the investigation of the death in this county of an African American," he said, stumbling over the extra syllables it took to be politically correct. "You're just a prop down here, son, and nothing more."

"Well, then, this prop would like, and is entitled to, copies of all your reports pertaining to the death of Michael Wright, starting with the autopsy."

Van Horn sighed and glanced at Wally, who gave a shrug of censure, as if to say, *You're the one who's indulging this.* This was Van Horn's mess to clean.

"I want to see it, too," Randie said.

She had not introduced herself, nor had Van Horn asked who she was, but it hadn't been necessary. The sheriff apologized for his earlier statement and offered his condolences for her loss. Then he said to Darren, "I'll see what can be done. Dallas has the body"—he said before softening his language—"uh . . . your husband, ma'am. I don't think the medical examiner there has completed the autopsy."

Darren knew Van Horn was stalling, that the autopsy was already done when Greg called him yesterday, but he had Wilson's order in his head. *Play by the rules.* So he said, as nicely as he could, "I'd also like to formally request from your department a copy of Missy Dale's autopsy when it's completed."

"Maybe I didn't make myself clear enough. Wilson put you on to monitor the Wright deal. But Missy is a local girl, born in Shelby County." Behind him, Wally was nodding his approval. "And we know how to take care of our own."

"I think you know those murders are connected," Darren said.

"Oh, I know. I know how they're connected, too," Wally huffed. "One of Geneva's people getting it in their head some lynching-type deal is going on when ain't a bit of evidence to that whatsoever. And they took one of ours for one of theirs. Parker, you know

Geneva attracts all kinds of trouble over there. Last two killings we had in this town was kin to her."

The sheriff pursed his lips but didn't agree one way or the other.

"Michael wasn't one of 'theirs,'" Darren said. "Wasn't even from around here."

"He hasn't been to Texas in years," said Randie, who was without an answer as to why he had driven nearly a thousand miles to Lark. The question was a locked door for which she knew she should hold the key, and the same look of guilt wrenched her face as it had last night when Darren asked *why*. Why didn't she know her husband well enough to know what had brought him here?

Darren looked from Van Horn to the owner of Jeff's Juice House.

"Was Missy Dale working Wednesday night?" he asked Wally.

"I'm reviewing the staffing records now," Van Horn said, as if looking up who was working at a bar in a town of fewer than two hundred people might take him weeks. Darren felt a heat rise up from inside, flushing his neck at the collar line.

"Look," he said, keeping his tone on a slim tightrope between indignation and due deference, trying to keep his anger in check. "The night he disappeared, Michael was at the icehouse where Missy Dale worked. And now those same two people are dead. Tell me you don't find that significant."

"So," Van Horn said. "You think some cracker shitheads saw Michael and Missy talking that night and followed him out of the icehouse?"

"I didn't say anything about Michael and Missy talking, but interesting that you did," he said. "And I'm just talking about *one* cracker shithead."

"Michael was with this other girl?" Randie said.

She glanced at Darren with a hurt look on her face, either about

Michael or the fact that she thought this was another thing Darren had withheld from her.

She sounded more heartsick than angry when she said, "Darren?"

It was jarring to hear her call him by his first name, which no one in Texas would ever do, not when he was wearing the badge. It was a sign of supreme disrespect. But from her lips, it made him feel more himself, made this personal.

"Don't make a bit of difference if he was," Van Horn said. "Everything we got says the man was robbed. The way you're telling it, if somebody gave that boy a licking out in the woods, then that car ought to been found sitting out on FM 19. Somebody would have seen it when the sun come up. But that car is probably chopped up in Dallas somewhere by now." He'd gone pink in the face.

"Keith Dale," Darren said. "Where was he Wednesday night?"

Van Horn crossed his arms. "I plan on talking to him about Missy, but it ain't none of your concern. One ain't got nothing to do with the other, son."

"Ranger," Darren said, correcting Van Horn.

Van Horn's jaw clenched. "Ranger," he said with a tense nod.

"He ABT?" Darren asked. "I know Keith did a stint in Huntsville."

Randie looked back and forth between Darren and the sheriff. "ABT?"

"Aryan Brotherhood of Texas."

"This county's clean of that kind of trash," Wally said. Van Horn blanched but said nothing. The mention of the ABT changed things, and it silenced him.

"Aryan Brotherhood?" Randie said. Her face had gone slack, eyes widened in alarm. She looked younger all of a sudden, almost child-like in the realization that some monsters are real. "Are you talking about the Klan?"

"Worse. It's the Klan with money and semiautomatic weapons," Darren explained.

"They're under control in my county," the sheriff said, "and I told Wilson this ain't me opening the door to a bunch of feds rolling through, coming after the Brotherhood. We're focused on the girl right now, my number one priority."

He caught the widow's eye, but he didn't take back the sentiment.

"Let me talk to Geneva," Wally said to Van Horn. "You know she and my family go a long way back. I'm aimed to help any way I can, and she trusts me."

"Leave that woman alone."

Darren turned to see that Laura had entered the room again. The child was on the carpet, down by her ankles, scooting on the butt of a thick diaper.

"We're talking serious here, Laura," Wally said. "Go on."

The little boy pulled himself to standing and toddled toward the sofa and Randie, and Laura bent down and scooped him up in her arms. To the sheriff, Wally said, "Let me see if I can get her to come clean about some of the rough characters coming out of her place who might have been hopped up and looking for trouble Sunday night."

"It's not natural, the way you stay after her," Laura said.

The boy swatted at her earring, then put his hand in his mouth to work his teething gums, slobber raining down on Laura's checkered shirt. The look she gave Wally was somewhere between a reprimand and a plea. Darren took notice of both it and the way Wally averted his gaze, quickly turning back to the sheriff. "Geneva's cafe is downstream of your icehouse, Wally," he said, letting the sheriff know his investigation had already begun. He remembered Wendy's words yesterday. *Everybody know Missy was coming out of Wally's icehouse.* "Missy Dale could just as easily have been killed out there, left in the bayou, and her body drifted down." Wally stared at Van Horn, perhaps waiting for him to cough up an alternative theory. Darren plucked a business card from his wallet and handed it to the sheriff. "I'll be waiting on that autopsy," he said.

11.

HE HAD Greg on the phone by the time they got in his truck. "I need that autopsy. Missy's, too, if you can get it." Randie shut the passenger-side door as Darren turned over the Chevy's engine. "Lieutenant's got me on this thing now, but I could use an outside assist while the sheriff is taking his sweet time."

"What turned Wilson around?" Greg said.

"The wife—" Darren started. He felt Randie in the seat next to him and started over. "A reporter started asking questions. That was enough."

"Should I drive up there?" Greg asked. "Get my supervisor to approve a cursory look around? If you're getting pushback from local law enforcement—"

"*I'm* local law enforcement now." He glanced at Randie in the passenger seat. He was saying it as much to her as he was to Greg. He was making her a promise. "This is my case now, whether Van Horn knows it or not."

"The Bureau might have an interest here," Greg said.

Darren remembered how this had started, Greg fishing for a professional come-up. Greg wanted out from behind that desk, and Darren knew it. But he wouldn't put that ahead of the need to handle this situation right, and that did not include bringing in a federal agent.

He said, "I don't think that's a good idea, another outsider coming in right now—and federal, at that. You know how these county folk can be. But I do need you to get me more about Keith Dale's time in Huntsville—his cell blocks, known associates, any write-ups, and any connection to the Brotherhood."

Greg mumbled something, either a *yes* or a *no,* that Darren couldn't hear over the engine. What *was* clear was Greg's disappointment, his anger, even, at being cast out of a case he opened, a case for which Darren was now sending him on errands, keeping him behind the very desk he hated. Irked, he seemed to enjoy the next thing that came out of his mouth. "Lisa called."

"What'd you tell her?"

"That I didn't know where you were."

"Shit." He'd already told her he was doing a job for Greg.

Now she would think he was lying.

The second he hung up with Greg, he meant to call her.

But Randie lit into him before he could dial her number. "You had access to Michael's autopsy this whole time? Why did you even bother talking to that podunk sheriff? Why go in there hat in hand, begging for information?"

"There's just a way things are done, a certain protocol that's wise to follow when you're dealing with these East Texas sheriffs," he said.

Randie bit off a bitter laugh. "You and Michael," she said as Darren pulled up to the highway, waiting to safely cross. She stared out the side window at the rural landscape, the pines and the red dirt, the pickup trucks on the highway, rifles racked in back windows, and Darren felt a feral heat coming from her direction. "He was always saying Texas this and Texas that. How it isn't that bad. Michael was always making excuses for these racists down here, had some kind of twisted nostalgia about growing up in the country that made him blind to all the rest of the bullshit down here."

"It's not making excuses," Darren said. "It's knowing that *I'm here, too*. I'm Texas, too. They don't get to decide what this place is," he said, nodding his head toward Wally's mansion behind them. "This is my home, too." He was speaking for a man who no longer could, but he was also speaking for himself. "As for Van Horn, it doesn't hurt to make him think we're following the rules."

But Randie was unmoved, alight with a quiet fury.

"He should never have come down here," she said, her hands balled into fists, the bottoms of which were pressed into the thighs of her jeans, as if she were holding tight to an invisible buoy, as if she believed her anger at Michael might keep her from sinking into the tide of grief that had only begun to lick at her toes. "What the hell did he think was going to happen in a place like this?"

"Coming home is not asking for it."

"This was not his home," she said.

But it was, and Darren understood that in a way Randie didn't. Not Lark, of course, but this thin slice of the state that had built both of them, Darren and Michael. The red dirt of East Texas ran in both their veins. Darren knew the power of home, knew what it meant to stand on the land where your forefathers had forged your future out of dirt, knew the power of what could be loved up by hand, how a harvest could change a fate. He knew what it felt like to stand on the back porch of his family homestead in Camilla and feel the breath of his ancestors in the trees, feel the power of gratitude in every stray breeze. He wanted to say all this and more to Randie. But she was closed off by then, sitting rigid, her chin jutted forward in an aggrieved anger that would never hold. God help her, Darren thought, when that wall comes down and the hurt comes calling.

It all circled back to Geneva's, any hope Darren had of stopping a racial witch hunt for Missy Dale's killer, and going back there was his best chance to get justice for Michael Wright, get answers about his last hours on earth.

Michael had been in the cafe, Wendy said.

Darren chased that lead, driving straight from Wally's to the cafe's parking lot across the highway. He'd just pulled into a space on the other side of the gas pump when his cell phone rang. Lisa's photo popped on the screen, a shot from a trip they took to Mexico when she graduated law school. Her kohl-lined eyes peeked out at him from behind the brim of a wide straw hat. Randie saw the image, too. She stared at it a beat too long, then nodded when he asked her to give him a minute. He stepped out to answer the call, leaning against the truck bed, the heel of his right boot resting on one of the Chevy's rear tires.

"What are you doing, Darren?" Lisa said. She sounded tired in a way that he knew didn't bode well for him; her patience had run thin. He'd burned through what little goodwill he had by not driving to Houston last night.

"Wilson called me in on something."

"You turned in your badge, Darren."

"No, I didn't." He refused to add the equivocal *not yet*.

"I thought you and Clayton talked," she said. "About school."

"If there's something you want to ask me, just ask me, Lis. You don't have to use my uncle to do it."

She sighed and said, "I don't want to do this again."

"Neither do I," he said, thinking she meant have this fight again. "I got two dead bodies out here, Lisa. I got people looking to me to make something right out here." He glanced at Randie, watched her through the cab's back window. She was staring straight ahead at the front of the cafe, at the cinched curtains in the windows and the sign out front advertising fried pies.

"And you have a wife who's alive *here*."

"You kicked me out. What did you expect me to do?"

"Well, now I'm asking you to come home."

"No."

The answer was immediate, and he meant it, but it didn't stop the feeling that he'd crossed a line past which he couldn't quite breathe right, the air around him thin and useless, like he couldn't get enough of it into his chest. "Lisa—" She hung up on him just as Randie opened her door and stepped out of the truck.

Wendy was sitting on a woven lawn chair, its yellow and blue threads fraying and swaying in the fall breeze. She was cracking pecans over a paper bag. At her feet were a handful of objects laid out on a blanket: a sewing machine, dusty Coke bottles, an old guitar accompanied by a sign that read STRINGS NOT INCLUDED, a smattering of tin cans, and a few mother-of-pearl pill cases. On top of a Mercury parked nearby was another sign: TAKE A PIECE OF TEXAS HOME WITH YOU. Randie was studying the makeshift bazaar when Darren came from around the side of his truck. Wendy nodded at the familiar face, then caught sight of the badge on his chest. "That thing real?" she said. "Not, I'll pay you thirty dollars for it."

"It's real," he said. "Ranger Darren Mathews, ma'am."

"Well, ain't this some shit."

She turned to see Randie eyeing a flat round tin, the green label rusted over in spots. Wendy pointed to it and said, "That belonged to my mama."

"And you're selling it?" Randie said.

"What I need a tin of hair grease from 1949 for?" Wendy said, popping the meat of a pecan into her mouth. She was dressed head to toe in red, and her crimson lipstick had stained her front teeth. "Lady come through here about a week ago and paid me ten dollars for a can just like it. Shit, I believe my mama paid ten cents." She started on a new pecan, cracking the shell with a silver nutcracker. "You see something you like, let me know."

"We're here about Michael Wright," Darren said.

"Who?"

"The black man who was killed."

"Oh, no," Wendy said, studying Randie. "You not kin to him, are you?"

"He was my—"

Darren stopped her, wanting to disperse information only when and how he saw fit. "Did you see him when he was here, talk to him any?" he asked Wendy.

"Naw. That was Geneva," she said, just as something on the highway got her attention. Her face fell, skin going slack, and Darren saw she might be even older than he realized. He watched her expression go from naked fright to outrage. He turned to follow her gaze. "Now, looka here," she said. There was a blue Dodge truck creeping along 59, going at a stalker's pace of barely forty miles an hour, passing by the cafe. The driver was white, but in profile Darren couldn't see much of his face. "That's three times now," she said.

"The truck?"

Wendy nodded. "Keith Dale."

"That's Keith Dale?" Randie said, turning in time to see his truck's tail end disappear up the road as the truck picked up speed, gunning past Geneva's. "He was at the icehouse last night," she said, turning to Darren, trying to understand what it meant, seeing Keith here. It wasn't good, Darren knew that much.

"He ain't the only one, neither," Wendy said. "Bunch of them down Wally's way been riding up from the icehouse, eyeballing the place, making sure Geneva know they watching. I told her she could hold on to my pistol till all this blows over, but she got her twelve-gauge loaded under the cash register."

Darren stared off after the truck, wondering would it turn around.

He thought, *Why is Keith Dale not being interrogated right now?*

He grabbed Randie by the arm. "Let's get you inside."

He opened the door for her, then turned to Wendy. He'd meant her, too. But the old lady's answer to his concern lay behind a fold in her skirt that she lifted to reveal the .22 in her lap. Didn't look like it could kill a mosquito, but it was all she needed to say, *Not running me from my place of business.* Her corner of Geneva's parking lot wouldn't go down without a fight. Darren hoped like hell he could solve this case before there was another murder in Lark.

Geneva was behind the counter wrapping a plate with foil. She set it inside a cardboard box on the countertop, the words *Heinz ketchup* printed on it. She wiped her hands on her apron, this one a starburst pattern of yellow and orange, then lifted the lid of the pastry case. The cafe warmed with the smell of butter, sugar, and canned fruit, peach and pear. Huxley was at his usual seat with his newspaper. Next to him was a young black girl in her early twenties. She had a milky skin tone that was just short of high yellow, and she had her nose in a bridal magazine. As Geneva wrapped a few fried pies in foil, the girl pointed to a couture gown in the magazine and said, "Grandma, what you think of this one?" Geneva gave the most cursory glance and shrugged.

"That looks like a white sandwich board."

The girl sucked her teeth and turned the page.

Geneva saw Randie and said, "Can I help you?"

The girl turned and immediately took an interest in the stranger. She studied Randie from head to toe, the black jeans, the fine linen T-shirt rolled at the elbows, the tiny gold hoops she was wearing. "I like your hair," she said.

Randie gave a faint nod, but Darren wasn't altogether sure she'd heard the girl. She was staring at the cafe's insides. The Christmas calendars and the rusting license plates. The jukebox lit up with the color blue. Lightnin' Hopkins making his guitar cry, while across the cafe's linoleum floor, the barber, the middle-aged, fair-skinned black man, ran a pair of clippers along the hairline of a teenage boy. The smell of hair grease mixed with the smell of bacon grease coming out of the kitchen, and Darren felt his tongue thicken, could almost feel the pork fat coat the insides of his mouth. For reasons that made no sense to him, Randie still had that camera hanging off her shoulder, keeping it close. Darren felt her hand twitch toward it, felt her instinct to put a filter between her and the thing right in front of her, to create distance between herself and the small-town folks in East Texas. She looked like a tourist, but Geneva knew better.

"You from Dallas?" the girl said eagerly.

"No, Faith, she ain't from Dallas," Geneva said, looking not so much at Randie as at the man who had walked in behind her. "Ain't that right, Ranger?"

Darren nodded in her direction. "Ma'am," he said.

"I don't know what kind of game you're playing, but I don't cotton to people lying to my face, young man, not in my place of business."

"Just doing my job, ma'am, the way I know how."

"You could have said something when you were in here yesterday, but you came in here, no badge, ain't said a word about Ranger this or that, knowing I took you for a customer. You let them send you in here to blend in with us, thinking we'd say something in front of you we wouldn't in front of Van Horn."

"Nobody sent me, ma'am," Darren said. "And if you're willing to answer a few questions, maybe I can help you out with the sheriff and keep him at bay."

"Missy Dale wasn't nowhere around here Sunday night, and Van Horn knows it. That's my statement, top to bottom."

"You can talk to him or you can talk to me."

"I'll take my chance with the devil I know," Geneva said.

It stung, Darren could admit, to be held in such ill regard by this woman for whom he was only trying to do some good. The apron, the scent of the food surrounding Geneva, the discerning gaze—it was a tableau of black maternal warmth that tickled a hunger in Darren that he sometimes forgot was there. The most his mother had served him out of her kitchen was cans of Pearl beer. He'd had his first drink at her feet, in fact, on the steps of her trailer. He was thirteen, and by then Clayton was teaching con law at UT in Austin and spending most of the work week up there. Left on his own for days at a time, he'd ride his bike to his mother's place, something Clayton would have frowned upon. Bell would let him have one beer for every four or five she had, and they would talk—about school, which she'd pretend to listen to, and about girls, which interested her much more. Bell was a romantic, and she wanted her son to be a gentleman. *You make sure you buy her dinner before,* she said repeatedly, looking out for a future sweetheart whom Darren couldn't even imagine at the time. Clayton sent him to high school in Houston as much to give him a four-star education as to get him the hell away from his mother's influence. But it held just the same. The night he had sex for the first time—with Lisa, then his girlfriend—he spent every cent he'd ever saved at a chain restaurant at West Oaks Mall. *Whatever you want.*

He heard a voice behind him say loudly, "That's mine."

It was a bark that came out of Randie's mouth, and both Darren and Geneva turned, Darren utterly uncomprehending of what had just happened, why Randie looked like she'd seen a ghost, why her breathing had changed.

"That's mine," she said again. She was staring at the booth farthest from the door, which had its own mini decor. The wall above it was papered with concert bills from blues shows fifty years old. Lightnin' Hopkins at the Eldorado Ballroom, in Houston. Albert Collins headlining a Third Ward revue. Bobby "Blue" Bland on stage with a new band in Dallas. A show at the Club Pow Pow featuring Joe "Petey Pie" Sweet. And just above the booth, on a low shelf, sat a 1955 Gibson Les Paul, the blond wood scratched and fading on one side. This is what had Randie spooked—what Darren now saw had her hands shaking.

"I beg your pardon?" Geneva said.

"That's from my house. It's mine. I mean, it was Michael's." She walked toward the booth, reaching to grab the guitar on the shelf.

"Don't you dare."

Randie heard something in Geneva's voice that stopped her cold.

"That belonged to my husband," the older woman said. "And it's gon' stay right there."

She dropped condiment packets in the box of food, then lifted the whole thing and started across the cafe. She asked Huxley if he had any mail to get out, then hollered at Faith on her way to the door. "You coming?" she asked.

Faith rolled her eyes. "Waste of food," she said softly.

"She's still your mama," Geneva said, to which Faith gave no reply.

The bell on the door jingled as Geneva headed out. Darren reached for the woman's arm, grabbing her wrist. He felt bone through her papery skin.

"Just tell me, ma'am. Just tell us if Michael Wright was here."

Geneva looked at him and said, "You saw the guitar, didn't you?"

With that she pushed past him and out the door, the bell tinkling behind her. Outside, he heard the engine of her Pontiac kick into gear. He watched for a few seconds as she steered the boat of a car around toward the highway, pulling out and taking off down 59. "Where is she going?" Darren asked. Huxley raised an eyebrow but said nothing. Faith sighed and closed her bridal magazine.

"Gatesville," she said.

"Gatesville?"

Darren didn't know a soul who went to Gatesville for any reason other than to visit someone in the custody of the Texas Department of Criminal Justice. The town had eight prisons, five of which housed only women.

"She going to see someone on the inside?"

Faith stood and said, "My mama been in Hilltop Unit for two years."

She walked to the large mirror all the way on the other side of the cafe, squeezing past the barber's chair and the man cutting hair to look at her reflection. She lifted her wavy hair and piled it on the top of her head, then turned to Randie, the fashionable woman from out of town. "What you think? With some baby's breath on top? Rodney's saying he'll pay for me to get it professionally done in Timpson before the wedding."

In Geneva's absence, Randie went for the guitar. She crossed to the far booth, sliding in and kneeling on the cushion so she could reach the Les Paul on the shelf. "I wouldn't if I were you," Huxley said, and again Randie froze. She looked at Darren, who shook his head softly. They needed Geneva. He watched as Huxley closed his newspaper and tucked it under his arm. "Betty'll have my tail if I don't get home for lunch at least one day this week," the older man said.

Darren asked him, "Were you here on Wednesday, sir?"

"I'm always here."

"Did you see my husband?" Randie said.

Huxley stood and looked at her. "I'm sorry for your loss, ma'am. But the answers to what happened to your husband ain't around here. All I know, he came in around five, six in the evening, ate a little piece. Wednesdays is catfish. He and Geneva talked some, but Tim and I was in a card game, and I wasn't listening much. I heard something about him renting a room in her trailer back there, but he left, and then he just didn't come back. And now they saying he was up to that icehouse. That's where y'all need to be looking at things."

"But why?" Darren said, asking the question of Randie as much as of the old man. "Why would Michael just up and leave and go to the icehouse?" Of course Darren had done the same thing yesterday, hunting for a drink.

"I don't know," Huxley said. "But Lil' Joe used to hang around that bar, and look what happened to him."

"Leave my mama out of it," Faith snapped.

"Who's Lil' Joe?" Darren asked.

From the mirror, Faith said, "My daddy."

Before Darren could ask what had happened to Faith's daddy and what her mother had to do with it, his cell phone dinged in his pants pocket. It was a text from Greg: *sent u autopsy.*

12.

HE TOLD Randie he had to make a call, mumbling something about his lieutenant, anything to grant him a few minutes alone to read the medical examiner's report. He could not take in the information and protect her from it at the same time. He would tell her what he had to and no more. He left as a John Lee Hooker record dropped on the jukebox, and Randie sank into the booth below the guitar, staring at the Les Paul. *Bluebird, bluebird, take this letter down South for me,* Hooker sang as Darren opened the cafe's front door, the bell clinking behind him. The air outside stung the sweat breaking out across his forehead. He stepped into the cab of his truck, warm from the midday sun. The file came attached to an e-mail that reported that Missy Dale's final examination was still in progress at the Dallas County Medical Examiner's office.

Darren opened the file on Michael Wright.

The pictures hit him first. Skin a waxy, purplish gray, body bloated beyond recognition as a member of the species known as man. The two days Michael had spent in the water—before being discovered by a white farmer on the other side of the bayou from the icehouse—had destroyed the body as well as a lot of the physical evidence, as was noted on the first page of the written report. But there was still visible trauma to the left side of Michael's head at the time of the forensic exam, skin torn and bruised near his eye and a deep gash above his ear. He'd been beaten badly, enough to fracture his skull in two places, by blunt force from an object that was hypothesized to be about the width of a baseball bat but with defined edges, sharp enough to cut through skin, with enough force to break bone. The medical examiner, a woman named Aimee Kwon, noted that there were wood fibers embedded so deeply in the tissue around the injuries that, even though the body had been submerged in water for days, medical tweezers were required to remove them. They bore a resemblance to the pulp of unfinished pine but would require testing for the medical examiner to be certain. Because of the decomposition in the cranial cavity, the medical examiner could not be sure if the blow to Michael's head would have immediately incapacitated him or if he would have been able to walk of his own accord to the bayou's edge. His blood alcohol level was a .02, which means he'd had one drink, maybe not even finished it. Darren didn't think alcohol was a factor, and neither did the medical examiner. She'd ruled it out. There was enough bayou water in Michael's lungs to conclude that he'd drowned. But whether he'd fallen in the bayou on his own or been dragged to the water while unconscious was beyond the scope of the report. Absent more information from a Shelby County investigation, the manner of death was listed as undetermined. It was officially neither an accident nor a homicide. Darren, who'd stood in the shallow, muddy water, believed someone had to have dragged Michael's limp, prostrate body and tossed it into the bayou. And now, more than ever, he believed he knew who that someone was.

* * *

He walked Randie through it as gently as he could. He steered her away from the pictures and most of the written report. He was surprised that she trusted him enough to not press the issue. She was as quiet as he'd ever heard her. She listened to his words, his recitation from memory of the autopsy findings. She nodded but asked very few questions. Laying her head against the passenger-side window at one point, she cried. She said nothing except that she thought she was going to throw up, but when she opened the door and leaned her head over the gray pavement, nothing came. There was no relief, and she retreated back inside the cab, wiping a thin line of spit from her bottom lip. Whatever emotional sickness was locked inside her continued to roil. She put her black ankle boots on the seat, lifting her knees so she could hug them tightly, making her body an anchor against a pain that was literally shaking her. Darren said her name softly: "Randie." He went to touch her shoulder but stopped himself. "Let me take it from here, okay? There's no reason for you to put yourself through this. Take your husband home and lay him to rest. I promise you I will find the person who did this to Michael."

She released her knees and sat up straight. "I'm not going anywhere."

"Randie, I need you to let me do my job."

"I'm not leaving until there's an arrest. I'm not leaving him," she said, as if Michael's soul would stay in Lark forever if she didn't see this through. She'd hardened again, and the anger calmed and focused her; it made the shaking stop.

"Fine. But there are some things I need to do on my own." Randie shot him a look, a question implicit in the raise of her eyebrow. "I'm going back to that icehouse," he said. "And you can't just walk in there."

"Neither can you."

"I'm not going *in*."

Since they'd left her rental car at the motel—where Darren was no longer welcome—he let her drive his truck, with strict instructions that she was to return to pick him up as soon as she got a text from him or after an hour had passed, whichever came first. She dropped him on FM 19, along the narrow patch of woods between the farm road and the icehouse. He hopped out of the Chevy and walked through the thicket of blackjack and post oak trees, edging sideways through the branches, leaves falling at his touch. He walked until he came to a clearing around back of the icehouse. Country music was coming through the bar's walls and spilling outside. Waylon Jennings talking about starting over in Luckenbach, Texas. Darren listened for the sound of the Chevy's engine fading but couldn't hear anything above the twanged-up love song. He waited until he thought Randie was long gone.

There was a propane tank and a generator behind the icehouse, plus a smoker that had pine needles resting on top, the bottom having rusted out years ago. Next to a plastic lawn chair was an overturned paint bucket on top of which sat a chipped glass ashtray, the edge sharp enough to break skin. This close to the woods, the pine scent was sweet, but it was fighting a losing battle with the smell of trash and stale beer in the bottles piled inside a huge black trash can, dead flies stuck to the lid. Darren tucked a loose cigarette into his shirt pocket, and he waited. It was coming on three in the afternoon, and the sun had danced to the other side of the highway. Behind Jeff's Juice House, a breeze swirled, lifting a few stray paper receipts no one had bothered to pick out of the knots of grass. There were small plastic ziplock bags on the ground, too, some old and ground into the dirt, small enough to hold buttons or loose change or rocks of crystal meth. Where the Aryan Brotherhood was present, drugs usually followed. Darren bent down and picked one up with his handkerchief, pocketing potential evidence. He kept an eye on the bar's back door, and he waited.

To pass the time, he took out his phone and looked up Joe Sweet, whose name had been mentioned three times since Darren had rolled into town. Joe "Petey Pie" Sweet, according to his *Wikipedia* page, was born Joseph Sweet on a farm outside Fayette, Mississippi, in 1939, one of eleven children. His older brother, Nathan, taught him to play guitar, and by the time he was twelve, Joe was playing juke joints he wasn't old enough to drink in. He left Mississippi with two of his brothers in the late fifties, settling first in Gary, Indiana, then later in Chicago, the mecca for Delta blues, homeboys from the Deep South bringing their music up north. Joe soon fell in with Muddy Waters and a young Buddy Guy, played in a band with Little Walter, and had a regular gig doing session work for the Chess brothers. He toured some, joining Bobby "Blue" Bland's group, but never broke out on his own. He stopped touring and recording in the late sixties, and he was killed in a robbery in Lark, Texas, in 2010, at the age of seventy-one. He had been married from 1968 until his death to Geneva Sweet. Together they had only one son, Joe Sweet Jr., who died in 2013.

Out of curiosity, Darren clicked on a few other pages and pulled up pictures of a dark-skinned black man who favored skinny ties and a close-cropped afro. Darren's mind kept swirling back to something. *We ain't had nothing like this around here since Joe died.* Followed by Tim asking provocatively, *Which one?* They were dead— Geneva's husband and her son, Faith's father.

Her two Joes, both gone.

★   ★   ★

The back door to the icehouse opened suddenly, and Darren looked up to see the bartender from last night step outside, lighting a smoke before she looked up and saw Darren. She didn't break stride when she laid eyes on him, just exhaled a line of smoke through her nose and said, "You ain't supposed to be back here. Brady sees you sniffing around, he'll kick your ass *and* mine."

"That your boss?"

"Wally's the boss," she said. "Brady's just the manager."

"He know what kind of people come in this bar?"

"I know he don't want *you* coming in here."

"I'm talking about the Brotherhood, ma'am," he said, thinking that a woman like this—today wearing a mesh T-shirt over a dingy white tank top, more sores and pimples cascading down her neck—doesn't hear the word *ma'am* on the regular and that a little deference wouldn't hurt. "I'm talking about the dudes with the ABT tattoos in there, that big one who kicked us off the property last night."

"That *is* Brady," she said.

She glanced over her shoulder.

The back door to the icehouse was slightly ajar, propped open with a rock.

Darren could hear the clank of dishes from the kitchen.

"And Wally knows?" he said, sounding naive to his own ears.

"Wally ain't exactly marched on Washington," she said, and he wondered how old she was. If meth had laid those lines on her face, there was no way to tell; the drug ran on its own time. He watched her suck on her cigarette while taking a good, long look at his badge. It scared her—maybe more than Brady did.

"You want to ask me something, you better go on and do it before my break is up." She glanced twice more at the door, shifting from one foot to the other every two seconds, one hand or another reaching for her hair or mouth as she chewed on her thumbnail. She wore slip-on Keds that had sullied to a grayish brown, and the skin above them was dry and pale.

"Keith Dale?" Darren said. "Is he in the Brotherhood?"

"I'm not club secretary."

Darren gave her a knowing look, planted his boot heels in the dirt to suggest he wasn't going anywhere. "He hangs out here," she allowed, stubbing out her cigarette after a deep drag and a cough. Then she shrugged. "A lot of people come to this bar. It's a nice place. Keith ain't special."

"Was he here on Wednesday night?"

"*I* didn't see him," she said, looking over his head toward the pine tops, pointedly avoiding eye contact. Darren felt there was more in there, right under the surface. But absent anything else to smoke, she turned to go back inside.

He offered her the loose cigarette in his pocket, delivering carrot and stick as a twofer. "Brady dealing crystal out of here?" he said. "Van Horn might look the other way. But as a Ranger, I can't. Not with the feds pushing us for information all the time. You might be holding right now for all I know," he said, making a point of scanning the lines of her body for any bulges in her tight jeans. She immediately blanched, shaking her head and holding out her hands defensively, Darren's Camel between her fingers. He leaned in close to light it, looking into her hazel eyes as the smoke she exhaled curled around them. He'd gotten under her skin now. He felt her weighing her options. On the other side of the bayou, someone was smoking venison two weeks ahead of hunting season. Darren smelled the sweet burn of pecan wood. "'Cause you're flirting with your own indictment if you helping them hide any drug shit back there."

"I don't know anything about that," she said flatly. She ran a hand through her thin, greasy hair and sighed in surrender. "Look, Keith usually comes in from the lumber mill in enough time to get a beer and drive Missy home when her shift is up. But if he's held up in Timpson, she'll just walk home. They live right off FM 19, the farm road that runs on the other side of them trees," she said, pointing to the shrug of woods through which Darren had just come. "Honest to God, swear on my babies, I didn't see Keith Dale that night."

"And who waited on the stranger?"

"Who?"

But she knew what he was talking about.

"What's your name, ma'am?" Darren said. He was direct but not rude. But neither would he let her forget he was law enforcement. Some of this just wasn't going to be voluntary. When she hesitated, he pressed her again. "I asked for your name."

"Lynn."

"Lynn, tell me who waited on the black man."

She sighed, then finally spit it out. "Missy."

She studied her cigarette, as if she could tell time by nicotine. One and a half cigarettes meant her break was definitely over. "Listen, I can't be out here no more. Don't mean you no offense, but I'll catch hell for talking to a cop."

"Didn't you already talk to the sheriff about this?"

"He ain't asked no questions about that black fellow until *after* Missy died," she said, stubbing out the second cigarette. "Was just in here this morning."

So that's why he'd been late to Wally's house, Darren thought;

he'd been playing catch-up, trying to pretend he'd been working on the Michael Wright homicide all along. "And what'd you tell him?" he asked her.

"What I told you—that she waited on him."

"The black man? Michael?" he said, clarifying.

She nodded. "Lot of folks didn't like seeing the two of them talking."

"Talking?" It was the same thing Van Horn had said.

"For at least an hour. Missy actually sat at his table for a bit. I had to tell her to leave. She was twenty minutes past her shift and hadn't clocked out yet."

"She leave alone?" Darren said.

Michael had rented the spare room in Geneva's trailer but never returned.

"It wasn't any of my business," she said, equivocating.

"I'm going to need you to say it, Lynn."

She picked at a sore under her chin. "Yeah, I saw her walk out with him."

"You're sure?"

She nodded.

Darren shook his head to himself. He didn't want it to be true, could hardly imagine a world where a man who'd been with Randie would mess around with a junior-college dropout from a tiny Texas backwater. And he certainly didn't want the job of telling Randie about this part of the case.

"And what about Keith?" he said. "You said he never came in the bar?"

"No. I said I didn't see him. But he might have peeked his head in. If he don't see her, sometimes he'll catch her walking home and pick her up on the farm road. He would have been looking for her," she said before an ugly bitterness came over her. She spit out her last words. "Some folks never learn."

Darren didn't immediately understand what she meant. But he had a picture now, a theory. Keith could have come upon his wife and a stranger, a black man, together on the farm road. It was as close as Darren had been able to put Keith near Michael Wright. But he'd have to walk away from here with something concrete— on paper if he could get it—if he was going to sway Wilson to keep pressing, to look at Keith Dale as the number one person of interest.

"Does Brady work off a schedule, printed up somewhere?" he asked. "I mean, I don't need to know what else is in his office," he said, casually raising the specter of a drug case just to keep the wheels good and greased, "but I need that schedule, Lynn. For Wednesday night especially. It's very important." He didn't mention that she'd have to give an affidavit attesting to everything she just said for any of it to count as evidence. But she was nodding as she went back inside, so he didn't push it. He texted Randie to come for him. If she'd parked at Geneva's like he'd told her to, she'd be here within a few minutes.

The back door to the icehouse opened again.

Too fast, he thought. *Way too fast.*

He knew it was trouble even before he looked up and saw not Lynn's nicotine-stained fingers, offering evidence at his mere request, but rather Brady's fist traveling at the speed of a fastball. *Should have known it wouldn't be that easy.* The thought burst like a firecracker in his brain as the first hit landed under his chin.

He flew back, knocking over the trash can on his way to the ground. He flipped the latch on his holster and had his Colt in hand before he scrambled back to his feet. But when he took aim, Brady already had a .357 pointed at him. And he hadn't come alone. It took Darren a moment to place the white man in the sweat-stained ball cap standing next to Brady. It was Keith Dale. Brady offered him the kill shot with a callousness that shot adrenaline like hot acid through Darren's veins. "This is your bag if you want it, Keith," Brady said, a lopsided and eerily confident grin on his face. "I can jump you in after this."

Darren felt breath-choking panic over what he recognized as Brotherhood talk. Brady tilted his gaze in Keith's direction, wanting his protégé to grasp the magnitude of the moment, the gift that Brady was offering. Keith gave out a tough hoot of a laugh. Brady grew serious and said, "Do it for Ronnie Malvo."

The name ricocheted through Darren's skull.

Ronnie "Redrum" Malvo, the man who'd trespassed on Mack's property last month and come up dead two days later. Through whatever Brotherhood social media pages were out there, Facebook and Reddit threads, news of Darren's tangential connection to Malvo's death must have traveled to Shelby County. Darren was officially a marked man who was about to lose his life if he didn't act now.

He kicked the .357 out of Brady's hand, knocking it two feet to his left. Brady made a move for it, but Darren had the Colt pointed at his head in a matter of seconds. The badge gave him the right to shoot. But if helping Mack had gotten him suspended, shooting a man who'd been effectively disarmed would end his career. He was basically in a standoff with himself. His hesitation embarrassed and infuriated him.

Brady scolded Keith. "Should have shot ol' boy when you had the chance." But Darren had the upper hand now, held both men under the Colt's sway. He eyed Keith from hat to work boots. His knuckles were scratched, and there was a bruise across the top of his right hand as well as another on his cheek just below his left eye. It had blossomed into a buttercup yellow with faint traces of purple at the center. *A few days old.* "How'd you get those bruises, Keith?"

Keith eyed him with contempt and spat at Darren's feet. "Fuck you."

"Don't you say another word," Brady said. "Van Horn's got this."

Darren heard the sirens then.

A few hundred yards away, maybe, and coming closer.

Facedown in the dirt, Darren's phone was beeping repeatedly. Randie was waiting for him, he remembered. At least he hoped she was.

But no: here she came now, behind the wheel of his truck.

She had never gone back to Geneva's but had instead lingered at the edge of the icehouse's parking lot, waiting for him. And now she was nosing his truck around the side of the squat building, barely able to steer the wide load on the uneven dirt. She slammed on the brakes so hard that red clouds of dirt swirled above the earth. Darren could hardly see her face over the steering wheel.

When she saw the guns, Randie screamed.

Her panic made Brady jumpy. He was eyeing the pistol at his feet. This could go left, Darren knew, real quick, and he didn't want Randie caught in any crossfire. He needed to get her out of here now. Darren kept his .45 trained on Brady and Keith as he grabbed his phone and made a dash for the truck. The sirens were coming closer as he climbed in beside Randie. Brady went for his gun, and Darren screamed at her, "Drive!" She was so rattled that she gunned the engine, sending them flying forward. Another few yards and she would have driven them straight into the bayou. In order to turn the Chevy around, she had to swing the truck back toward the icehouse. For one brief, terrifying second, they came face-to-face with Brady standing in front of the Chevy, the gun's barrel pointed directly at them. Randie saw him through the windshield and completely froze, stuck in the middle of her three-point maneuver, her fingers gripping the steering wheel. "Take your foot off the brake, Randie," Darren said, coaching her through her fear as he yanked the wheel to point the front tires straight toward the highway. "Go now," he said. *"Drive."* She hit the gas, lurching them forward, Darren bracing himself against the dashboard. She hunched over the steering wheel as she squeezed the wide truck through the narrow passage between the wooded field and the side of the icehouse.

Behind them, Darren heard two unmistakable pops.

One shot took out the mirror on Darren's side.

The other caught one of the rear tires.

As they drove through the parking lot, they passed Van Horn coming in from the highway. As his squad car moved over the gravel, he locked eyes with Darren. At the sight of a cop, Randie hesitated, but Darren told her to keep driving before Brady landed a shot that mattered, before he killed them both.

13.

THEY DIDN'T stop till they got over the county line. Darren instructed Randie to pull into the parking lot of a bowling alley in Garrison. He was a cop running from the law, and much as he appreciated the ridiculousness of it, much as it galled him, he was not about to stop and explain himself to a sheriff he technically outranked. A verbal standoff with local law enforcement over pecking order would piss off Lieutenant Wilson and earn a mark against his name that Darren couldn't afford, not after just getting his badge back. Let Van Horn deal with the reckless gunplay out of Wally's place. Darren was not going to be questioned about the way he was running an investigation the sheriff had all but dumped at his feet.

He ordered Randie out of the car. She was lit with terror, her limbs like live wires she couldn't stop from quivering. He had to tell her twice to stand back from the Chevy while he changed the rear tire that a bullet had shot clean through. On the ground, fixing the spare into place, he scraped his right shoulder on concrete and tore a pin-size hole in the fabric of his shirt. He sweated as he worked, lines of it running down his back. Randie shivered as nightfall crept closer. She'd dumped the white coat and was wearing only her T-shirt and jeans. He had the spare in place in less than fifteen minutes and got on the phone with his lieutenant right afterward. He wanted a warrant on the grounds of potential drug possession with intent to sell, using the Brotherhood connection as probable cause. While he was searching Wally's icehouse he'd seize Missy's work schedule. It was the kind of bait and switch cops did all the time. But Wilson was furious.

"Ranger, you've got less than twelve hours before some stringer from Chicago touches down on Texas soil, sniffing around, and you're dicking around about meth sales? You practically begged me for this, remember? You're there to gather evidence on the Michael Wright homicide, and that's all."

"I'm telling you it's connected to the Missy Dale murder."

"You don't know that."

Darren explained his strategy: they could use the drug issue to get inside; they could bury a request for employee schedules in the warrant. It was potential evidence that could put the two deceased together on the same night, the very night Michael Wright disappeared. But Wilson wasn't having it.

"This is not a drug case."

"Wait," Darren said. "When I was working the task force, I wasn't allowed to bring up race crimes, and now I'm in the middle of a race crime, and suddenly you don't want me to bring up drugs?" Randie was standing on the other side of the truck's cab, leaned against the door. She'd heard every word.

"You don't know this is a race crime," Wilson said.

"Are you fucking kidding me?"

"Watch it, Darren."

"Why is it so hard for you to admit what's right in front of your face? I'm in this town that's swarming with members of the Aryan Brotherhood, and two of them tried to make a trophy out of my ass tonight."

"What?"

Darren stopped himself. He hadn't told his lieutenant about the shooting; some part of him didn't trust his department to back him in this situation. If he said a word about Ronnie Malvo, with a grand jury indictment still hanging in the air, Wilson would pull him out of there instantly, and Randie would be on her own. Wilson's end of the line went silent, save for the soft trill of phones ringing in the background. Darren remembered the quiet hush of the sensibly carpeted Houston headquarters, how civilized the public corruption investigations and assists in the world of white-collar crime seemed as he stood on cracked asphalt in a shitheel town on the outskirts of Shelby County, having just been shot at by a member of the Aryan Brotherhood. He told Lieutenant Wilson he was working on a few leads, then got off the phone as quickly as he could, cursing under his breath. Randie crossed her arms over her chest.

"What now?"

Darren told the only truth he knew right then. "I need a drink."

He tossed his tools into the narrow backseat, then started for the bowling alley. Randie seemed confused at first but followed him anyway. Because the bar inside the bowling alley had only beer and wine—and *fuck that*—they made a quick turnaround to the truck and ended up at a tin-roofed joint up the highway. This side of the county line, he could breathe a little more deeply. They were playing blues when Darren held the door open for Randie, a Koko Taylor song filling the one-room bar and dance hall. It was black folks mostly, wrapping up a late afternoon of day-drinking. There were a few men in T-shirts setting up for some kind of a show tonight, bringing in drum kits and portable speakers.

Darren tried to remember what day it was, how long it had been since Greg had called him about the two murders in Lark. Some part of him knew he was edging around a mistake sitting inside this bar, that the heat from the run-in with Brady and Keith Dale was blurring his judgment. It wasn't yet six o'clock: the sun was still setting when they'd left the parking lot. If Randie didn't have anything, he thought he could keep it to one drink. But she met his bourbon with an order for a vodka martini, which somehow came back as two shots of vodka mixed with Sprite and a maraschino cherry tossed in. Randie took a sip, made a face, then drank half of it. They sat in silence for a bit. The music played as two men in their sixties wearing nearly identical checkered shirts played dominoes at the next table, the pieces clinking musically against the wooden tabletop, matching time with the blue notes pouring out of the speakers. Darren was trying to figure out another way into the icehouse, another way to prove Missy's whereabouts on Wednesday night, to verify Lynn's story, when Randie pushed her drink a few inches away and crossed her arms. She spoke so softly that Darren had to lean forward, setting his elbows on the sticky table. The whole thing tilted, startling Darren and nearly upending Randie's drink. But she didn't flinch.

"I was leaving him," she said. "I never said it. But he knew. I was setting him free." She lifted her drink and took a big gulp. The admission weighed her down, sinking her shoulders, the hot shame of it caving her chest. "I never should have married him. I didn't mean it. The love...yes. The life...no."

"This isn't your fault, Randie," he said. "You didn't do this."

He'd been trained in this particularly difficult area of police work, and he knew that folks grappling with sudden death often blame themselves to some degree, even when it makes no sense. He'd felt such a stab of guilt after his uncle William's death—even though he'd been nowhere near the traffic stop that took his life, wasn't even in the state—that he'd lost a few weeks in a nearly blinding depression over the loss of his favorite uncle, the man he'd considered his North Star, the light by which his life was guided. He didn't sleep or eat with any regularity, and his grades suffered, making the decision to leave law school that much easier. William had been killed by a suspect he'd pulled over for expired tags, shot twice in the face as soon as he approached the driver's window. It wasn't fair, and it wasn't Darren's fault. And joining the Rangers wouldn't bring William back. He knew all that. But years later, he was still wearing the badge.

"I'm the reason he came here," Randie said finally.

"What do you mean?" He remembered the scene in Geneva's suddenly, the tense moment playing out right before he got the medical examiner's report. "The guitar," he said, trying to follow. "Michael was bringing it to Lark?"

"He was chasing a love story."

"I don't understand."

"He must have told me a dozen times," she said, a bittersweet smile finding its way to her lips. "The story behind that guitar. He grew up with it. It's what he wanted to believe about us. A love that turns your life around in a single day, a love that changes everything." She reached across the table for her drink and downed the rest. "His uncle, Booker, used to tell the story all the time."

"Booker Wright?" He'd seen the name on Joe Sweet's *Wikipedia* page.

She nodded and ran her finger around the rim of her glass, repeating the name. "Booker."

He played bass in a band with Joe Sweet. That's the way the story always began, she said. Sometime around 1967, Booker and Joe were doing a string of gigs with Bobby Bland. Starting in Detroit, Gary, and Columbus, up north, then down through Missouri, Kansas City, and Joplin, then on to Little Rock. They were heading into Houston that summer, had a few dates set for the Eldorado Room and the Pin-Up Club. They'd met in Chicago in the late fifties, Joe and Booker, and had played as a team for most of their careers, either doing session work for local labels that produced rhythm and blues or crashing chitlin' circuit tours, playing backup for Etta James and Wilson Pickett, Johnnie Taylor and O. V. Wright, even one time jumping on a run of shows with Otis Redding in Atlanta and the Carolinas. They were men who roamed, forever on one highway or another, off to the next town, the next gig, sleeping in motels that would rent to colored folks or in their car—a '59 Impala they shared the note on. Neither was married, though Booker kept girls in several cities, and neither was looking. It was music first and where they could make a dollar second. They hopped on Highway 59 just outside Texarkana, heading south to Houston, speeding through the East Texas woods, where Booker was raised. He and Joe were in the first car, some other cats from Bobby's band following behind, chasing a dream, too. Multiple telegrams had made their way to Don Robey, and there was talk he could get them a spot on a revue he was putting together, something steady around Houston. They thought Robey might actually let them lay something down on wax, recording under their own band name, the Joe Sweet Midnight Revelers.

It looked for all the world like this was their big break, a shot at signing with Peacock Records. A new sharkskin suit or two had been purchased, and pairs of Stacy Adams had been polished in the front seat of the Impala, Booker with a kit at his feet, brush and polish in hand, as Joe drove them down Highway 59.

And this is where the story always took its turn, the way Booker told it. *Joe ain't ever make it to Houston,* he told Michael, who told Randie, who told Darren now, sitting across from him in a one-room juke joint not that far from the one Joe and Booker rolled up to one July night forty-some years earlier.

It was called Geneva's, and it resembled a very well-constructed shack, with sanded wooden slats and scalloped shingles on a roof that was strung with tiny colored bulbs. It had been built by hand, the kind of homey place that looked like it catered to Negro folk traveling on the north–south main line in and out of East Texas. There was no gas pump back then; there was barely what you could call a kitchen, just a pit out back and four burners on a mint-green porcelain stove. And no staff, of course. Just a woman called Geneva who opened the door for them at a quarter past eleven at night, even though she had already closed. There were six in their party, and they were hungry and not ready to make the rest of their trek through Klan country, where city law met its ugly, racist cousin in the faces of small-town cops and rural sheriffs—not on an empty stomach, at least. Geneva fried up a few pork chops with onions and thinly sliced potatoes and let them root around in the cooler she kept out back. For three quarters, they could each have a couple of beers and a nip or two of the gin she didn't have a license for.

Wasn't long before they got to jamming a little, once Geneva said she didn't mind a little music. She wasn't but a few months past twenty-one years old, and a party was all right by her. She owned a few blues records herself but had never gone past Timpson, had never seen a live show, so this was something. Joe had his guitar out first, the Gibson Les Paul on which so many people's fates turned—Joe's and then Michael's and now Randie's and Darren's. Geneva stopped dead in her tracks when she heard him play.

Joe was nearing thirty. He was a dark-skinned man in a pale blue cotton shirt rolled to his elbows, and the ropy muscles in his forearms danced with each note he picked. He was playing a piece of a Lightnin' Hopkins number, *Better make it up in your mind, baby . . . little girl, do you know you traveling a little too slow,* and he kept his eyes on Geneva as she set a steaming plate in front of him, his nearly black eyes peering into her wide, oval ones, lit gold from the gas lamps dangling overhead. As Joe sang the words to her, Booker watched what was happening, felt a current tickle the air around them, felt the one-room cafe grow warm, damp with the breath of seven people packed in a tiny shack on a summer night—five people too many, by the looks on Joe's and Geneva's faces. Never in his whole life had Booker seen two people home in on each other like that. Time Joe walked in, Geneva never took her eyes off him, and he watched her move as she cooked, the way she ducked her head to the beat while flipping meat, twirling onions in pork fat. He picked that guitar and watched her hips sway in a damp chambray dress. Tommy and Bones, runaways from Bobby's band, played a set next while Booker got good and drunk, double-fisting Joe's untouched beers and the flask they kept in the Impala's glove box as Houston slowly slipped away.

He didn't remember losing track of Joe, only that at some point the food had been eaten and the plates were still sitting on the table. Bones, Tommy, and Amon Richmond, another one of Bobby's boys, were talking about getting back on the highway, thought they could make it to Houston by sunrise, unless ol' girl had a place they could stay. Because of the booze, Booker couldn't remember if he was sent outside to ask Geneva if they could crash on her floor or to tell Joe it was time to leave. He didn't even really remember how he knew they were outside—except where else could they be?—and anyway he had to relieve himself in a way that felt epic. He was just getting his fly down when he saw the two of them backed up against an oak tree, Joe's shirt sticking to the skin on his back and sweat running down Geneva's neck as Joe ran a hand up under her thin cotton dress. Booker felt weird holding his johnson while this was going on, and he quickly slipped back inside. Joe came into the cafe a few minutes later and said he wasn't going to Houston. They were welcome to spend the night—at this Geneva nodded, already acting like it was her decision as much as his—but Joe was staying in Lark.

It broke Booker's heart in a way he wouldn't understand for years to come. It was a betrayal first and foremost; there would be no Joe Sweet Midnight Revelers now. But it also lit up some deficit Booker felt in his own life: of all the women he had bedded, pressed up against in the nighttime, not one of them would he want to look at come sunrise. He hoped Joe didn't wake up with any regrets, but either way, Booker wouldn't be around to see it, didn't even want to look him in the eye by daylight. Joe let him keep the car, and in the frantic rush to pack the Impala—grown men avoiding any moment of silence that might be filled with talk of hurt feelings— Joe's Les Paul got packed back into the car. Booker was about ten miles outside Space City before he realized it was in the backseat.

There were good intentions over the years, plans to return it, but over the rest of his career, whether his front mind knew he was do- ing it or not, he never found himself on Highway 59 again—not through East Texas, at least. In fact none of the Wrights returned to Texas. There was always another way to Chicago, his adopted home; the heart always has a workaround. Joe Sweet was like a brother to him, and it was a loss that ate at him for years, compounded greatly when he heard that Joe died before Booker ever got a chance to make peace. When Booker got diagnosed with stage 4 lung cancer, he left the guitar to his nephew, along with a note about a pretty brown lady down in East Texas to whom it rightly belonged.

"That's beautiful," Darren said.

Randie shrugged. She was into her second drink by now, and he was cozying up to his third, right on the line between a nice time and a mistake. "Too good to be true," she said flatly. But Darren didn't buy her cynicism. Joe and Geneva, they'd made it more than forty years; it was real, and they both knew it, even if they didn't recognize that kind of loving devotion in their own lives.

"Not a romantic, huh?" he said, picking beneath the surface of her doubt, wondering what made a woman hear a story like that and turn her back on it.

"I resent it, that's all."

"Why?"

"Telling that story was a way for Michael to suggest I didn't love him enough to leave the road for *him*," she said. "It was manipulative and unfair."

Darren found himself taking Michael's side, not realizing until the words were coming out of his mouth how much they sounded like Lisa's. "Maybe it was just love. Maybe he just wanted you home as much as he could have you there."

At least he wanted to believe that's what Lisa wanted. She'd accepted the idea of him as a Ranger behind a desk, but joining the task force, his push to do more work in the field, had changed something between them. The boots and the truck, the shining five-point star, it was all of a piece of Lone Star swagger that drew a stark contrast between the young law student she'd married and the man life had demanded he become. It terrified him to consider that maybe their marriage had been built on conditions in fine print he never bothered to study, requirements his wife had buried beneath a thousand kisses, a thousand times she said she loved him. "Maybe he wasn't forcing you to make a choice," he said, a wistful hope in his expression that lay naked his own unease around the subject of marital constancy. He looked across the table at Randie, smiling tightly, attempting to play the moment light but failing. By then the band was playing a Sam Cooke song, a slow drag hoping to freeze a moment in time. *To say it's time to go, and she says, yes, I know, but just stay one minute more.*

Darren felt something painful settle in his gut then, saw clearly what he'd been previously unable to face, as if the truth had pulled up a seat at the table and offered to buy the next round. His eyes watered slightly, blurring the neon beer signs on the walls into a kaleidoscope of liquid color. He felt at sea against a rising tide, and he gripped the half-empty glass of bourbon in his hand tightly.

Randie nodded at the ring on his left hand. "What about you?"

She was opening a door, he knew; it was an invitation to talk if he wanted to. Her hand inched the slightest bit across the table, and he had a panicked thought that she might reach out and touch him, that the simplest kindness would break him and make him say things out loud he still didn't want to believe. He and Lisa— he wasn't sure they were going to make it. He leaned back in his chair and built a dam for the rising emotion from the loose stones in another man's marriage, pivoting back to the case.

"There's something I need to tell you."

There was a blues-filled beat of silence before she spoke.

"The white girl," she said, shrugging as if she knew this was coming.

"I don't know if anything happened," he said carefully.

"Wouldn't be the first time," she said.

He suddenly remembered Lynn's words out back of the icehouse. *Some people never learn.*

"White women?" he asked.

"Does it matter?"

"Around here it does."

Randie sighed and looked away. In profile, she looked younger somehow. By daylight hours, he'd put her at thirty-six or thirty-seven, but in this darkened bar, the low light kissed by amber and rose from the neon signs, the skin on her face was so smooth, and her features so tiny, that she looked girlish, even more so when she raised her glass to the bartender, a plump girl in her twenties who was talking on one phone while texting on another. Darren laid a hand on Randie's arm to stop her. He couldn't come back from a fourth drink, but neither could he resist if it showed up at his table. He was still touching her arm when Randie said, "There were women—black, white, who knows? I don't know how many. He never said, and I never asked." She fell silent for a long moment, glancing toward the guitarist on stage, a man in his seventies wearing a gray wide-lapel suit. "I was gone a lot."

"None of this is your fault, Randie."

"Never said it was."

"I'm not trying to hurt you." But he *had* been trying to deflect his own pain. He said softly, "I just wanted to let you know there may be some connection between your husband and another woman."

"I knew that was a possibility when I got on the plane," she said. "And I'm still here."

She ordered another drink anyway, and so did he, as he told her his suspicion that Michael left the bar with Missy, that Keith had found them on the farm road, that this was where the initial confrontation had taken place.

Something in the story still didn't fit.

He felt it like a ghost limb, something missing on his body, an itch he wanted to get at but couldn't. The bourbon and the music, the heat rising from the bodies in the room dancing to a Jackie Wilson song the band was playing. It all swirled, and he couldn't get his thoughts together.

At one point Randie said something he couldn't hear above the bass player, and he'd had to lean in so close that strands of her hair brushed his cheek. She turned and, her lips sticky from her sweet drink, whispered in his ear.

"I was a shitty wife."

Darren placed a hand on her back. She leaned in so he could return a whisper in her ear. "There is sufficient evidence that I've been a shitty husband."

14.

THEY QUIT drinking shortly after the band's first set because it had grown loud and difficult to get the bartender's attention. So they were both still walking straight when they left the roadside bar. Still, Darren tossed the keys to Randie and asked her to drive. She was a drink behind him, and that seemed like sound enough logic, until they arrived at the Chevy, parked on the other side of the gravel lot. She looked so small standing beside the driver's-side door that he couldn't believe he'd *ever* let her behind the wheel. The Chevy was parked on the north side of the building, which was painted a deep blue that nearly blended with the night sky around it. The bar had only a single exterior light, a tin barn light affixed over the front door. The light was too weak to turn corners, which is why he didn't see the blood at first. He actually smelled it before he saw it. This had less to do with his law enforcement training than with his boyhood in Camilla, where his uncles, if one or both of them was lucky enough to bag a buck for the season, used to drain deer carcasses off the back porch, letting the iron-rich blood soak the grass and making Darren hold the hose to run the waste down the hill behind the house, a river of blood that sank into the earth and left a copper-scented tinge in the air until the next hard rain.

Tonight there was a bunch of it leaking out of the driver's side of the truck. Darren told Randie to step back. He'd lost his flashlight in the bayou. He had another one inside the truck, of course, but he wasn't touching anything until he knew what this was. He used the flashlight on his phone to brighten the scene. There were fat drops of blood, dried nearly black, on the pebbles and gravel stones by the left side of the truck, but there was nothing on the door itself.

"What *is* that?" Randie said.

Darren didn't answer. Instead he pulled out the tail of his shirt and used the fabric to cover his hand while he opened the door. Soon as he did, the head of a red fox flopped out along the side of the truck. Its throat had been slit, and blood was starting to gum up around the wound, black clumps of it clinging to the animal's fur. Someone had slit the fox's throat and placed it in the cab of Darren's truck. Randie screamed when she saw it, and again Darren told her to step away from the car. "Don't touch anything," he said. His mind was racing as he turned and looked both ways up and down Highway 59, as he scanned every inch of the bar's parking lot. He saw no one, heard only the music inside the bar, the bass and drums thrumming against his rib cage. He was struck less by the symbolism of the sacrificed animal—the wily fox punished for his cunning, his trespass into woods not his own—than he was with the realization that he and Randie had been followed, the possibility that they were being tracked. He flipped the latch on his holster, making sure the Colt was at the ready, then he dragged the carcass from the truck with his bare hands, ruining his last good shirt. He tore it off and stood breathing heavily in his undershirt as he laid the animal in the tall grass at the edge of the parking lot. Using rags he kept in a lockbox in the bed of his truck, he wiped off as much of the blood as he could and, in the process, confirmed his suspicion that the fox had been slaughtered elsewhere and then carefully placed in his truck, which had been entered without the least sign of a break-in. But somebody over the county line had blood on his hands tonight.

This time of night, he could think of only one place to go to get the mess inside his car cleaned up, the one place in Shelby County where he thought few questions would be asked and where the color of his skin might afford some cover—which, even with the badge, he felt he could use on a night like this. He didn't feel like explaining the blood to an attendant at a well-lit truck stop in Garrison or Timpson. He made Randie drive—even though she was shaky and unsure she could manage—so he could ride in the bed of the truck. Out in the open, the wind stinging his eyes at seventy miles an hour, he kept watch on the highway as it slid away in the dark behind them. The loaded Colt in his lap, he made sure no one was behind them, and he prayed for Randie to steer them to safety.

The cafe was open but empty save for Geneva's granddaughter, Faith, who was sitting in one of the booths typing on a Dell laptop the size of a coffee-table book, and Isaac, who was sweeping up knots of hair by the green barber's chair when Darren walked in, traces of blood on his undershirt and the front of his pants.

Faith looked up and gasped.

Darren said, "Your grandmother here?"

Faith looked at Randie, who had come in behind him, her curls tangled like a fluff of black cotton from the drive; she'd had to ride with both windows rolled down to keep from vomiting the Sprite and the vodka and chunks of jarred red cherries. She and Darren were both breathing heavily, as if they'd run the five miles across the county line from Garrison. "Lock the door," Darren said. Faith stood and complied, ringing the tiny bell as she turned the brass key in the door lock. Again Darren said, "Where's Geneva?" He was already walking behind the counter when Faith said her grandmother was in the kitchen.

Darren pushed open the swinging door to the other room, where Dennis, Geneva's cook, was tying up a black garbage bag, dark liquid leaking out of the bottom, and Geneva was setting pork chops in tinfoil and placing them in Tupperware containers. She had an industrial-size Frigidaire that took up most of the small kitchen, nearly bumping edges with the eight-burner stove. When she closed the refrigerator door, she saw Darren and the blood.

"What in the devil?" she said, taking a step back and glancing anxiously at Dennis while Darren scanned the kitchen for cleaning supplies.

A second later, a blast from a rifle shook the walls.

They heard an explosion of shattering glass from the other room and Faith screaming in a way that filled Darren with dread. He lifted the .45 from its holster and pushed through the kitchen door. Faith was standing by the door to the cafe, which had a crater the size of a baseball just above the handle on which the brass bell was still trembling. "Move," Darren said, pushing her aside.

Randie was crouching on the floor underneath the counter. He fought the urge to go to her. Instead he raised his pistol and went outside just as a pair of red taillights slipped out of Geneva's parking lot, drifting away and up the highway. *North*, Darren noted. Weapon drawn, he checked the parking lot and the weeds surrounding the cafe. He made sure to check for anyone lurking behind Geneva's place, feeling exposed in the dark as he walked the uneven patchwork of grass and clumps of dirt and weeds, his eyes unable to see by the dim light of night, unsure even in which direction he should look. His heart hammered in his chest; his breath came in short, ragged bursts. The lights were on inside the trailer out back, but the rooms were empty. He went through them one by one. Three bedrooms and a narrow kitchen, the fridge and stove an olive green, the whole place done up in a reddish-orange shag carpet. This was Geneva's home, all six hundred square feet of it, and it held her scent, a mix of sandalwood and sugar.

He remembered that Wendy said something about Geneva and a shotgun.

On his return to the cafe, he told her to keep a handful of shells in her apron pocket, to keep the twelve-gauge at the ready; it was going to be that kind of night. He checked on the others next. Isaac was mumbling, over and over, "Ain't see 'em coming, sir," as he wrung his ashy hands. He made a humming noise between each word and was rocking from heel to toe, heel to toe on both feet. He wore ill-fitting slacks and penny loafers, the fake leather peeling at the seams. Darren wondered if the man was mentally challenged—if he was, in the parlance of East Texas, *touched*. The moment she saw Geneva, Faith ran to her grandmother, who wrapped her arms around the girl. The older woman was just coming out of the kitchen, Dennis at her heels. His eyes were lit on fire, his jaw squared in rage. "I knew this was coming," he said. Darren turned to Randie finally. He holstered his weapon and, without thinking, put both hands on her shoulders. He checked to see if she was hurt. He searched for injury, either from a wayward shotgun pellet or flying glass, either of which could put an eye out, could nick an artery or vein. But she appeared unharmed.

She threw her arms around him, holding on as she might have held to a piece of driftwood in raging waters, a lifeline that might slip through her fingers. She clung so tightly he could feel her racing heart through the thin cotton of his undershirt, could feel her tears dampen the skin on his chest, for something in Randie broke then. This night had opened a valve past mere grief, had touched a fear that burrowed beneath the skin of any colored person below the shadow of the Mason-Dixon Line. She was terrified and shaking in his arms. Darren whispered to tell her, "I'm here." *I'm here, too.* Like his people, Mathews men going back generations, he was not going to be run off. As he held the man's wife, Darren doubled down on his vow to catch Michael's killer.

Wasn't but a minute past midnight, and the lights were still on in the front room of Wally's house, across the highway. Darren put Geneva, Faith, and Randie in the trailer out back, with Dennis and the shotgun in a lawn chair out front. Dennis was more than happy to take on Darren's role of protector. Isaac, despite Darren's many protests, took off for home on foot. Geneva told Darren to let him, that there was no reasoning with Isaac when he got spooked. Darren reluctantly let him go, then climbed in his bloody truck and made the short trip across the highway. The gate to Monticello was still open, and Van Horn's squad car was parked in the circular driveway.

Darren hopped out of his truck and banged on the front door.

Wally opened it a few seconds later, and Darren pushed past him, over the door's threshold. Wally looked into his living room and said, "Parker, we got us a live one here. Smelled the bourbon on him before he hit the door."

Van Horn stood from behind the dining-room table, where pa-

pers and files and a mug of coffee sat next to a desktop computer
that had clearly been deposited there for the sheriff's purposes.
There were cords running every which way and coming to rest in a
tangled pile at Van Horn's feet. The sheriff saw the blood on Darren's clothes, the fact that he wasn't wearing his shirt or his badge.
Wally let out a whistle. "You didn't hear that shot?" Darren said.
"Right across the highway, and you're sitting in here drinking coffee and not doing a damn thing."

"Watch your language, son."

"*Ranger,*" Darren said.

"What shot?" Wally said, but his head turned in the direction
of his front window, through which he could see Geneva's cafe, a
telling gesture.

"Not ten minutes ago, somebody shot through the front of
Geneva's."

Wally said, "That's a shame."

But Van Horn was less dismissive. He hiked up his pants and
went to grab his car keys from the corner of the dining-room table.
"I'll have a look."

Darren said the perpetrator was long gone and gave a description
of the back end of a pickup truck, the size and shape of the taillights. It'd been too dark to read the license plate, but he thought
he saw the number 2, maybe 5.

"How much have you been drinking, *Ranger?*" the sheriff said.

"I know what I saw."

"Like I said, I'll take a look."

"I can look for a rifle shell, but if you go after 'em now, you
might find a gun that's still warm. I suggest you start looking in
and around Wally's bar."

"You the one brought trouble up there," Wally said.

"It was two of them tried to jump me today, tried to shoot my ass."

"That's not the way I heard it."

"Wally, stay out of this," Van Horn said. To Darren, he said, "We got an eyewitness said you were the one out there waving a pistol around."

"After an assault on an officer."

The sheriff nodded toward Darren's undershirt, stained with the rust-brown traces of blood. "And you identified yourself as such? Had a badge visible? 'Cause this could all be tossed up to a misunderstanding. Looking like you do mighta confused—"

"This," he said, referring to the blood on his clothes, "is after some piece of shit tailed me out to Garrison and dumped a dead animal in my truck."

"Well, I can't do nothing about that. You was over the county line."

"Getting lit, apparently," Wally added.

Darren felt sober as a stone. He balled his left hand and rapped his fist hard on the cherry wood of the dining-room table. "Somebody's waging a terror campaign, trying to stop me from looking into the murder of Michael Wright."

"That shooting at Geneva's don't have nothing to do with you," Wally said. "A local girl was killed out back of her place, and it's just stirring up long-held feelings about the kind of folks coming in and out of her place. Folks gon' sure use this as a way to push her out. If she'd sell it to me, I could make her comfortable for the rest of her life, and she ain't have to fool with standing on her feet twelve hours a day. But Geneva don't know when to cut her losses."

"You're worried about the folks coming through her place when you got members of the most violent gang in the state spilling out of your icehouse? Two of whom pulled a gun on me tonight while mentioning Brotherhood business with the Rangers?"

They'd said Ronnie Malvo.

"We have an eyewitness who said no such thing took place," Wally said.

We, Darren noted. He seemed to already know a hell of a lot about an incident he didn't see. He wondered what else Wally knew about Brady and Keith.

"You know they're ABT?" he said.

"Who?"

"Brady, your manager, and Keith Dale."

Van Horn got a sense of where this might be headed and said, "I heard from Brady that things got a little heated, but that's a serious accusation."

"And based on what?" Wally said. "A few tattoos?"

"I worked the fed task force investigating the Brotherhood. I know more than a little bit about their goings-on. The guns and the drugs," he said, looking at Wally, making sure the possibility wasn't lost on him that either one of these things could be moving through his icehouse.

"And I happen to know you were removed from that task force," Wally said. "Had your badge suspended until you miraculously arrived in Lark."

So he got it like that, huh? Darren thought.

Apparently Wally had enough juice to dig deep into Darren's department and come up with his personnel record. He wondered again about Wally's business dealings, what put him in this five-thousand-square-foot house, how and from which direction he was connected to law enforcement, on the up-and-up or the down and dirty. Was he merely letting the Brotherhood drink in his icehouse or was there more to the story? Wally had a smug look on his face as he said, "And you in here drunk and looking like an alley cat. It ain't a wonder they took your badge."

From the other side of the house, a child cried.

Keith's son, Darren remembered. He couldn't understand what that boy was still doing here, why he'd been left here by his father and his grandparents.

"I'm not drunk," Darren said.

But he smelled like it, and he looked like hell.

He turned to Sheriff Van Horn and said, "I want Keith Dale."

"I'm not about to arrest a man on your say-so."

"I want a sit-down, that's all," Darren said. "I want an interview."

Van Horn pretended to consider the request, but he knew he couldn't very well deny this of a Texas Ranger investigating the case. Darren didn't even need to make the request, but he wanted a setting only the sheriff could provide.

"Lark don't have no police force," Van Horn said, "but I'd be happy to let you talk to the man here, with me present, of course."

He looked to Wally to confirm this was okay.

Darren shook his head. "I want it at the sheriff's office in Center."

"As long as I'm there, too," Van Horn said. "Not turning this into a free-for-all. I'll allow it only if you keep the questioning along a very strict line."

Van Horn could *allow* all he wanted to for all Darren cared.

He was about to get Keith Dale in an interrogation room.

15.

HE GRABBED a plastic bucket and a bunch of rags from Geneva's kitchen, filling one with water and splashes of bleach and tucking the others in a bunch under his arm. Then he walked outside. Working by the glow of his headlights reflecting off the cafe's front windows, he scrubbed down the front seat of the truck with the doctored water, sopping up rags and wiping and then dropping them on the pavement when they got too soaked to do more than spread the blood around. He was ever mindful of the sanctity of Geneva's place, not wanting to leave puddles of blood in her parking lot, not knowing where or whether she kept a hose around the place. He worked in silence, ear to the road for any passing cars on the highway, the Colt .45 at his hip. He'd propped the broken front door open, which is why he didn't hear Faith come out. He caught a flash in his peripheral vision and had his hand on the butt of his weapon before he heard her voice. "You should try ammonia on the carpets," she said. Walking closer to the truck, she caught a whiff of the bleach and said, "But you can't mix it with the bleach or you're liable to fall out. Still, for blood, ammonia's better on rugs."

"You shouldn't be out here," he said. "Randie okay?"

"She and Grandmama sleep," she said before bending over and picking up two of the rags. Not squeamish in the least, she walked to the edge of the parking lot and squeezed the smelly pink water into the weeds. When she returned the rags ready for reuse, she looked at him and said, "You like her?"

"Randie?" he asked, though he'd known whom she meant.

"I never met a widow young as her."

"It's a terrible thing that happened," he said, leaving it at that. He wasn't entirely sure what she meant by the question or how he should answer.

"I never met a Texas Ranger, either."

Darren turned from the open driver's-side door and looked at Faith. She was a small girl, petite, with fine features. Her lips and her hair were the two biggest things about her, giving her a doll-like quality even though she had to be at least eighteen to be getting married. Her lipstick had faded hours ago and had left a pink stain, and she chewed on her bottom lip, wanting to say more. He thanked her for wringing the rags, and she said, "It's salt and baking soda to get blood out of clothes. I can wash yours if you want."

"You know a lot about cleaning up blood, young lady," he said.

He was trying to play the moment light, searching for some levity on this dark night, but the look on Faith's face made him sorry he'd said anything at all.

"I've had to clean my fair share."

He wasn't sure if there was more she had to say or if he wanted to hear it.

He asked her a generic question instead.

"You live in the back with your grandmother?"

"I do now. I was at Wiley College before this. It's in Marshall."

He knew Wiley. Most black folks in East Texas did. Wiley, Prairie View A&M, and Texas Southern University were hallmarks of black collegiate education going back generations. His uncles got matching bachelor's degrees from Prairie View; Duke, Darren's father, had been accepted to TSU, in Houston, but deferred so he could follow in his big brother William's footsteps by doing a tour of duty in Vietnam.

"What'd you study?"

"I was a public relations major," she said. "Wasn't gon' be in this town forever. I always thought I'd end up in Dallas or Houston somewhere."

"Still can, can't you?" he said. He'd gotten most of the dried blood off the seat, though it had taken a lot of sweat and effort. The carpets were left, and he thought to simply toss them into the truck bed until he could get the Chevy detailed, whenever that would be. "A PR degree—you can take that just about anywhere."

"I never got my degree."

There was a brief moment when he chose to leave it there.

She was a nice girl, but she had small-town problems that didn't interest him while he was cleaning blood out of his truck in the middle of the night. He didn't want a story. He asked about something to eat. It was coming on eight hours since he'd had anything in his belly besides bourbon. Faith walked toward the kitchen, and Darren followed, asking as he set down the bucket and rags where he could get some plywood to fix up the front door. Faith told him to check out back, and he did, riffling through vegetable crates and a collection of old soda bottles—grape Nehi and Coca-Cola— and newspapers stacked in a damp cardboard box. There were more cardboard boxes, broken down and leaning against the Dumpster.

Darren grabbed a handful of these and a roll of duct tape from a shelf high above the kitchen sink. While Faith heated up a couple of pork chops on the stove, Darren jerry-rigged a cover for the front door, leaving the bell in place, free to swing and sing for Geneva's customers. He could smell the pork fat sizzling on the bone and nearly tore into the meat with his hands when Faith set a plate across from him on the counter. She poured him a Dr Pepper. He wanted a beer at the very least, but he considered himself on duty now and wanted to be alert. Faith leaned against the counter from the other side, near the cash register, and watched him eat. He finished and wanted more, but he didn't want to trouble the girl more than he already had. "That woman ruined my life, my mama," she said suddenly and with a heaping dose of drama and bitter spite. She seemed pleased to have a captive audience in Darren. "That's why I didn't want to go with my grandmama to Gatesville, if you were wondering."

He wasn't.

He sipped the soda and belched.

"When word got up to Wiley that my mama shot my daddy, you know those girls threw me off the AKA line without even giving me a chance to explain. I just kind of fell apart after that, couldn't keep up with my grades, nothing. That's why I didn't finish. I didn't flunk out or anything. I was just too ashamed. It's bad enough I had to tell Rodney it's just gon' be Grandmama at the wedding. His daddy offered to walk me down the aisle, but that ain't proper."

Darren dropped his napkin on top of the bones on his plate, staring at the grease soaking through the paper as he said, "I'm sorry. What did you say?"

"There was a story on it in the Houston paper," Faith said, genuinely confused when she added, "I thought you knew," as if a one-inch piece in the back of a Houston newspaper would have caught and held Darren's attention.

A few years ago, Faith said, her mother, Mary Sweet, snuck up on her husband, Joe, soaking in the tub. There was only one bathroom in the two-bedroom house Faith grew up in, an A-frame wood cabin about a half of a mile from Geneva's cafe. The bathroom was at the back of the house, and Mary was able to sneak up on Lil' Joe without his hearing a thing over the radio that was sitting on a chair next to the bathtub. She was holding a pistol and a grudge, and she was prepared to force a reckoning. Lil' Joe was stark naked, and Mary was wearing one of Lil' Joe's Houston Rockets T-shirts like a dress. What followed could be trusted only to the degree that you were willing to believe a convicted felon.

Mary pointed the pistol at her husband's forehead while grabbing the radio by its handle. She held it over the water, making sure the cord was still plugged into the wall. The gun in one hand, the radio held over the water in the other, she said, "Which way you want it? 'Cause either way, I'm through."

Lil' Joe, who was fair-skinned, like Faith, and had a tiny gap between his front teeth and dark brown curls that were damp and sticking against his neck at the water line, smiled at his wife of twenty years, misreading the moment as emotional theater. He'd been sleeping with the other woman for more than a year, and Mary hadn't ever done a thing about it, never did more than suck her teeth behind his back. He had a cigarillo clamped between his back teeth, and he didn't bother to remove it when he told Mary point-blank, "Well, I guess you better go ahead and shoot me, then." He talked tough, but the second Mary dropped the radio on the pink bathroom rug and cocked the .22, Lil' Joe jumped out of the water and knocked Mary down as he ran toward the front of the house. He had gotten almost to the front door when she shot him three times in the back.

After her mother was arrested, Faith cleaned up the scene herself, weeping on her hands and knees, because there was no one else to do it for her. Geneva was so shattered by the loss of her son so soon after her husband, Joe, had been shot in a cafe robbery that she closed the restaurant for a week, something she hadn't done when Joe was killed. They had to sell the house anyway, with Lil' Joe and Mary both gone. And since she'd left school, Faith had been living in the trailer with her grandmother. "Rodney says after the wedding we gon' find a little place all to ourselves."

"Why'd she do it?"

"Daddy took up with a white girl," Faith said. "He used to hang out at Wally's place, the icehouse up the way, before it got to be so much hate coming out of there, and the two of them used to run around some, parking on FM 19."

Darren remembered Huxley's sage words. *Lil' Joe used to hang around that bar, and look what happened to him,* he'd said. And on their heels, he heard Lynn's husky condemnation of Missy talking to Michael. *Some folks never learn.*

Their voices landed in harmony in his head.

"And the white girl?" he said, even though by then he'd already guessed.

"Missy Dale."

Faith picked up Darren's plate and took it through the kitchen door. Darren stood off the vinyl-topped stool and walked around the counter to follow her. The water was running in the sink, and Faith used a ratty sponge to hand-wash Darren's plate. He was momentarily at a loss for words. "He thought he was slick, Daddy did," Faith said. "Sometimes men act like they don't know who washing they clothes." She set the plate and fork on a drying rack and said, "Speaking of which, you get out of those pants and shirt and I'll clean 'em."

"Did you know her?" he asked. "Missy?"

"No. We were the same age, went to the same high school in Timpson, but I never said a word to her. She never spoke to me; our worlds never crossed," she said, ignoring or not realizing the irony of what she was saying. She wiped her hands on a dish towel and thanked him for fixing her grandmother's door.

Darren realized that he'd never seen a picture of Missy Dale, just a tail of blond hair peeking from beneath the white sheet that had covered the body on the morning he rolled into town. "Was she a pretty girl?" he asked.

Faith shrugged and said, "They don't always have to be."

Darren didn't get more than two hours of sleep, trading guard shifts with Dennis until the sun came up. When he woke for good, he found his clothes, still warm from the iron, pressed and resting on the arm of the corduroy love seat in Geneva's living room. The trailer was still and silent, no sign of Geneva or Randie, and outside, the braided nylon lawn chair was empty. He'd woken up thinking about the kid, Keith Jr., who was, it seemed, living in Wallace Jefferson's house. Now that he knew about the relationship between her son and Missy Dale, there were questions he wanted to ask Geneva. But overhead, clouds were rolling in from the east, thick and threaded with charcoal, threatening rain. If he wanted to dust the Chevy for prints, the time was now. He should have done it last night; there was a lot about last night he should have done differently. He wasn't hungover, saved by the greasy pork chops he ate after midnight, but there was a haze at the edge of his memory, not so much in his recall of the events—the blood and the shooting and the confrontation in Wally's house—but rather in his access to roads not taken, ways he could have handled himself better.

He worked from a kit he kept inside the truck, moving in silence around the Chevy as he dusted, focusing mostly on the driver's-side door handle, especially the area around the lock, which had been expertly disabled. He was just moving to the passenger-side door, picking up a few latent prints that belonged to either Randie or persons yet unknown, when the first drops began to fall. He locked the kit and evidence cards he'd collected inside his truck and ran across the parking lot to Geneva's front door. The cardboard patch was damp but holding under the slight overhang of the cafe's roof. Inside, the place was packed—more customers in Geneva's than Darren had ever seen, including Huxley and Tim, on his return trip from Chicago, as well as faces he'd never seen before. The booths were all occupied, so that the only open seat Randie could find was in the barber's chair on the other side of the cafe. Isaac was not in his usual spot, nor did Darren see any sign of Faith. He asked about her, speaking to Geneva over the countertop, hoping to work his way toward their conversation last night, the news he'd learned about her late son and his romance with Missy.

"Sleep," Geneva said in response. She had her hands full, turning out order after order from the kitchen, and aside from nodding once to the patched-up front door and saying "'Preciate that, son," she ignored him completely. There was no way to get her alone to talk about something so sensitive—unless Darren were to use his badge to compel her to talk. He'd rather approach her as a friend, one to whom she *wanted* to confess her son's affairs. And anyway, when Randie saw him enter, she hopped off the barber's chair and came quickly to his side, asking to get out of there. She wanted a ride to the motel so she could shower and change her clothes. The talk with Geneva about Lil' Joe and Missy would have to wait.

Once they were outside and in the truck's cab, which still smelled of bleach, Randie buckled her seat belt and said, "Was that real?" She had twin half-moon shadows under her eyes. "Did any of last night really happen?"

"All of it," he said.

He let her use the shower first. If he had to, he could make do with only a few splashes of cold water on his face, running a finger of toothpaste across his teeth. There was a toothbrush sealed in plastic that came with the room, but Darren made sure to save that for Randie. Instead he washed his hands and scrubbed his face with a small pink bar of soap, aware of the door between the sink and the bathroom, which was cracked open. He heard the water behind the curtain, felt the hot steam drifting across the few feet that separated him from the woman in the shower. He felt things he wasn't proud of, felt a stirring in a place that was less sordid than it was tender, a warmth beneath his breastbone. Right or wrong, he was embarrassed by his affection for her. He felt an intense obligation to shield her from harm that was equal to his commitment to avenge her husband's death. He wanted to make her wrong about Texas, wanted her to know it as a place that did not fell black men and get away with it. He dried his face on a rough towel, folding it back neatly so Randie could use it, too.

His phone was ringing on the edge of the queen bed.

It was Wilson.

He had a time and a place for the Dale interview—two o'clock at the sheriff's office in Center, per Darren's request—along with

explicit instructions. Darren was to do his job thoroughly while offering due deference to local law enforcement at all times, which
meant backing off questions of which Sheriff Van Horn disap-
proved. The murder of Missy Dale remained solely under the sheriff's purview until adequate evidence arose that linked it to the
death of Michael Wright. "Not gon' get that if I can't talk to the
man," Darren said.

"Nobody saying you can't talk to the man. I respect Van Horn
for not blocking you on this, and you owe him a little back. Just
be mindful we got to work with these local departments long after this is over. Rangers can't afford to get a reputation for not
respecting their authority. And if I'm supposed to go to bat for
you with the higher-ups at headquarters in Austin, I need to be
able to tell them that you've toed the line, that you're not a loose
cannon."

"You know me better than that."

"I know you, that's right. And I'm asking you to respect your
limits out there. The thing with the local girl is delicate. Prelim-
inary results came out of the medical examiner's office early this
morning that's changed some things."

"Like what?"

"I'm not at liberty to say."

"But you know?"

"When and if the time is right, Van Horn promised to share the
findings."

"Have you seen it?" Darren asked. "The autopsy?"

Wilson fell silent on the other end. Darren heard the water turn
off in the bathroom, heard the screech of a tight faucet handle as
Randie's shower ended.

"There's a concern about your connection with the woman who

runs the black cafe out there. Ginny's or Genevieve's, is it? Older black woman?"

"Geneva. What does Missy's autopsy have to do with her?"

"When and if the time is right," Wilson said. "Van Horn promised."

Darren hung up the phone just as Randie was coming out of the bathroom, reaching as quickly as she could for the towel resting on the edge of the sink and wrapping it around herself before she stepped out fully from the bathroom. Darren turned his head, mumbling, "I'm sorry." Randie said she could dress in the bathroom, but Darren said that wouldn't be necessary. He stepped outside and watched the rain that was falling now in fat gray drops, streams of it twisting like ropes as it ran off the eaves, splashing the asphalt in front of the spot where his truck was parked and dotting the toes of his boots with water. He dialed Greg's desk phone at the Bureau, listening as it rang.

That's when he saw the other car in the parking lot. It was a gray Buick sedan, and there was a white man in his thirties, with close-cropped dark brown hair, behind the wheel. He was parked near to the motel lobby, but the nose of his vehicle was pointed at the door in front of which Darren was standing. He'd watched Darren come out of Randie's room, and now the man's driver's-side door opened. Darren put his hand on the butt of the Colt and called for him to halt his approach. The man either didn't hear him or didn't care, because he kept walking. The young man wore a plaid button-down shirt underneath a brown sport coat. He had Rockports on his feet. He was wearing glasses, but maybe he was due for a checkup, because it wasn't until he got just a few feet away from Darren that he seemed to register the gun and the badge on Darren's chest. The man stopped cold, dropping a scuffed leather messenger bag on the wet pavement. He was younger than Darren originally thought. There was no way this kid had seen three decades.

He reached for something behind his back, and Darren felt all the blood in his body rush to his trigger finger. He felt a shooter's high, a power that made him feel trippy, that made his senses of sight and sound sharpen and reason recede into the distant gray. He made a quick scan: the messenger bag, the ill-fitting khaki pants. Darren lowered the gun at the exact moment the man pulled a leather billfold from his back pocket. Darren let out a breath he didn't know he'd been holding, felt his heart explode with relief. The man produced identification before Darren could ask for it. When Randie stepped out of the room a few minutes later, Darren introduced her to Chris Wozniak of the *Chicago Tribune*. The outside world had arrived in Lark, and it had some questions.

16.

IF CHRIS WOZNIAK was at all curious as to why the Texas Ranger investigating Randie's husband's death had walked out of her motel room at nine o'clock in the morning, he kept it to himself. Twice he looked at Randie and asked, "And you're the widow?" as if he had to make sure. He offered his condolences and said he'd like the chance to interview her as well. "You know Teresa Martin, my editor said." Randie nodded but didn't make eye contact.

"We were at SAIC together. The Art Institute of Chicago," she added for Darren's benefit. She was wearing a pair of black pants and a crimson, crepe-paper-thin T-shirt. She was shivering and had her arms crossed tightly across her chest. Darren had an impulse to go inside the room to find her white coat, but this was October in Texas, and it would be eighty degrees before noon.

"I know the school," he said. "I lived in Chicago for a few years."

She looked at him strangely, as if the information didn't line up with the boots and badge the man in front of her was wearing. "You did?" she asked.

Darren nodded. "I went to law school at U of C."

Law school didn't fit, either. But the mention of it made her smile.

"Michael went to U of C," she said.

"Yeah, yeah," Wozniak said. "I want to get into all that. The victim's background...and interesting that you guys have that in common," he said to Darren as he reached into the messenger bag for a pen and pad. He jotted down a quick note, then turned back to Darren, who was shocked that he seemed so callous in front of the dead man's wife. "Look," the reporter said. "I've got a camera crew coming. Later today, I hope. And I'd love to get a sense of the basic facts at this stage, not to mention a sense of the lay of the land, so to speak. There was something about some redneck bar in town." He glanced at Randie. There was more he wanted to poke at here, but not in front of her. "I can drive."

He had a digital camcorder in his rental car and wanted to get pictures of the crime scene as soon as possible, thought Darren could fill him in on the drive over. But Darren wanted to get back to Geneva's, wanted to dig around this newly discovered deeper connection between Missy Dale and the world of Geneva's cafe. It felt as revelatory as the fact that Michael had likely spent his last hours at Wally's icehouse. These two establishments, on opposite ends of town and separated by a quarter mile of highway, were like twin poles in the story of these two murders: it was impossible to understand one without the other. And now Van Horn was holding some new piece of information that involved Geneva. Darren didn't know what that could be.

He didn't like the idea of leaving Randie alone with this dude. But more than ever, he felt that the rifle shot through Geneva's cafe last night was meant for him. The Aryan Brotherhood of Texas had an enemy in Shelby County, and he might actually be putting

Randie in danger the more time they spent together. As he looked out across the parking lot—empty save for his truck and Randie's and Wozniak's rentals—he scanned the slick highway running in front of the motel, rainwater sluicing into weed-choked ditches, and came up with a plan. He was not about to share any piece of the puzzle with a reporter until he understood how it fit into the bigger picture. And right now he didn't have the bigger picture. He wanted to know more about Missy and Lil' Joe, Geneva's son. A thought had been forming in his head since last night. If Keith Dale knew about his wife and Lil' Joe, who's to say he didn't take out on Michael Wright the fury he never got a chance to take out on Lil' Joe? It offered an explanation for the sequence of the killings that felt right to Darren. Keith comes upon Michael and his wife leaving the icehouse on the farm road, and he kills the black man he thought was messing with her. Two days later, he murders his wife in a fit of rage. Both bodies found in the same muddy water. Why Keith waited two days to kill his wife Darren couldn't say. But he'd get into the timeline when he had Keith in the box at the sheriff's office later.

He wanted to talk to Geneva first.

He gave Randie a pleading look as he told Wozniak that it was Rangers protocol to give the deceased's family a chance to speak with the press before the department made an official state-ment. The lie made no sense. But he was over six feet tall and wearing a badge and gun, which made for a convincing package. Wozniak didn't question it. Randie would stay behind with the reporter, talking about Michael and what she knew—or, frankly, didn't know—about his trip to Texas. Darren put no restrictions on it. It was her story to tell. And it would buy him time. She asked when he would be back and looked, for a moment, undone by the idea of being without him. He didn't mention the Keith Dale interview in front of the reporter, but he looked at her and made a promise. He'd be back soon.

Wendy was out front of the cafe when he pulled the Chevy into the parking lot, which was still full. Geneva's was as busy as it had been when he left with Randie this morning, if not more so, and he wasn't sure how easy it would be to get Geneva alone. The topic was delicate and private. *Unless it ain't,* he thought. Lark was a tiny little dot of a town. Everyone at Geneva's seemed to know about Lil' Joe hanging out at the icehouse, and Lynn, the bartender, had hinted at a predilection for black men on Missy's part. Maybe Missy and Lil' Joe's relationship was common knowledge, even if it was rarely spoken of.

"You still putt-putting around here?" Wendy said.

She had a can of beer in her lap along with the rusty .22, keeping watch over the day's wares: jelly jars and cast-iron pots, a wooden wig stand, and a yellow-and-red Coca-Cola crate probably thirty years old. It was clearly stuff she'd found lying around her house, items that, placed on a quilt by a colorful old lady, took on enough historical significance to earn a little pocket change. Darren admired the swindle. "You know they ain't gon' let you arrest nobody over that killing, neither one of 'em," she said. The rain had stopped for now, and two clouds broke away from each other, clearing the way for a snatch of sun.

Wendy shielded her eyes.

Darren smiled and said, "All the more reason you ought to feel free to tell me the truth." Then with no preamble, he said, "So that child is Lil' Joe's, right?"

"Well, lookie who woke up sharp this morning."

"And Geneva knows?"

Wendy looked at him as if he were slow.

"Keith, too?" he asked.

"He gave that boy his name, but that ain't fooling nobody."

"Why the hell is Van Horn asking for lists of Geneva's customers, folks passing through town, when the dead woman's husband was raising another man's child?" Darren asked. A child Keith and his family seemed to have fobbed off on Wally and Laura Jefferson, a retroactive renouncing of a boy who wasn't blood? Wendy waved him to her right so she wouldn't have to stare into the sun behind him. He stood under the roof's overhang, and in the little bit of shade it provided, he saw that Wendy's eyes were a paler brown than he'd thought, a rich honey color. She said, "You a Texas boy, you know how this story goes."

It was Wally who started telling tales, she told him.

"He holds a mean grudge."

Wendy was certain he'd steered the sheriff in a direction that served *him*.

"See, Wallace Jefferson's people built this town," she said.

Lark had begun as a plantation more than a hundred and seventy years ago. That's the old house there, she said, nodding toward Wally's place across the highway and the dome of Monticello. Wally's people fancied themselves some distant relation of the nation's third president, saw themselves as direct heirs to American history. And like ol' Thomas, they prospered as slave owners, clear of conscience and flush with cash. Juneteenth switched things around for them, but not that much; there was always a new way to make a dollar. Most black folks living in Lark came from sharecropping families, trading their physical enslavement for the crushing debt that came with tenant farming, a leap from the frying pan into the fire, from the certainty of hell to the slow, hot torture of hope.

The Jefferson family made a good piece of money when the state paved a brand-new highway right through the center of town. Wendy supposed it was just good business sense that kept Wally in fancy trucks and diamond rings a generation later. That and the fact that Wally still owned almost 90 percent of the land in this little corner of the county—all except Geneva's place. Darren wondered how a young single black woman was able to buy property off the highway in the 1960s. "That," Wendy said, "is the story I'm trying to tell you."

Geneva Marie Meeks never made it past eleventh grade, which was the year her daddy got sick and could no longer tend his ten little acres of cotton. Her mother and brothers pitched in, but still the family fell behind, far enough for them to decide that even the youngest, Geneva, would have to work. She could always cook, had been feeding her family of six since she was barely tall enough to reach the top shelf in the cupboard, so she took a job in the Jeffersons' kitchen—making breakfast, lunch, and dinner six days a week as well as bag lunches for young Wallace Jefferson III, who was in high school up to Timpson and had a little Ford Fairlane his daddy bought him so he could breeze up and down the highway in style twice a day. Wally had always been a little too fussed over, made to think he was more special than he was. But he idolized his father and everything about him, from the way he cinched his britches tight at the waist, held up by a sterling silver buckle, to the gentlemanly way he carried himself around town, holding open doors for ladies and never saying the word *nigger* in mixed company. Wallace Jefferson II, whom folks called Jeff, was on his second wife by then. After his first wife, Wally's mother, had passed suddenly, he'd taken to frequenting church socials as far away as Marshall and Dallas looking for a decent girl to marry, to make his house a home again. But the second Mrs. Wallace Jefferson II, Phyllis Slatterly of Longview, didn't last, having greatly overestimated the joys of plantation living in the twentieth century. She quickly grew bored in a town of only a couple hundred people, many of whom were too black and poor to admire her station in life to the degree she felt her title as Mrs. Wallace Jefferson II deserved. Besides, she had to drive nearly two hundred miles to Dallas to spend Jeff's money in any way that was satisfying. She didn't last but eighteen months before fleeing and having the marriage annulled in the courthouse in her hometown. Jeff let her go and raised his boys—Wally and his younger brother, Trent, who died in a car accident during his freshman year at Texas A&M—on his own. He made peace with his life as a bachelor, and he gave up on love. Which was why he was in no way prepared for having Geneva in his house.

She was too young for him, he knew that.

In fact it was not lost on him the looks his son Wally gave Geneva when she passed through any room in the house he was in or the way Wally would bring her a cold Coke all the way from Timpson and ask her to take a break and sit on the back steps with him. They were close in age, Wally and Geneva, if not in temperament. Even at eighteen he was a blowhard, a boy who didn't quite fill out his shoes, who loved to brag about money he hadn't earned. Geneva was a quiet girl, smart and funny, if you caught her in the right mood, and she knew about hard work. Two or three nights a week she'd stay late prepping food so she could come in a little later the next day—which meant extra time she could spend cooking for her own family.

They got to talking that way, the elder Jefferson and Geneva. Late at night, Jeff, a whiskey on the kitchen table, would watch

Geneva knead dough for dumplings or wash collards leaf by leaf to make sure she got all the cabbage worms. He offered to help a few times, but she told him to sit down, and he did.

They talked about school. Did she miss it? *Yes.*

They talked about her daddy. Was he getting any better? *No.*

They talked about Jeff's first wife and how he still cried sometimes.

Some nights they traded stories and family lore, his ancestors versus hers.

He'd have left it alone, but goddamn, she was pretty.

"And she'll tell you," Wendy said. "She'll tell you she fell for him, too."

Jeff took to driving Geneva home on the nights she stayed late. She didn't live more than a mile away, but he started to feel strange letting her walk out the door after midnight. And he started to feel strange in other ways, too. A lick of heat up and down his neck when she looked at him. A terrible ache below the waist if she was standing too close. And a yearning to touch her everywhere, to know what those curls would feel like wrapped around his fingers.

One night she told her mama the Jeffersons wanted her to work through the night, and when Jeff climbed into his pickup truck to drive her home as usual, she told him to park somewhere instead. He looked at her across the cab and felt a rush of blood through his whole body. Knowing what was about to happen, he chewed on his fingernails as he drove them out to the very edge of the land on which his mansion sat. He had never been with a colored girl, so when he tasted her for the first time, a kiss that lasted near about an hour, he was too ignorant to know if it was black or Geneva that tasted so sweet.

It was her first time, and he told himself to take it slow.

But he couldn't help what happened. Soon the truck was shaking in the middle of that field, Jeff with one hand pressed against the damp passenger-side window and the other cupping her left hip. They rocked each other, and Geneva screamed and bit his earlobe and prayed in gratitude. It was over in less than ten minutes, and they lay together in the front of the truck till the sun came up.

It's possible Wally didn't know what had happened when he came down for breakfast the next day and Geneva "arrived" for work wearing the same clothes as she'd been wearing the day before. But what he *did* know is that shortly after that fateful night, his father, without explaining a word about it, starting building a small shack right across the highway from their home. He built it by hand, paying Isaac, who used to do yard work for the Jefferson family, five extra dollars a week to saw lumber. Isaac wasn't but around twelve at the time, as thickheaded as he is now, Wendy said. Wally first thought it was a house for Geneva, which was bad enough, but a cafe on his family's land galled the boy much worse. His daddy had built a business for the girl he loved. Jeff hand-painted the sign with her name on it, and it was Geneva's idea to string up some lights on the building, make her place colorful and inviting. It was the only colored place for miles back then, and she and Jeff made a good profit, enough for her family to finally give up tenant farming. When her daddy finally passed from the cancer, she laid him to rest in a satin-lined coffin, had money enough for a marble headstone and a sea of flowers—lilies, her mother's favorite. They were an odd family of sorts, Jeff staying for meals at the restaurant, eating at the same table as the colored family who used to work for him, and Wally refusing to join him.

Anybody who looked at it would say they were happy, Geneva and Jeff.

And then came Joe.

The night she told Jeff about the music man, Joe had already been staying in the back room of the cafe for two days. Those two had fallen hard and pledged true to each other from the very first they met. And Joe was through hiding.

She sat Jeff at the nicest table and brought him a slice of lemon meringue pie and a glass of whiskey, neither of which he touched. He saw her with the much younger and much blacker man and asked one question. "This what you want, 'Neva?" And when she said it was, he pushed back from the table.

"Fine, then."

Those were the last words he ever said to her.

Joe bought out the place with his music money, and Jeff, God bless him, was dead within a year. And yet here Geneva was, still making good money off Wally's land, least that's the way he saw it. She had stolen it from him, and for decades he'd been on her to sell it to him, not that he would do anything except tear it down. "It's just the principle of the thing with him, you understand."

"And how soon after Joe arrived was Lil' Joe born?"

It was as delicately as Darren could think to put it.

"Child, I don't know nothing about all them dates," Wendy said. "But if you asking if Lil' Joe is kin to Joe, then the answer is no. Didn't matter much. Joe loved that boy just like he was his own. They don't make 'em like Joe no more."

"So Wally and Lil' Joe were brothers?"

"You pretty quick," she said with a wink.

"That baby—my God, Missy's kid is Wally's nephew. Does Wally know?" He'd had Keith Jr. staying in his house since the murder.

"I don't know what that man know."

A heavyset black woman walked out of Geneva's picking at her teeth with a red toothpick. She glanced at Wendy's wares laid out next to the door, leaned in for a closer look, then thought better of it and waddled to her burgundy Honda Civic. The car tilted heavily to the left when she got behind the driver's seat, and Wendy said, "I have a girdle in my car. Bet she'd have bought that."

As the Honda backed up and pulled out of the parking lot, Darren saw a curious sight. A Shelby County squad car pulling off the highway with its lights on, flashing blue and white. The siren was off, and Darren felt a disconnect between sound and speed that made it seem like the world around him was moving in slow motion. A second squad car pulled in behind the first, and they both parked at the edge of Geneva's lot. When Van Horn stepped out of the first car, Wendy whistled a low note. Darren felt a sinking feeling in his chest, a stone of hope lost down a well, gravity playing out its game of inevitability. It was always going to lead to this, wasn't it? Somebody in Geneva's going down for Missy's murder? He put out a hand before Van Horn could get to the door. "What's going on?" he asked, watching as two deputies climbed out of the second vehicle. What could possibly require this much manpower? Van Horn told Darren to stand back, that this didn't have a thing to do with him, then he walked into Geneva's followed by the two deputies, who leaned against the wall near the jukebox. The sheriff's men stood, armed and at the ready, as Darren entered. Behind the counter, Geneva looked up and saw Darren and the county men at the same time, and she looked confused, as if they'd arrived together, as if there had been a coordinated effort.

"Geneva," Van Horn said. "Let's do this nice and easy, hear?"

He asked her to come from behind the counter with her hands out in front of her. Then he nodded to one of his men, a fellow younger and fatter than Van Horn. He lifted the cuffs off his belt and waited patiently for Geneva to come forward. She stared at the scene before her as if it had materialized for her entertainment, as if the men were bad actors working with a less-than-stellar script.

"Parker, what in the hell is this shit?"

"Geneva, don't talk," Darren said. "Don't say anything."

"We taking you in for Missy's murder," the sheriff said.

Huxley swung around in his seat, and Tim got to his feet. "Are y'all crazy?" Tim said. "What cause y'all got to believe Geneva killed Missy?"

"We have evidence to suggest Mrs. Sweet was the last to see her alive."

"What—did I rape her, too?" Geneva said.

The deputy holding the cuffs said, "We no longer believe she was raped."

"That's enough." Van Horn snapped at his deputy for speaking out of turn and ordered him to cuff the woman immediately. Both Huxley and Tim tried to block the deputy's advance on Geneva. "I can fit three in them cars," the sheriff said, and Huxley and Tim backed off. The deputy went behind the counter and—rather gently, Darren thought—placed Geneva's thin wrists in metal handcuffs. The kitchen door opened, and Faith walked out and screamed.

"What are y'all doing to my grandmama?"

Darren looked from her to Huxley and Tim and finally to Geneva as she passed him, her wrists shackled behind her back. The deputy kept a firm hand on her shoulder. Darren followed them outside, watching as the cop ducked Geneva's head so she wouldn't hit the car's door frame. She stopped and threw a glance back at her business, at the place around which her entire life revolved.

"Huxley," she said. He'd come out with Tim and a few of her other customers to watch what was happening. "Close up the shop and call that lawyer up in Timpson, the one who come around when Joe got shot." Then she looked at Darren. Her bottom lip quivered, and it was the first crack he'd seen in her steely facade, the first he knew she was terrified. "Don't talk, no matter what," he told her, calling on his legal training. Then he made a promise he wasn't sure he could keep. "I'm going to get you out of this." She nodded as she slid into the caged backseat.

Part Four

17.

THE MISSY DALE autopsy was a point of pride now that Sheriff Van Horn had his arrest. Oh, he was all too happy to share the findings with Darren now, might have gift-wrapped them if he could, so smug was he about this turn of events, proud to have closed at least one murder case, even if it meant arresting a woman in her late sixties for reasons that made not a lick of sense to Darren.

The sheriff's station was wood-paneled and ice cold, or at least the room where Van Horn put him was. The carpeting was flat and gray and torn up by boot heels in places. There were junior football league pictures on the walls—a team sponsored by the Shelby County sheriff's department, the boys growing from tots to teens in the photos—as well as a wall calendar featuring state wildflowers, October's picture a grove of red-and-yellow Indian blankets. Darren sat below the calendar at a table on top of which a secretary had laid a doily next to the Mr. Coffee machine as a place setting for Styrofoam cups and sugar cubes. Darren pushed it all aside and opened the file in front of him.

The pictures were less gruesome than those of Michael Wright—

less bloody, at least. Unlike Michael's, Missy's face appeared as it had in life: round with an acne-scarred chin, but a pretty girl, all in all, or what passed for beauty in small-town Texas. Blond alone would get you far in these parts, and Missy had thick golden strands of it, without any roots showing. There wasn't a mark on her above the neck. Her eyes were closed, as if she were sleeping, on the edge of a dream that had just turned bad. It was what lay below her jawline that told the real story. There were fingernail scratches up and down both sides of her neck, where she'd tried to fight off her attacker. Darren could see the imprint of the fingers that had strangled her. The bruises were wine red and deep midnight blue, and the skin around them was freckled with a constellation of broken capillaries. According to the medical examiner, Missy had spent less time in the acidic water of the Attoyac Bayou than Michael Wright had. There was no trace of the Attoyac in her lungs—no bayou water or silt—which meant she was dead when she went in. The cause of death was listed as asphyxiation by manual strangulation. Her hyoid bone had been fractured in two places. The manner of death was listed as homicide.

The bayou had been a set piece, Darren saw now, a staging that was meant to suggest a link between Missy's murder and that of Michael Wright, to assert causality where perhaps there was none. It was a clever ruse. Hadn't Van Horn been working under that very assumption—that one murder had been in retaliation for the other? But what any of this had to do with Geneva Darren didn't know—until he got to the second-to-last page. Buried down at the bottom, beneath a notation of her blood alcohol level, zero percent, the contents of Missy's stomach told a secret about how she'd spent the last hours of her life.

* * *

"Van Horn got some nerve," Geneva said when Darren finally got in to see her. They'd already processed her at the jail in the county courthouse, had removed her apron and wedding ring. She kept a thin gold-plated wristwatch in her pocket to prevent flour and grease from gumming up the gold band, and they'd taken that, too. Her lawyer was a portly white fellow with a shock of white hair that was both receding and reaching for the ceiling at the same time. He had the look of defense attorneys everywhere, with a sartorial nod to an antiauthority streak. Around Austin, Darren's uncle Clayton was known for his collection of unruly socks—plaids and polka dots and stripes that he mixed and matched proudly. Frederick Hodge, counsel for Mrs. Sweet, wore a pearl-button western-style shirt beneath his suit jacket and a pair of square-toe boots that had no place in professional society. He had done his best to keep his client from speaking with additional law enforcement personnel, but Van Horn liked the idea of giving Darren free rein with Geneva, especially since the visiting room for any man or woman without a bar card was closely monitored.

"Talk away," he'd said.

The room was small, and the air was close, thick with the faintly sweet scent of mildew. There were water spots on the ceiling, brown stains that looked like sick clouds. "He's got some nerve," Geneva repeated, wringing her hands.

"Nerve? Or probable cause?"

Geneva's eyes narrowed as she glanced over Darren's shoulder. There were two deputies watching them, monitoring the exchange from behind the smudged glass of a window cut into the plaster wall. Darren was being careful about what he said, but he also felt himself toeing close to the edge of his loyalty to a woman he didn't know—not really. She'd felt like home, like the women he'd grown

up around in Camilla, women who were the embodiment of the
mother figure who was missing in his life, and he worried he'd let
it cloud his judgment, had potentially mistaken a maternal countenance for a peaceful heart.

"This is bad, Geneva."

"That lawyer say they can't hold me much longer. It's all just
circumstantial. They just panicked 'cause it's been three days, and
they still don't know who done it or what happened. He says they
can't—"

"Your lawyer hasn't seen the autopsy yet." He took the other seat
at the table, setting himself directly across from her so he could
watch her face when he listed the partially digested food removed
from Missy Dale's stomach and small intestine: beef and beef fat,
the latter in a quantity significant enough to suggest what is col-
loquially referred to as oxtails; purple-hull peas; raw green tomato
and vinegar; fried dough and powdered sugar; canned peaches and
cane syrup. Save for the pastry, it was the exact meal he'd had at
Geneva's—the same day Missy's body had been discovered not even
a hundred yards from the cafe.

"Still circumstantial," she said hotly.

She'd lived through two homicides and believed she knew a
thing or two about criminal liability. He could see she'd grown
calmer and ever more steady since being put in the back of a squad
car. Something new had settled into the feathered lines around her
eyes, the tight set of her dry, cracked lips. It was pure indignation.
It made Darren furious, the degree to which she misunderstood her
position here. "You lied to me," he said.

"No. I simply ain't told you things wasn't your business to
know."

"But you saw Missy the night she died."

"And what if I did?"

"You didn't think to tell anybody that?"

"You keeping secrets your damn self." She crossed her arms, sharp elbows pressing against the table. "Didn't say you was a Ranger when you came steady strutting around and ain't said a word about being suspended."

So Wally and Geneva had talked. For the life of him, Darren couldn't understand their relationship. It was nakedly adversarial but also strangely familial in the way they tolerated each other, accepted each other, even. Whether either of them liked it or not, there was no getting around it: they *were* family.

"I'm trying to help you," Darren said.

"Not wearing that badge you not."

"I'm not Van Horn, Geneva."

She considered this but wasn't in the least bit impressed.

"I know about your grandson," he said finally.

"Then you ought to know that's what got her killed."

"Keith?"

"Who else?"

"They're going to say you were the last one to see her."

"I had every right," she said, slamming her fist on the tabletop. Darren was wrong. It wasn't indignation radiating off her slim body. It was rage. She pushed herself back from the table, which had patches of bald wood where the shellac was peeling off. She nearly knocked over her chair. "I had every right to see my grandson. I will always respect that about Missy. She did what she could to let me see him, in a way that wouldn't rub it in Keith's face. She came by my trailer now and then, usually when she thought Keith would be late coming from the mill in Timpson. He picked up overtime a few times a month."

"What did you talk about?" he asked. "You and Missy?"

In his mind, he heard his uncle Clayton's voice: *Find a crack in the timeline, son.* Darren had worked at a free legal clinic in Cook County the summer after his first year in law school and used to keep Clayton on the phone late at night while they dissected some of the difficult cases Darren had come across. It was the closest they'd ever been—when Darren was in law school—and right now he needed Clayton's influence more than William's. The autopsy reported the digestion of the contents of Missy's stomach as "advanced"; some of the food had made its way into her small intestine. It was estimated she'd eaten as long as four hours prior to death. So unless she and Geneva had sat and talked for hours in her trailer before Geneva just up and strangled her, it was possible and *probable* that Missy had gone somewhere after she left Geneva's.

Geneva sighed and said, "She knew she was running out of time."

Still standing, she seemed to sink a little in her knees as she talked about Missy and the baby. "Blond as that boy is, his true color was coming through. Missy had been panicky about that for a while. This summer she had him in long sleeves so much, hot as it is, that he got a little heat stroke, had to be run up to the pediatrician in Timpson several times. I told her to quit all that. She was going to suffocate the child. I even bought him a bunch of little-tyke clothes with the legs and arms out. I told her to blame his color on the sun, like folks been doing for a hundred years. Wasn't nobody going to make a fuss about it 'cept for Keith. And he already gave the boy his name, so she ain't have nothing to worry about. I told her that every time she brought him by. We argued sometimes, I'll admit. But mostly Missy let us be. She watched my TV while me and the little one caught up on things." Here

Geneva's face lit up. "I bounce him on my knee, same as I used to do with Lil' Joe. He likes that. Likes my sugar cookies, too." She sighed and dropped back into the chair. "With Missy gone, I don't know if they're going to let me see him again."

"He's been staying at Wally's."

"I know."

This seemed to bother her almost as much as the idea of not seeing her grandson at all; that Wally had unlimited access to the boy rankled her. "He's probably happy to see me 'bout to rot away in here."

"Give me something so I can challenge them." Darren nodded at the deputies over his shoulder, Van Horn's men watching from the adjacent room. "What time did she leave your trailer? Did she say anything that might have given you an idea of where she was heading when she left?"

"I know where she went," Geneva said, so plainly that Darren wasn't sure he'd heard correctly or that she knew what she was saying. "I drove her home."

"Home?"

"Home."

"And Keith was there?" he asked, remembering how neatly his initial suspicions lined up with Geneva's theory of why Missy was murdered.

"His truck was."

"So he was the last one to see her?"

"I don't have no proof of that. It ain't exactly like I walked her to the door and rang the bell, got asked in for a glass of tea. I've never been inside. I just like to make sure she and the little one get home safe. I started keeping a car seat in my trunk so I could ferry them home. It's sitting in my backseat right now."

200 • ATTICA LOCKE

"Why the hell didn't you say something?"

"Keith didn't see me. Wouldn't be nothing but my word against his."

"But if Van Horn knew, he would have questioned Keith first thing."

"You been here long enough to know that's not necessarily true."

She looked down at her hands, which were resting in her lap. She picked at a pill of wool at the bottom of her oversize sweater. "Besides," she said, "Missy truly believed no one knew the boy wasn't Keith's. It was a secret that mattered to her. And fresh after she died, I didn't want to put her business in the street."

There were rules of decorum in place that she hadn't wanted to upend in the wake of the young girl's death; she didn't think it was her place to *out* Missy when the girl could no longer speak for herself. She'd promised to keep her secret when she was alive and had tried to honor the kindness Missy had shown Geneva—letting her see her grandson—by not saying a word to anyone. That this had ultimately protected Keith was a price Geneva was now paying. But Darren wasn't raised in Lark, didn't know these people. *Screw decorum,* he thought. Van Horn had arrested the wrong person, and Darren wasn't going to let it stand.

18.

THE LUMBER mill where Keith Dale worked was on the north side of the town of Timpson, on the way toward Carthage and Marshall. It sat on ten acres that ran alongside Highway 59. According to the foreman on duty when Darren called, Keith Dale was in fact at the job site today. He was in the middle of his shift at the finishing plant, near the back of the mill, where his team oversaw the pallets of stacked wood as they came off the conveyor belt from processing and were then wrapped in a white plastic sleeve that had "Timpson Timber Holdings" printed on it. The foreman offered to escort Ranger Mathews to Keith's exact location—"Did they find the one who killed his wife?"—but Darren said that wouldn't be necessary. *Oh, I found him,* he thought as he parked his silver Chevy in the lot behind the twenty-foot front gate, the letters TTH casting a shadow across his windshield. There was a row of semis idling near the warehouse where Darren was heading, oversize trucks waiting for forklifts to load pallets of finished wood onto their flatbed trailers. As far as Darren could see in either direction, there was no open land on the entire property that wasn't filled with stacks of

202 • ATTICA LOCKE

raw pine being stored out under the sun, scenting air still damp from the rain with the milky sweetness of freshly cut wood. He had walked out of the sheriff's office without so much as a word to Van Horn about where he was going. He told himself that he and Keith were just going to talk, that he was just making sure he got the interview he feared wouldn't materialize in the wake of Geneva's arrest.

The warehouse was about a third the size of a football field and was open on two sides. Darren stepped past an idle forklift, the driver waiting on a signal from another worker. The man stared at Darren—at his pressed shirt and slacks, not to mention the star on his chest—walking among a dozen men in fluorescent yellow safety vests and hard hats, their work boots caked in dirt and mud. Darren found Keith clear on the other side of the warehouse lay-ing a plastic sheet of Timpson Timber Holdings packaging across a four-foot-wide pallet of planks of raw pine, each two by four inches. *Blunt-force trauma. Skull fractures. Wood fibers embedded in the skin.* The hair on Darren's arms shot clear up out of his skin as he stood in front of the man who, he was now sure, had killed Michael Wright—the man who had beaten him within an inch of his life then tossed him into a shallow, watery grave. He had never been more certain, and he knew that the moment required him to free himself of Wilson's rules.

"Keith Dale," he called out.

Several men turned to stare before he did. In fact Keith was one of the last men to take notice of the black Ranger in their midst. When he did, a slow grin spread across his face. Under the yellow hard hat, his skin was sallow and even more sinister looking, the smile playing as pure menace. Unlike his coworkers, who regarded Darren's arrival in the warehouse with a kind of bemused awe because of the many things that didn't line up at first glance—*A black Ranger? Here?*—Keith Dale seemed almost tickled by what he took as absurd.

"I already know they got that old lady for killing Missy."

Two of the men near him glanced at each other, one attempting a mournful pat on Keith's back, a gesture of male solicitude that Keith shrugged off.

"Know you tried to put it on me, too."

"I'd like you to step outside with me," Darren said. Keith would get more difficult the larger and whiter his audience became. There was one black guy in the corner who chose to keep working despite the drama playing before him.

"I don't think so," Keith said. He stepped away from the pallet he'd been wrapping and lifted off his right glove, then his left. He tucked them into the back pocket of his faded, grease-streaked jeans. There was a threat in the gesture, as if he were prepping for something for which he'd need physical dexterity. Darren took a step forward, making clear he was standing his ground.

"I want to ask you a few questions, Keith."

"I don't have to answer nothing you say."

"Afraid that's not true."

Keith looked at a few of his buddies, and his smile widened. Darren saw teeth, sharp and white, with tobacco stains at the gums. Keith was enjoying himself, said the next bit loud so that the black guy in the corner could hear, too.

"Turn your nigger ass around and get out of my place of business."

Darren swallowed it, because one *nigger* wasn't worth it.

He could take one *nigger* if it meant keeping the upper hand.

Firmly, he said, "That's not going to happen. I need you to come with me to the sheriff's office in Center. Time we sat for a proper interview."

"I ain't going nowhere with you."

"I'd rather you come nice and easy, not make a scene in front of your people here," Darren said. "Otherwise I got to do this the hard way."

"The hell you will."

The hard way meant cuffs, a pair of which he'd made sure to clip to his belt. But there was another hard way, too: if Keith wanted to show out in front of his buddies, Darren would give them a show. "I know about your son," he said.

Keith's whole body went rigid. His eyes darted left, then right, trying to gauge if any of the men around him knew what Darren was talking about, if anything on their faces gave away their knowledge of the gossip, if it had made it all the way up here.

"Keith Junior is not *your* junior, is he?"

"Shut up."

"Let's go, Keith. We can talk when we get down to the station."

He was giving him an out, but Keith refused to move. He stepped even closer to Darren, and when one of his buddies whispered his name and grabbed him by the arm to keep him from doing something stupid, Keith told him to fuck off. The guy, a man in his early thirties with a reddish beard and a rather girlish tattoo of a thorny rose on his forearm, called Keith an asshole and walked off.

"What happened?" Darren said. "Were you afraid Missy was going to tell on you, that she was going to tell everyone what you did to Michael Wright?"

"I never saw that man before in my life."

"Sure you did, Keith. You saw him and your wife on the farm

road. You caught your wife out there with a black man, and you didn't care which black man it was, but somebody was going to pay for making a fool out of you."

"Now, wait a minute. I didn't have nothing to do with that."

The mention of the Wright murder, the one for which there was no person in Shelby County currently under arrest—combined with the fact that several more men inside the warehouse had inched away from him—shook something loose in Keith. The warehouse fell silent except for the continual chugging of the conveyor belt shooting out pallets of lumber every forty-five seconds. They were starting to stack up at the bottom of the belt because all activity in the room had ceased; no one was working. Even the black guy had finally given in to the spectacle. Darren was reaching for his cuffs when he saw Keith grab hold of the nearest two-by-four. He swung hard as somebody screamed, "Keith!"

Darren ducked, and the board hit him in the shoulder.

The pain sent him to his knees. Keith lifted the two-by-four again, but before he could take another swing, Darren raised his gun and shot over Keith's shoulder, shattering an overhead light. Glass rained down to the warehouse floor. Keith flinched and finally dropped the plank. He looked around the room, again trying to gauge his standing among the men around him. Most of them wouldn't look him in the eye, and Keith, shamed not so much by his behavior as by the secrets that had spilled in the warehouse, lowered his head.

Darren pulled out his cuffs and locked the man's wrists in place.

"Assault on an officer," he said. "Now I gotta take you in."

"Sit down."

He pointed Keith, still cuffed, to a chair opposite the door in the tiny interrogation room, four plaster walls and a round table, hardly big enough for a decent card game. The ceiling was low, and Keith, who had maybe an inch on Darren, could have reached up and touched it without the cuffs. Van Horn entered behind them, already reaching for the handcuff keys on his belt.

"What in the hell do you think you're doing?" he barked.

Keith held out his shackled wrists to Van Horn, confident in the sheriff's ability to put a stop to this, banking on Van Horn's rage at Darren for making an arrest in this county without his say-so. The older man had been on Darren's heels since he'd entered the station and walked Keith through the building without a word of explanation. Van Horn had nearly exploded. Now he reached for Keith's wrists and tried to fit his key into Darren's Ranger-issued cuffs.

"This man is under arrest," Darren said.

"On whose authority?"

"Mine."

"This nigger come down to my job," Keith said, his hair mashed against his damp scalp in the shape of the hard hat Darren had torn from his head when he shoved him into his truck. "Running his mouth about things that ain't no business of his, talking about my private life—asking for it, far as I'm concerned."

Van Horn's face reddened. "What did you do, Keith?"

"He swung a piece of timber at my head, a two-by-four that looks a hell of a lot like the weapon that beat Michael Wright within an inch of his life. Take those cuffs off, Sheriff, and I'll arrest you for interfering with a state investigation."

Van Horn let out a bullish sigh, a weak protest, before he finally relented.

Exasperated, or just plumb worn out from the high tide of adrenaline that had washed over him, he grabbed a second chair and with great drama planted it a few feet away from the table, making a show of letting Darren run this. He pulled a handkerchief from his pants pocket and wiped his brow.

"I didn't kill that black man," Keith said, looking at Van Horn, "and nothing y'all say can make it true."

"Well, jumping a Texas Ranger ain't doing a whole lot for your defense."

Darren told Van Horn to back off. "I got this."

He again pointed to Keith. "Sit."

"You making a bigger mess than the one we started out with," the sheriff muttered to either Keith or Darren. It was hard to tell where his loyalties lay. "Answer the man's questions so we can be done with this."

"It's simple, Keith," Darren said. "Nobody can account for Missy's whereabouts from the time she left Geneva's till she was found the next morning. So how come you didn't call anybody? Your wife was missing for nearly twelve hours, you with a little one at home, and you got up the next day and went to work like normal, even though your wife hadn't come home the night before."

Van Horn sat straight up as if someone had pulled a string that kept his spine from going slack. "Now, wait a minute," he said. "I agreed to let you ask the boy about the Chicago fellow. But we made an arrest on the other deal. Geneva Sweet's been booked and everything. We not treading old water."

But Darren didn't let up.

"Unless she *did* come home," he said.

He searched Keith's impassive face. The man's skin was flushed, but his expression otherwise betrayed nothing. Keith looked to Van Horn, his presumed ally. "That's enough, Ranger," Van Horn said. "This is still my department."

"Geneva Sweet swears she dropped Missy off at your cabin the night she died," Darren said. "She says your truck was sitting right there in the driveway. Which means *you* were the last to see your wife alive."

"That truck don't mean nothing."

"Stop talking, Keith," Van Horn said. It was the first time Darren had ever heard a cop utter those words during an interrogation. It was frankly stunning to Darren, the sheriff's repeated impulse to shield this young man.

"She saw you, Keith," Darren said.

"You're lying."

He was.

He was trying to see if Keith would trip up.

"And she says you saw her."

"I thought you was in here trying to find Michael Wright's killer," Van Horn said. He laid a hand on the table in Keith's direction, a signal Darren couldn't read. But he felt something conspiratorial in the gesture, Van Horn offering reassurance of his absolute authority in this sheriff's department.

"I *am* looking for Michael Wright's killer," Darren said. "But I'm also trying to make sure Geneva doesn't go down for something she didn't do."

"I knew this was some black bullshit," Keith said. "You see how they stick up for each other?"

"She liked Missy, Keith," Darren said. "And she loved your son. I don't think she would have ever taken the boy's mother from him." He let that last piece hang in the air made sticky by the sweat coming off Keith's body, rings of it soaking the pits of his denim work shirt. At the mention of his son, his jaw squared. Darren could count the veins running like swollen rivers across Keith's forehead.

The man smiled to show off how little Darren had gotten to him.

"Look, we know about the relationship between Missy and Joe Junior," Van Horn said. "As far as my department is concerned, Missy's relationship with Geneva's son and the baby that came out of it—that's all potential motive for Mrs. Sweet committing the crime. She harbored a grudge over the death of her son."

He delivered it with a prosecutor's flair for carving a story out of any old block of wood. Darren was quick to remind him: "Missy didn't shoot Lil' Joe."

"No, but if she'd kept her legs closed, he'd still be alive," Keith said.

The smile was gone, and in its place Keith wore a look of utter contempt, married with rage as poorly caged as a bull in a rusty pen. His body had raised the temperature in the room by a few degrees. Van Horn was flushed now.

"Can the same be said for Michael Wright?" Darren said. "If Missy hadn't fooled with him, would he still be—"

"I didn't kill that man."

"But you did beat him up."

It was a shot across an open field. Darren waited to see would it land.

Keith said nothing for a long time, so that the only sound in the room was the buzzing of the fluorescent bulb overhead and the rise and fall of Van Horn's breath, laboring under the pressure of a belly that had asserted its dominance in middle age. He was very nearly panting. Darren asked Keith directly, "Did you see your wife and Michael out on the farm road Wednesday night?"

Keith didn't flinch, was no more bothered than if Darren were inquiring about the best route to Dallas. "What difference does it make?"

"Keith," Van Horn said his name softly, a warning or a plea.

"You saw another black man with your wife, and you beat him up."

"I didn't kill him."

"So you *did* beat him, then?"

"That's not what I said."

"I still ain't heard you deny any of it," Van Horn said. It was a hint, an invisible lifeline for a young man whose ill temper threatened to undo him at any moment. Keith suddenly pushed back from the table, hard enough that the front legs of his chair briefly lifted off the linoleum. They touched back down with enough force to make Keith's teeth click together, as if he were chewing stones. He looked past Darren to the other white man in the room. "What would you have done, Sheriff?" He crossed his arms, the muscles like ropes taut with tension. Darren searched for tattoos, the *SS* or the shape of the state of Texas branded with the Aryan Brotherhood's initials, and was surprised to see Keith's skin smooth except for sunspots and a few moles.

Van Horn, salty over Keith's refusal to heed his guidance, left him at sea.

"I don't know, son," Van Horn said. "My wife sleeps at home."

The balance of power in the room had shifted.

Keith felt it before Darren did.

"Sheriff, you know I ain't had nothing to do with any of this."

"DA puts you on the stand when this thing goes to trial, and the other side asks where you were the night your wife went missing, why you didn't call me or even Missy's parents, what are you gon' say, son?" Van Horn asked him.

"You gon' let this fucking roach turn you around about me?"

"Truth is," Van Horn said, "I got two murders, and your name is coming up too close to both of them."

"Must have shamed you," Darren said. "Claiming a son that ain't yours, a boy that's gon' grow up looking a lot more like me than you can stand."

"You got this all wrong. Keith Junior is my son. I love that boy, period."

"I bet that crew down at the icehouse don't see it that way. Can you even claim ABT if you're raising a half-breed? Or did Missy take that from you, too?"

It was the first mention of the Brotherhood, and you would have thought Van Horn had discovered a mound of fire ants under his chair. He leaped to his feet and said, "Now wait a minute. We had a deal. This is a local crime. In Shelby County. We not opening doors on a statewide investigation, let alone allowing some federal task force in the back door." He looked at Keith—rather sternly, Darren thought, like a coach dealing with a running back he can't keep in a straight line. "You don't have to say nothing about that, Keith."

But Keith wasn't listening. He'd hung his head a little and was shaking it back and forth. "It didn't have nothing to do with Junior," he said roughly.

"What?" Darren said. "What didn't have anything to do with Junior?"

Keith ignored him. He asked Van Horn for a cigarette and a Coke, as if it finally dawned on him that he was going to be here for a while. Van Horn wasn't about to leave them alone together, so the Coke was a no go. Darren offered Keith a smoke from the pack in his pocket. He tossed a matchbook on the table. It was from the icehouse. Keith set the cigarette between his dry lips and lit it.

"I know you got the boy staying at Wallace Jefferson's place."

"What else I'm supposed to do?" Keith said. "Her people ain't claim him, and mine's all the way to Montgomery. Laura, Mrs. Jefferson, she offered to take the boy for a bit, and with Missy gone, I ain't had no other kind of help. So I—"

"What about the child's grandmother? Geneva?"

"That was all Missy. I didn't want the boy around them kind of people."

"You mean his family?"

"I mean niggers," he said. Then, realizing he was enjoying a spot of nicotine thanks to the largesse of one of those said niggers, he muttered, "No offense."

"What happened, Keith?" Van Horn said. "Were you home when she got back from Geneva's place? If it was a fight that got out of hand, we can work with that, make everybody see you ain't mean to kill her." He shot Darren a look, cop to cop, that asked for the baton. *He'll never tell it to you,* his face said.

"I never even hit that girl once since I met her, and we been together since junior year. She just wouldn't stop, wouldn't stop going on and on about it."

"Going on about what, son?" Van Horn asked.

"I wasn't going back. Wasn't no way in hell I was going back."

"Going back where?"

"The Walls," he said, meaning the correctional facility in Huntsville.

"Then tell us something we can work with, Keith, something to keep your time down, keep a needle out of your arm," Van Horn said. "If it was an accident, son, both of 'em . . . the black fellow, and then Missy, then maybe we can—"

"I didn't kill him!" He stubbed out the cigarette directly on the wooden table. The smoke curled into nothing around his head. He ran his fingers through his greasy hair. "That's why I needed Missy to keep her fucking mouth shut." They had walked him up to the line, and neither officer spoke. Darren was afraid to make any sudden movements for fear the spell would break.

Keith set his hands on the tabletop. Without the work gloves, they appeared calloused and dry. The backs of his hands had scratches—thin red lines where she'd gotten him, Darren thought. Those were the marks of Missy fighting for her life. Keith rubbed at them absently. "I loved her," he said. "She just wouldn't stop, wouldn't stop, saying we was both going to jail 'cause I beat up the wrong nigger. And you're right," he said, looking at Van Horn. "It did get a little out of hand, that's all. I ain't mean to kill nobody, just needed her to shut up about it."

Then he looked at the black Ranger and said, "But I swear I left that man alive on the farm road. I drug him out the car, all that, got a few licks in, and I'll admit I had some bad ideas. I grabbed a two-by-four from the truck, I did. But Missy took to hollering like she was about to lose her mind, and something just come over me then, like a voice in my head said *stop*. And I did, quit it right then. I dropped the stick, and we climbed in the truck, and we *left*."

Van Horn sighed, the sound like the hiss of bad brakes; he was on a ride that had taken an unexpected turn. He glared at Keith as if he'd been betrayed.

"I don't understand," Darren said. "If you didn't kill Michael Wright, why were you so worried about getting caught?"

"Because of that car."

Darren felt his head go light.

"The car," he said. It was the thing that had been bothering him this whole time, the part that didn't fit. If it wasn't a robbery, where was the car?

"Missy was on me that night to go back and see was he okay. Time we stepped in the house she wouldn't let it alone. So finally, just to shut her up, we got back in the car, Keith Junior right in between us, and we went down FM 19," Keith said. "And sure as I'm sitting here, I'm telling you he was gone. I mean, not thirty minutes after we left him out there, the man and that car were gone."

19.

KEITH CAUGHT up with them on the farm road, the nigger and his wife, just a few acres from the house Keith paid the rent on every month. Later Missy would say, over and over, that he was just driving her home, that Keith had it all wrong; they had only been talking. But right then, Keith didn't care. He spun his wheels in the red dirt and sped out in front of the black car. Michael Wright had to slam on his brakes to keep from hitting the front end of Keith's truck, which was by then pointed in his direction. The nigger held up his hand, shielding his eyes against the blast of white light stabbing into the front seat of his car. He seemed genuinely confused as to what was happening, and that only fueled Keith's rage—that the man didn't even know enough to know he was doing something wrong, wasn't from around here and didn't know we don't play that shit down here. The lights on Keith's Dodge showed Illinois plates, the hood ornament a classy blue and white, the nigger too stupid to know he was driving the führer's favorite ride. *How you like them rims?* Keith himself had never been north of Oklahoma, thought the world outside Texas was a cesspool of race mixing and confusion about who built this country, spics and nigs with their hands out, begging for this, that, and the other, never doing a decent day's work in their lives, but even still they were coming for our jobs, coming for our wives and daughters. And now it was happening inside little ol' Lark, Texas. It was happening to him *again*.

Missy stumbled out of the car first. She had on a white T-shirt and a skirt with flowers running up the sides, and he couldn't help but think of the ease with which a hand could slide up her thigh. He saw his son's face suddenly and had to stop himself from revving the engine and taking them both out, toppling them like bowling pins. He'd caught her out here a couple of times before, one time only a few months before Junior was born. He knew there was a chance that baby wasn't his even before he came out purple and wet and screaming at the world. He'd have shot Lil' Joe Sweet himself if his woman, skinny little nigger bitch, hadn't done it first. Black or not, he couldn't help but respect her for the efficiency with which she had dealt with the problem. From the beginning, Keith had been hemmed in by his love for that girl and his son. He and Missy had been high school sweethearts. He'd taken her to his senior prom, had come back from Angelina College his freshman year so he could go to hers. They liked the same music, hunting, and fishing. She was a country girl, sweet but strong. First deer season they were together, he'd gone out with her and her dad on opening day and was floored when she downed a buck their first hour in the stand. And good Lord, she was pretty, green eyes and blond hair, a plump ass and a waist he could wrap an arm around. She was only the second girl he'd been with. One kiss and he was done. He'd married her as fast he could, found a small cabin they could rent. They wanted babies, lots of babies. Then he went away on drug charges, a twenty-six-month bid, and knew he'd lost her the first hour he was home. It was in the way she turned her mouth to the side when he went to kiss her. His lips landed on her cheek, and he knew she was done.

She held up her hands in front of her, the headlights making black shadows beneath her eyes, clouds of red dirt swirling at her feet. "No, Keith," she said. The crescent moon wasn't strong enough to muscle any light through the thick braid of pine trees and cottonwood, and the darkness beyond the circle of light around the two cars was absolute. "This ain't what you think," she said.

The nigger came out of the car next.

He said, "Just taking the lady home."

He wasn't scared, not yet, and that inflamed Keith even more.

He hopped out of the truck's cab and went for the nigger, grabbing him by the collar and slamming him against the shiny black car, worth more than Keith made in the last two years combined. The man's head hit the roofline of the car, and that's when he got really scared; he was alone on a dark farm road with two white folks, one of whom had him by the throat. The panic on his face whetted Keith's appetite for inflicting pain, and he hit the man square in the face. Behind him, Missy was yelling for Keith to stop. She ran from the other side of the car and beat two fists against his back. Keith hit the man again, with homicidal force. But the nigger didn't go all the way down. In fact before he even hit the ground, something seemed to snap in his posture, a surge of stress chemicals tilting toward the fight side of the fight-or-flight scale. He came up swinging, and Keith can admit the nigger landed a few good pops across his head, not enough to leave a scratch but enough to keep Keith from being fooled by the man's clothes, his smooth leather loafers. The nigger could fight, would get the best of Keith if he let him.

Keith reached down and caught a handful of dirt and threw it in his eyes. It was a dirty trick, but with no witness besides Missy, Keith didn't care.

It was enough to give him the upper hand. He went at the man with both fists, pummeling him from all sides, punching until skin broke, until he felt bone, until he could see blood on his knuckles by the light of the truck's headlamps.

"Stop it, Keith," Missy yelled, because the nigger could no longer speak for himself. Keith told his wife to get her nigger-loving ass in the truck right now. He stepped back a few feet, and both Missy and the nigger got the wrong idea, thought a retreat was in motion. She actually went to his side, tried to help the man to his feet. She didn't see Keith head to the back of his Dodge, didn't realize he'd fished a two-by-four from the truck bed until he was standing right over her and the man on the ground, telling Missy, "Get out the way."

He lifted the piece of solid wood and told the nigger to open his eyes. He wanted him to look at Keith when he said, "Stay the hell away from my wife."

"Damn it, Keith, don't you dare."

The nigger spit blood in the dirt. He raised a hand in defense. "I was just driving her home, man," he said, his voice a thick croak. "That's all."

Keith was seconds from landing the bar of wood on the man's skull when Missy jumped between them. "Do it and you'll have to kill me, too. You might could explain one dead, but I know you ain't smart enough to get out of two. 'Cause I'll tell—don't think I won't." The headlights were behind him, haloing his head, and Missy couldn't see his eyes for the shadows. "This ain't about Junior," she said. "This don't have nothing to do with that. He was just driving me home." And when Keith still didn't drop the weapon, she said, "You just got out, Keith."

The mention of the Walls cleared his head.

He dropped the two-by-four, gave the nigger one last kick in the gut, and spit on his head. Then he grabbed Missy and yanked her ass to the truck. The BMW's headlights were still on. They bore witness to Keith backing up the truck so he could turn around on the dirt road and head around the bend toward his cabin, farther up the road. The nigger was still breathing. "I swear."

"He's lying," Van Horn said. "Just like he's been lying from the beginning about Missy. He all but confessed in there." He'd unbuttoned the top of his shirt, and Darren could see how red his skin was, heating him from the inside out. Van Horn pulled a handkerchief from his slacks and wiped his brow.

"He only copped to Missy's murder," Darren said.

They were standing outside the interrogation room in a narrow hallway that shared the same chipped linoleum tiles, the same rows of too-bright fluorescent lights. Van Horn looked both chastened and relieved when he told Darren of his intention to have the district attorney file charges against Keith Dale.

"He killed her to cover up for the other," Van Horn said. "Then he put her body behind Geneva's, knowing I'd think one of her people did it, mad about that other fellow. I didn't know he had that much of the devil in him."

Darren couldn't believe the words about to come out of his mouth.

"I don't think he did it," he said. "At least not by himself."

Van Horn waved away the thought. "He killed that girl in cold blood."

"Missy, yes. But not Michael."

"You actually believe that shitheel?"

"There's somebody else." *Has to be.* Brady came to mind. Something about their run-in out back of the icehouse was sitting wrong with Darren.

"Wait a minute, now," Van Horn said. "You was hollering about Keith Dale being good for this from the time you crossed the county line."

"But where's the car?"

"Who the hell knows? Maybe he drove it into the Trinity River for all I know or care. But there's no way in hell he didn't finish the boy that night."

"Unless he didn't do it alone."

Van Horn shook his head and started down the hall, the heels of his black ropers clicking on the tiles, forcing Darren to follow him into his office, near the front of the station. Like the room Darren had sat in earlier while reading the grisly details of Missy Dale's autopsy, it was paneled in wood. But Van Horn's office was carpeted in a military gray that clashed with the cheap paneling. His desk was wide and pale oak and empty save for a phone, a brass paperweight, and the sandwich he had been eating when Darren walked into the station with Keith Dale in cuffs. It was homemade—deviled ham on thick slices of white bread, whisper-thin slices of tomato and red onion peeking out. There was a diet soda sitting beside it on the desk. Darren found himself scanning the room for family photos, looking for a ring on Van Horn's left hand. Seeing neither, he got a sudden image of the sheriff standing over his kitchen countertop in his shorts at dawn, making his lunch, and it unnerved him in a way that he couldn't quite put into words. He didn't want to see a man in this room, couldn't afford to see flesh behind that sheriff's badge. Van Horn closed the door behind Darren.

When the two men were alone, the sheriff said, "Look, you got the win. You brought him in, and folks ain't gon' forget that."

"Brady," Darren started.

"Who?"

"The manager at the icehouse. He offered Keith a kill. *Me*. He offered me." Darren felt his face flush at the mention of the incident. It was his lowest point as a Ranger, his lowest point as a man who'd been taught to stand his ground. "As an initiation into the Brotherhood."

"Look, I know you got a hard-on for the Brotherhood," Van Horn said, shutting him down. "I know you got kicked off that task force—"

"Not true."

"But this here is a domestic deal, that's all. Keith Dale got his panties in a bunch over his gal out there with another"—he paused where one particular word wanted to come out of hiding, but then settled on—"black man, and he went crazy, beat his ass and killed him, and then he was afraid Missy was gon' say something to somebody so he killed her to keep her quiet. This was a man with a wife he couldn't control who was gon' make sure he got the last word."

"But if he'd already killed Michael Wright, why would Brady have offered me as his chance to jump in the ABT? He should have already been initiated."

"You not listening, son," Van Horn said. He stood behind his desk, looked at his half-eaten lunch, then threw the whole thing in the trash. The sudden movement ignited the smell of the onions, and the air in the room soured. "Keith Dale is too chickenshit to be a member of the Brotherhood." He said it as if Keith had failed to qualify for active duty in the Marines, as if being a member of the Aryan Brotherhood of Texas was some kind of badge of honor.

"Look, I'm still point on this," Darren said.

"You were never point."

"The Rangers put me on the ground to investigate the murder of Michael Wright, and I have a duty to them and to my state to find the real killer."

"I'm ready to arrest Keith on both the Wright murder and Missy."

"You arrest Keith, and I'll tell the DA myself the case is shit. You put this on trial and lose, it'll look at best like you're incompetent and at worst like you're rushing to put this on Keith to avoid the ABT connection. And then you sure as shit will have the feds in this county before you can blink."

He knew that would get him. It seemed like any mention of the Aryan Brotherhood of Texas operating in Shelby County spooked Van Horn to hell.

"You want to let that boy walk out of here?"

"Hold him on assault charges for that stunt at the lumberyard. Give me some time to put together stronger evidence. If it's Keith, it's Keith. But if it's someone else got their hands in this thing, then give me time to find them."

"I hold him on assault charges, that means the only one I got for Missy's murder is Geneva Sweet," Van Horn said, "and she stays in lockup."

He thought of Geneva spending a night—alone, if she was lucky—in a rusty jail cell, a single cot chained to a cement wall, the floor cracked and stained with God knows what, bars not wide enough to stick a fist through. It had already been a few hours, but things would feel different come sundown, every sound in the night an ominous echo. He felt faintly ill at the thought of her spending the night there. He tried to remember what she was wearing. If the temperature dropped tonight, would those clothes be enough to keep her warm?

"Look, you can arrest Keith for Missy," he said. "I'm fine with that."

"Naw. You got me questioning everything now," Van Horn said with a sly smile. It was the card he had, and he laid it down hard. "Geneva Sweet stays in jail. I got forty-eight hours till I have to put her before a judge." He lifted the can of diet soda and downed whatever was swimming around the bottom of the can. He let loose a rough belch, then said plainly, "You got two days, Ranger."

20.

THE COURTHOUSE steps were slick with leftover rain, and the clouds overhead had conspired to shut out the sun, blanketing the sky with gray. East Texas decided to give fall a chance this afternoon, and the air had cooled considerably. For the first time since he'd been in Shelby County, Darren felt he ought to be wearing a sport coat or even the windbreaker he kept locked in his truck. He felt a shiver of wind inch its way beneath the thin cotton of his shirt.

He'd been trying to get in to see Geneva, to renew his promise that he was going to get her out of there; he just needed a little more time. But Van Horn had rescinded Darren's visiting privileges, and he never made it past the deputies on the third floor. He was hurrying to get to his truck and get back to Lark when he saw the *Tribune* reporter—Chris Wozniak—and Randie stepping out of the reporter's rental car, which was parked just a few spots from Darren's pickup in the courthouse parking lot. When she saw him, Randie practically ran from the passenger side of the Buick, breaking away from the reporter. "Darren, what is going on?" She nodded toward Wozniak. "He said Geneva's been arrested. For Missy. But then they brought in Keith Dale. Does that mean they're arresting him for Michael?" She was trembling, either from the drop in temperature or a turn of events that both pleased and confused her. She was wearing the cashmere coat again. It was soiled about the shoulders, dirtied after a few days in East Texas.

"I brought in Keith," Darren said. "But look, there are still some moving parts. We don't have all the facts at this point." He was embarrassed by the need to speak to her in the language of a cautious press release. Darren had very nearly offered Keith Dale to her as a promise, as the answer to the question of what had happened to her husband. Keith was the man Darren would bring to justice, ending this nightmare, and it seemed cruel to take that away from Randie when he had nothing to offer in its place. Wozniak hardly acknowledged Darren and walked quickly past both him and Randie on his way to the front doors of the courthouse. Darren called out to stop him. "Wait," he said. "Before you go in, there are some things you need to understand about what's going on, Chris. I'd like to get more information before making any comment on the case."

It was more than he'd said to Randie, and she grabbed his arm roughly when she sensed he was soft-pedaling. "Hey," she said. But he kept moving toward Wozniak. The man's pants had dried into a wrinkled mess, and he was clutching the messenger bag at his side as if he honestly believed Darren might snatch it. It was then Darren realized that something had changed between him and Wozniak, who, inches from the courthouse doors, spun around to Darren.

"I'm not dealing with the Rangers on this anymore."

"What?"

"Let me get this straight . . . a double homicide with serious racial overtones, a sheriff's department that initially gave short shrift to the killing of a black man, and the Texas Rangers send in an officer on suspension—"

"I'm not on suspension." But even as he asserted it, he wasn't sure it was true. He was currently wearing the badge merely by permission, not by right. His future with the Rangers hung on a grand jury in San Jacinto County.

"You know what I take from that?" Wozniak said. "That the Rangers were never really serious about getting to the bottom of this. You're no better than the good ol' boys out here. Actually you're worse, 'cause you don't even realize you're being used."

His words hit Darren in his gut, a sucker punch that flowered into sickening self-doubt, because he couldn't say for certain it wasn't true.

"The Rangers didn't send me in," he said. "It was a friend in the Justice Department who tipped me off to the murders in Lark."

"Greg Heglund. I know," Wozniak said. "He called me."

"He called you?"

"I'll be getting my information from the feds from now on."

Wozniak paused with his hands on the courthouse door, holding it open for a woman in pantyhose and Keds below the skirt of her suit who stepped outside to light a cigarette. He looked at Randie, who was standing behind Darren. "You coming?" he said. And when she didn't respond right away, he stormed into the building and let the glass door swing closed behind him.

"What the hell is going on, Darren?"

She'd hardly gotten her seat belt on before he swung into the parking lot of a liquor store a few blocks away, slamming the car into Park. What was Greg doing calling the *Tribune* reporter? Did he want a professional come-up so badly that he would interfere with what Darren was trying to do out here? He was starting out of the car when Randie said, "What are we doing here?"

He ignored the question as he climbed out of the truck.

It was three o'clock in the afternoon, and he was still in uniform, the button-down, boots, and badge, but the black lady behind the counter didn't bat an eye when he set down a twenty and a five for a bottle of Jim Beam, which was about the best he was going to get his hands on in this backwater. He had the plastic off the cap by the time he slid back into the front seat of the Chevy. Randie looked at him like she'd never seen him before, as if a stranger had stumbled into the wrong truck. As he uncapped the bottle and bit off two fingers, enjoying the burn as it went down, the flush that crept across his jaw and throat, she said, "I'm not comfortable with you drinking and driving."

He unceremoniously tossed her the keys, then got out of the truck, walking around to the passenger side while Randie slid across the front seat to drive.

By the time they were back on Highway 59, he made a show of capping the bottle, of the fact that it was just a little something he needed, that it didn't signify a problem so much as an itch for which the slightest scratch would do.

Randie had her hands gripped at ten and two on the steering wheel. She had not adjusted the seat for her height and was perched on the very edge so that her feet would meet the gas pedal and the brake. She didn't say anything until they got about a mile outside Lark. "They've got Keith in custody, and what? Now you suddenly don't think he did it?" she said. Darren, flush from the bourbon, rolled down his window to let in a noisy crack of air. It whistled by his ear and swirled around the truck's cab. He sat with that for a minute, his tongue slowed by the liquor, his heart weakened by a fear that he was letting this woman down.

As they pulled into the north end of town, they came on the ice-house first. Darren asked her twice to pull over, and when she didn't, he reached for the wheel himself. She shoved him back but eventually turned the truck into the icehouse's gravel parking lot and shut off the engine. It clicked as it cooled, and for a moment that was the only sound in the cab save for the distant thrum of drums and guitar, the warm twang of country music playing inside the bar.

Finally she spoke. "You better tell me what in the hell is going on right now," she said, reaching for the bottle of bourbon between them on the seat and tossing it into the cab's tiny backseat. "Don't you dare fall apart on me."

"There may be someone else involved."

It came out as a confession—or a plea for understanding, at least. He felt terribly insecure about the halt he'd put on Keith's arrest. *What if I'm wrong?*

"How?" But what she really meant was *why*. Why did he think there was someone else? He told her about the car, the missing BMW, Keith's tale of returning to the scene and finding both it and Michael gone, as if they'd simply vanished, as if the night had swallowed them whole. But Randie seemed less than impressed by this. It was the mention of the Aryan Brotherhood as a wealth of poten-tial accomplices, the fact that a handful of them were as comfortable inside Wally's icehouse as they were in their own living rooms, that got Randie's attention, that made her nod her head several times and gave him the faith to trust his instincts. There was more to this story, he knew. "I can smell the liquor on your breath," she said. His pulse quickened at the thought that she was close enough to smell

anything on his breath. It was a stirring he didn't want to name, so
he blamed it on the bourbon. As he reached for a water bottle in the
glove box, downing half of it, she said, "I don't think you should
go in there."

"Trust me: word has spread by now that Keith Dale is in lockup.
The Brotherhood is going to be itching to retaliate. I'm not interested in sitting around waiting on another shoot-out to happen
when I can walk in there and lay down a message right now. It's not
going down like that. Not on my watch."

The liquor had made him bold—or foolhardy.

Time was about to tell.

Randie waited in the truck.

Darren had made her turn the Chevy around so that it faced away
from the bar; that way she would see any car that pulled into the
parking lot. First sign of trouble, she was to honk the horn and hold
it, a siren call. In the rearview mirror, she watched Darren step on
to the porch and open the door to the bar.

Inside, he went to the jukebox first. He bent down and pulled
the thick black cord from the wall. The music vanished, and the
click of balls roaming the pool table was the only sound inside
the icehouse. The faces on the TVs, tuned to Fox News and the
Food Network in daylight hours, were mute witnesses to Darren
Mathews lifting the Colt .45 from his waist. He held the piece at
his side as he instructed the room to gather 'round. This time of
day, it wasn't but five people in the place: Lynn behind the bar; two
men at the pool table, both well past retirement age, Wranglers
baggy where their backsides had faded with time; a man sitting
alone at the bar, hunched over a bowl of chili, his T-shirt straining
against the spare tire around his waist; and Brady, who quickly as-

certained that he was without worthwhile backup and reached for the cell phone clipped to his waist.

Darren said, "Put it down."

He gestured the man forward, using the Colt as a punctuation mark on his repeated request. "Gather 'round," he said again. He ordered Brady and the woman out from behind the bar. Lynn didn't move until Brady did. And he only came forward after knocking the white boy at the bar on the back of the head and pushing him off his stool. He was the only other white man in the icehouse under the age of seventy, and Brady told him, "Wake the fuck up." He and the fat boy inched forward. Darren positioned himself so that his back was neither to the front door nor to the kitchen. He had no choice but to trust Lynn when she said no one else was back there. Leaving the room would give Brady time and the chance to do God knows what. That he hadn't grabbed the twelve-gauge behind the bar the second Darren walked in the door told him that the other men in here weren't part of Brady's clan. Otherwise he'd have already made a move, trusting that his ABT brothers would back any play, no matter how violent. It meant there was a chance Darren would get out of this alive. Brady crossed his meaty arms, the tattoos like flags crossed in the wind. Lynn was chewing on a corner of her bottom lip. The skin around her mouth was pink and red and crusted where she'd broken the skin, a festering wound she'd been working at for days. The older men had laid down their pool cues. Fat boy was looking longingly toward his chili.

One of the older men held up his hands, as if this were a stickup, as if he couldn't see or understand the five-point star on Darren's shirt. "We don't want no kind of trouble around here," he said. His billiards opponent nodded.

Darren directed everything he needed to say to Brady, the man who would spread the word to his brethren that Geneva's cafe was not to be touched, that any man who came near Randie or Darren with so much as a mean look would be shot on sight. "I hear about any kind of trouble for black folks anywhere in this town, I'm going to walk back in here and shoot the first cracker I see and say you had a gun. Hell, I'll put one in your hand. And a couple of bags of whatever in hell you got going on back in that office."

He was breaking about three different laws just talking like this. But he didn't care.

He wanted them to feel the same gut punch of fear he had when Brady had him cornered behind the icehouse, when Darren thought he might die.

"Now that we got that out of the way," he said.

"Goddamn it, Brady, just tell him about Keith," Lynn said. "He don't care about none of the rest of it."

"Shut your mouth," Brady said.

"I got kids, man. I can't get locked up."

"I know about Keith," Darren said. "Who else?"

Brady shot her a look, and whatever she was thinking she swallowed whole. "Wednesday night," Darren went on. "You said a bunch of folks didn't like seeing Missy and Michael talking. Who didn't like seeing them together?"

"Wasn't anybody in particular," she said. "I just meant this ain't the kind of place for that sort of thing." She looked at Brady, wanting to see whether that met with his approval. He gave her a tiny nod, and she smiled. Her hair was styled in a braid that ran down the side of her face, and she'd painted her nails blue, tiny pools of color set against cuticles that were torn and peeling. She smelled of grape gum and a body odor Darren couldn't quite call bad, but it sure as hell wasn't good.

"Keith came to pick up Missy," Darren said. "Somebody must have told him where she was, who she'd left with. So who did Keith talk to that night?"

Lynn opened her mouth to speak, but Brady put a hand on her arm.

She thought about it a second and said, "Actually, I didn't see Keith at all that night." It was delivered like a line from a script she'd recalled in the nick of time. Darren could see the relief on her face. It was Brady she was playing to, the one she wanted to please. She was as changeable as the weather, and right now the storm was coming from Brady's direction. She was more scared of him than she was of the distant idea that she might go to jail on drug charges she correctly guessed Darren didn't give a damn about. He was getting nowhere with this.

They drove around for more than an hour after that, searching every square inch of farmland and thicket wide enough to drive a car through. Darren nosed the Chevy up and down farm roads in Lark, mere dirt paths that cut through weedy fields. Twice he got out of the truck to poke around in abandoned buildings: a horse shed made of graying wood, whole planks of which had retired from their responsibilities and lay rotting in a choke of ryegrass on the ground; and an empty barn, its roof torn off by some Gulf-driven storm, something strong and mean enough to chart its wrath all the way from Houston. By the light of the graying sky, Darren checked for tire tracks in the dirt. There was nothing that time hadn't already done away with.

He got back in the truck without saying a word, and he drove.

He crossed the line into Nacogdoches County, poking around tiny Garrison, where they'd spent last night. Again he drove up and down back roads and through fields of tall grass, looking for the BMW, before doubling back and checking the same roads all over again. By the time he led them back to Highway 59 and they passed the juke joint, Randie said she felt sick. She remembered the dead animal and the blood and could smell it on her clothes, she said. She could smell it in every corner of the truck's cab. She pulled at her coat, unbuckling her seat belt so she could yank it off her. She rolled down the passenger-side window and stuck her face into the coming night with a kind of desperate hunger for air. She was gray and clammy, sweat breaking across her forehead.

"You're never going to find that car."

"I have to look," he said.

"You're not going to find the car. Because it's gone. Because it doesn't matter." Her words were nearly swallowed in the rush of wind through the window, and he worried she truly wasn't well. She wasn't making sense.

"If I don't at least look—"

"Keith is in jail, Darren. Why can't that be enough for you?"

She rolled up the window, and the suck of wind from the cab seemed to vacuum-seal them inside, and he, too, could smell the faint traces of animal rot.

She twisted around so far in her seat that she was facing him head-on.

"I'm tired, Darren," she said, her voice cracking slightly. "I want to go home. I want to get Michael in Dallas, and then I want to take him home."

"I'm not convinced it was Keith."

"I don't care."

"You want an innocent man charged with this?"

"He's not *innocent*."

Her voice was rubbed raw at the edges by an anger that was crawling up the inside of her throat. "He beat Michael, then he *left* him out there. Left him out there to die, for all we know. That's enough for me, Darren. You're never going to get anything better out of this redneck justice out here. So I want to take what I can get, and I want to take Michael home. You've got a man in lockup right now. Keith Dale is enough for me. I want an arrest, and then I want to go home." The grief was at her back door, scratching at the screen. It was coming for her, and she wanted so badly to break down in private that she was willing to take less than the truth to get out of this town, this county, this state, to get away from all this. It was selfish and shortsighted. For a Ranger, anything less than the truth was never going to be enough, and he told her so.

"This isn't about you." She nearly spit the words at him.

"Yes, it is," he said. "I made a promise to you, and whether he knew it or not, I made a promise to Michael from the time I pinned this badge to my chest."

"You made a promise to Geneva Sweet, too," she said. "But you're driving around in circles rather than face her people and tell them *you're* the reason she's not coming home tonight." With that she turned around and didn't look at him again, nor did she say a word when she lifted the bottle of Jim Beam from the backseat and took a large gulp of it herself. It must have stung going down, because her eyes watered, and then before he knew it, she was crying for real, the sound like a wounded animal trying to scratch its way out of her insides, a rain of tears and streams of snot streaking down her face. She heaved for air a couple of times, and Darren finally pulled off onto the shoulder of the highway and stopped the car. Before he could undo his seat belt, she fell across the seat into his arms, laying her head on his chest as she wept and wept and wept.

21.

RANDIE HADN'T eaten in nearly a day, and anyway, she was right.

He owed Faith an explanation, or at the very least a sense that her grandmother hadn't been abandoned. He only hoped she would understand what he was trying to do, the thorny path he was trying to walk. He was a man of the law, and he felt the tension of attempting to straddle both sides of it: he was trying to protect Geneva from wrongful arrest while trying to ensure that the real killer paid the price for what was done to Michael Wright. He prayed he wouldn't fail at one while trying to accomplish the other. *Pop,* he thought, calling out for his uncles by their shared pet name. *Help.* He nearly said it out loud. What he wouldn't give for the chance to sit this one down with his uncles at the dinner table, back when it was just the three of them, before William married Naomi and started his own family, before the brothers stopped speaking to each other. What he wouldn't give for the chance to go back in time, to sit around a pot of kidney bean stew, Clayton's specialty, and talk it out—to ask each of them, the lawyer and the lawman, what he should do, while the brothers argued and shared bites off a bottle of Tennessee whiskey. Darren used to sip glasses of apple juice as a kid, pretending it was the same smoky liquor that made his uncles flush with dreams of a world that was safe for black folks.

He hurt for Missy Dale, of course he did. But Missy Dale had folks looking out for her. The world was looking out for Missy Dale. Van Horn could get twenty Rangers out here tomorrow to gather evidence for Missy Dale simply by asking. No district attorney would drag his feet prosecuting the killer of Missy Dale. *Dateline* would come out to do a story on Missy Dale—*48 Hours* and *20/20,* too. But Wozniak was right: to solve the unexplained death of a black man in rural Texas, Wilson had sent in a single man with a tarnished badge. Darren was all Michael had. In fact Wilson hadn't even technically sent Darren: he had merely acquiesced to a situation that threatened to become a public relations problem for his department. It was quite literally the least he could do. It was Greg who'd first mentioned the murders in Lark, who had first said Michael Wright's name to Darren. He should call him. He never did get those Texas Department of Criminal Justice records on Keith Dale that he'd asked for. By the time he pulled into the parking lot at Geneva's, the sun was setting. Randie left the truck first, lifting the bottle of bourbon from the backseat and walking it into the cafe.

She chased it with sips of ice-cold Dr Pepper, kept a sweating bottle of it at her side as they waited for their food. Thin slices of pork, ringed in fat crisped in its own grease in the pan, dirty rice, and grilled onions, with pickled cabbage and sliced tomatoes on the side. The first two drinks went down on an empty stomach, and Randie grew strangely quiet, her fingertips grazing the tabletop in time to the slide guitar coming from the jukebox. She kept staring at the guitar mounted on the wall across from her booth, the Les Paul that had brought her husband down South. Darren stood at the front counter talking to Faith, who, against her grandmother's wishes, had kept the place open.

"She won't be in there long," he said to her and Huxley.

Wendy had the stool next to Huxley and sat hunched over a plate of baked chicken and sweet corn, pushing the food around on her plate as if it owed her money, as if it had personally insulted her. Twice she asked Faith for some salt—"Lawry's or something."

Darren told them, "I promise you I'm doing everything I can to get Geneva home." They had not yet heard that Keith Dale was spending the night in lockup as well, on potentially overlapping charges, and it bought Darren some goodwill, even if he felt a blush of shame over the fact that he wasn't telling them the whole story. The cafe patrons thinned as Darren and Randie ate heartily, washing the lot of it down with shots of Jim Beam. Wendy, in answer to no one but Freddie King on the jukebox, his guitar crying over some heartbreak or another, said, "It's a mess is what it is." And Huxley nodded as Faith poured him a second cup of coffee. "Geneva ain't even closed when Joe was killed."

"It was a robbery?" Darren said, his voice lilted in inquiry.

"First time Geneva had left Joe alone in years," Huxley said.

"Grandmama had taken me up to Timpson to look at dresses for my junior prom with my parents. Granddaddy was watching the place on his own." From the pocket of her grandmother's apron, made of cotton the color of blue hibiscus, she pulled a white rag and started wiping down the countertop.

"What happened?" Darren asked.

Randie, her face plump with alcohol, her tongue thick and slow, said, "He beat my husband. Keith did it." Wendy heard her and understood she was lost in something that was bigger than this moment. She stood on two spindly legs and crossed to the booth. Without a word, she slid across the vinyl seat next to Randie. She patted the younger woman's hand, then held it in hers.

"It was three of 'em that came in, the way we heard it," Huxley said.

"The way I heard it, too," Wendy said.

"Isaac said they came in after midnight."

Darren looked past Faith down the length of the cafe toward the tiny barbershop, which was empty at this hour, no guests in the swivel chair, not a single comb in the electric-blue bottle of Barbicide. There was no sign of Isaac.

Faith said, "He ain't been in. He's been spooked since they shot out the window."

"He kinda nervous-like, Isaac," Wendy added. "Funny in the head."

"Anyway," Huxley said, "Isaac said he was coming in from taking the trash out back when he heard the shots. Two, back-to-back, just like this." He rapped his knuckles on the Formica countertop in rapid succession, a one-two. "He said by the time he made it through the kitchen, he could just see the men making off in their car." He nodded toward the cafe windows. Beyond the gas pump and Darren's truck, the sky was dipped in blue, the honeyed sunset giving way to indigo as night crept slowly on. "It was three white men, he said."

Darren followed Huxley's gaze into the darkening night.

"How did he know the killers were white?" he said.

Huxley raised an eyebrow and looked at Wendy, who said to Darren, "Same way you knew the man who shot up that door was white." She gave a tiny shrug, as if to say, *Who else would it be?* "This ain't new." Darren had run outside only moments after the shooting. But he'd barely been able to make out even a few digits on the truck's license plate let alone see faces in the cab. It was history and circumstance that had filled in the rest.

"People loved that man," Wendy said, speaking of Joe. "For a lot of folks that live they life on the road, he and Geneva made this place home."

"He gave it all up for her," Huxley said. "The music, the big city."

Faith smiled and said, "Granddaddy set down roots for love."

"That man was Geneva's whole life," Wendy said.

"It broke her, what happened," Huxley said. "To the point that ain't none of us bring it up no more." He looked up from his coffee at Randie. "Before your husband came around, ain't nobody ask about Joe in a good long while."

Randie sat up in the booth, but it was Darren, sitting across from her in the booth, who spoke first. "Michael Wright was asking about that robbery?"

"That's what Geneva said."

"He was always doing that," Randie said softly. She pulled her hand from Wendy's and poured herself another shot. They were drinking out of ceramic shot glasses that had a picture of Big Tex in Dallas on them. Faith had fished them out of a rarely used cabinet in the kitchen. Randie sucked down the shot, skipping the soda back. By then her words were slurring. "I thought he should have gone into criminal law. I think he would have, maybe, if it weren't for me, if it weren't for money. He gave up stuff for me." She was getting teary again and talking in circles. Darren said her name, but it didn't stop her talking. "He always did that, made everything a case. He was drawn to criminal law. I should have done more to encourage him. I should have told him I loved him more. I should have told him he should follow—"

She stopped suddenly.

"I don't feel so good," she said, scooting out of the vinyl booth. The elderly Wendy was surprisingly spry and quick to her feet as she dodged out of the way. Randie made it all the way through the cardboard-covered front door and out past the lone gas pump before she kneeled and vomited everything. The bourbon and the pork and rice and the sticky sweet soda and acidic tomatoes and the cabbage soaked in vinegar and red peppers. It came out in milky pink waves, and the heaves shook her slim body, one after another. Darren rushed through the cafe's front door. Behind him, he heard the bell on the door tinkling as he grabbed Randie by her shoulders and helped her to her feet.

They were neither of them in a position to drive.

Faith gave them a room in the trailer out back. She said she felt weird about letting anyone sleep in her grandmother's room, even though Geneva was certainly not using it tonight, but Darren said he understood and told Randie he'd let her have the spare bedroom and he'd sleep on the couch. But as soon as Faith had finished setting out towels and clean sheets and gone back to close up the cafe, Randie asked Darren if he'd stay in the room with her, and he agreed. She lay on top of the bed in her clothes. And Darren sat on a nearly doll-size brass vanity stool that had no matching table or mirror—at least not in this tiny bedroom, with its walls paneled in wood veneer and its burnt-orange shag carpet. With no place else to put it, he set the bottle of bourbon at his feet. He knew better than to offer her any more, yet the Texas gentleman in him did so on re-flex. She shook her head and simply watched as he sucked down a piece straight from the bottle. Randie's hair was spread out around her on the pillow, thick black curls spilling like rivers undammed, and he thought he saw her close her eyes. But then she spoke. "Is that the reason you were suspended?"

The liquor, she meant.

He set the bottle at his feet and shook his head.

"This," he said. "This didn't really start, didn't really become a thing, a problem, or whatever, until the thing with Mack." It was the first he'd ever used the word *problem* in relation to his drinking. It made his head feel light, his world blurred at the edges, warming the effects of the bourbon in a way that wasn't entirely unpleasant. "I didn't start drinking like this until the thing with Mack got me in trouble, until the whole thing came between me and Lisa."

"I don't understand."

"It gave her an excuse, the suspension—an excuse to say I've been reckless, that the whole choice to join the Rangers was reckless in the first place," he said, explaining the night at Mack's house, in San Jacinto County, the incident that led to Darren's censure, the temporary suspension of his badge, and the potential indictment of a man who was just trying to protect his family. When he looked over again, she had closed her eyes for real this time, and he leaned over and pulled up a corner of the bedspread and laid it across her legs. She curled on her side, and Darren sat back on the brass stool. He was reaching for the bottle again when Randie sat up on her elbows and spoke suddenly.

"Why'd you do it?"

The question spooked Darren. He felt a spike of fear, a panic that he'd left himself exposed in some way, that she was talking about that night in San Jacinto County, until she clarified what she meant. "Why did you come back here? You had a way out. Michael had a way out. There was Purdue and then U of C for law school. He got out of Texas." She looked across the room at Darren. By the low light of the floor lamp in the corner of the room, a knockoff Tiffany deal with colored glass, he saw dark shadows beneath her eyes, and he felt incredibly tired all of a sudden, uncertain he could fight the feeling of a thickening of the blood in his veins, weighing his limbs. He wanted nothing right then so much as to lie down somewhere. He moved toward the door, heading for the couch in the other room. Randie called out for him to stop. "Lie with me," she said.

He hesitated in the doorway, his hand on the doorjamb, a bitter scent wafting up from the dampness of his armpits. He didn't care about the bottle anymore, didn't care about anything but resting his head somewhere, anywhere.

"Just lie down with me."

He left the bourbon in the sea of orange carpet and kicked off his boots. In his socks, he climbed across the crocheted bedspread and set his body within a few inches of Randie's. He rested his head on his arm and stared at the low ceiling. In his stocking feet, he could nearly touch it. On his back, tired as he was, the reach felt miles away. "Why did you come back here?"

"It's home."

The words didn't mean anything to Randie, who said she'd spent most of her life in the mid-Atlantic—DC and Baltimore, then Delaware, following her father's job in sales from town to town. When she was in high school, the family had settled in Ohio before finally moving to Illinois the summer before her senior year. She could barely remember the house she'd been born in, the city where she'd spent the first six years of her life. She'd gone back to DC right out of graduate school; her first job was a glorified internship at a political magazine. She'd looked for the row house where she'd been raised and gotten lost going up and down 16th Street, unable to remember if it was Northwest or Southwest where the Winstons had lived. It was an afternoon excursion, a lark; she'd taken photographs and stopped for a coffee at some hole-in-the wall cafe and made it to her apartment before nightfall, not sure if she'd walked past her own house. But deep down, it hadn't mattered to her if she found the building or not. The place didn't call to her, not the way Texas felt ever at hand for Michael—the way the land, or the memory of it, pulled at him. It was as if some part of him had never left the red dirt of East Texas, which Randie didn't understand.

You couldn't, Darren thought.

"But the truth is, he did leave. Because he knew this place wasn't for him. You made it all the way to the University of Chicago," she said, propping herself up by folding a thin pillow in half. "You could have gone anywhere."

"I did."

She nodded, staring at him in the dim light. "But why come back?"

"Jasper," he said softly.

He stared at the ceiling, lit yellow and blue by the lampshade. One of them would have to get up and turn off the light at some point if they planned to sleep. "Jasper," Randie said, rolling the name around her tongue. "I remember that. I was in my junior year of college. I had never seen anything like that in my lifetime, to drag a man like that. And I thought...*Texas.*"

"That was my September eleventh."

Randie didn't speak for a second, and Darren took his cell phone from his pocket and laid it on the floor by his leather holster and his boots. His wife hadn't called since he'd said he wasn't coming home. And some part of him knew that their next conversation would decide things he wasn't ready to face. He took a deep breath, gathering himself, as if he needed to pull from the same well of courage that had walked him out of law school just to say these words:

"It was a calling," he said. "It was a line in the sand for me, a line past which we just weren't gon' go, not on my watch. The badge was to say this land is my land, too, my state, my country, and I'm not gon' be run off. I can stand my ground, too. My people built this, and we're not going anywhere. I set my sight on the Aryan Brotherhood of Texas, among others, and I turned my life over to the Texas Rangers, to this badge," he said, pointing to the star on his chest. And when Randie grew silent and the honeyed light too dim to read her expression, he said, "She didn't understand, either." He lifted his body and rolled to the edge of the bed, which was as far as he needed to go to be able to reach up and turn off the floor lamp. "Lisa *doesn't* understand what this is for me. I mean, she knows what goes on in rural Texas. She thinks the work matters, but she wants it to be someone else's fight. She wants me home every night."

"I don't blame her," Randie said.

Darren finally closed his eyes. He heard the creak of the mattress springs as Randie turned and faced the wall on the other side of the bed. "I don't mean you any offense," she whispered into the dark. "But whatever you're trying to do down here, the shit isn't working. He should never have come back home."

22.

WILSON WOKE him again.

For a good thirty seconds, he thought he was still dreaming. He couldn't place the room or the woman sleeping next to him, a woman whose breath he felt across the lower half of his face, as her body was curled toward him, her head turned up, just an inch or so from his shoulder. *Lisa,* he thought. But the hair brushing against his neck was all wrong, thick where Lisa's was thin and straight, and her skin smelled yeasty and sour, unlike the vanilla scent of the expensive creams his wife favored. *Randie.* He whispered her name before he understood what his lieutenant was saying. She exhaled and rolled away from him, her body turned toward the opposite wall. Darren sat up and threw his legs over the side of the bed. He shifted the cell phone he didn't remember answering, cradling it against his neck. Wilson was speaking, mid-bark. "I need you to get out to Center right away," he said. "They're doing this thing at the courthouse there, and headquarters in Austin wants you on camera."

"What the hell are you talking about?"

"The press conference."

"What press conference?"

"Tell me, Ranger, that you've been trapped under a fallen tree for the past four hours and you haven't been willfully ignoring my calls all morning."

Darren looked down at his phone. It was barely past nine in the morning, and there were eight voice-mail notifications, all starting shortly after 5:00 a.m. He recognized Wilson's number as well as Greg's. Greg had made at least three of those calls from his desk at the Houston office of the FBI. Darren had apparently slept through the whole thing. "Wait," he said, rubbing the crust from his eyes and unbunching the fabric between his legs. "Who's having a press conference?"

"They arrested Keith Dale."

"For the murder of his wife?"

"For both murders."

"No," Darren said, standing. "No. Van Horn is giving me more time on the Michael Wright case. He promised he wouldn't make a move until—"

"Ranger, you made your case," Wilson said, sounding unsure what the problem was. He'd misread the lack of enthusiasm in Darren's voice for indignation, his junior officer fishing for an apology of some sort. Wilson huffed out a breath of exasperation. "I missed this one, okay? You got your arrest."

"Based on what?"

"They got a confession."

"That's not true," Darren said. He started toward the bedroom door, stepping out so as not to wake Randie, but as he closed the door, he looked back and saw she'd already awakened and was sitting up and looking at him. "I was in the room," he said, shutting the bedroom door and leaning against the wall of the narrow hall-way that led to the two other bedrooms. "He said he beat the guy, that's it."

"Van Horn likes him for both."

"Something's missing," Darren said. "The car, for one thing."

"There's always pieces that don't fit; you know that."

"If he did it, I'm not sure he did it alone. There could be some larger ABT connection in all this. The icehouse out there is a Brotherhood stronghold. Wallace Jefferson is clearly aware of, if not outright sanctioning, members of a criminal gang fraternizing at his establishment. If we dig a little deeper—"

"Look, this is the exact thing the county and the feds don't want."

"The feds?" Darren said, remembering the calls from Greg.

"This is some backwards-ass cracker shit, Mathews, and you know it," Wilson said. "You called it from day one. And the last thing we need is the idea that the Aryan Brotherhood is running out of control in East Texas or that we got blacks and whites killing each other in this state. All the protests that's been going on in the rest of the country—Texas don't need nothing like that down here. Folks are still smarting over the cop shootings in Dallas. Let's don't start ourselves a race war over one dumb redneck in Shelby County. As of right now, there's not a stitch of evidence the Brotherhood had a hand in this, so let's take a win where we got one and not turn this into a bigger crusade."

Still, something was wrong.

Darren felt it, even as he felt he had no other choice but to meet his boss at the courthouse in Center, Texas, the county seat, where Wilson had, with spectacular forethought, brought along a clean white shirt and a pressed pair of black pants from Darren's bottom desk drawer in Houston. He changed in the first-floor men's room, located just outside the county clerk's office, where there was a line of folks waiting to apply for marriage licenses and get copies of birth certificates.

Inside the men's room, Darren dressed quickly, as Wilson had said they wouldn't start without him. He tucked in the shirt and smoothed the front of the pants, which had an awful sheen from being pressed too many times. He couldn't remember how long the clothes had been sitting in his drawer, and it shamed him the thrill he got knowing that his desk hadn't been cleared out in his absence, that he might yet be welcomed back to the Rangers, for real this time. He guessed he had Michael Wright to thank for that, and the perverse gratitude he felt was tainted by an awful guilt, a heavy weight anchoring the lower half of his body in place. He still, up until the moment he slid his Stetson on his head, wasn't sure he could go through with it. If he did this thing—walked out there and let them use his black face to tell a bank of reporters that there was nothing to see here, that they'd found their man, that the death of a black man from Chicago and a local white woman was no more than a domestic matter, the Rangers and the county having brought in a black officer to investigate and ensure sensitivity to the racial issues at play—if he just gave in to the simplicity of it, Keith Dale as nothing more than a jealous husband who'd lost control, if he could take the win, like Wilson said, he could get his badge back and go home. The bathroom door opened, and Greg poked his head in. "D," he said, smiling when their eyes met.

He was shorter than Darren.

But then again, most people were.

He was wearing a navy blue suit, cut slim across a torso that wasn't as slim as it used to be. It gave Greg the appearance of an adolescent boy squeezed into his only good suit for a funeral no one saw coming, a suit he'd long ago outgrown. His mood was also wrong for the occasion, enlivened where it should have been sober. He went in for a hug, but Darren was stiff and awkward, and Greg settled for a pat on his friend's back. "You came through, man, big-time."

"The Bureau sent you?"

Greg nodded. "Once my supervisor heard I was the one who gave you a tip on the double homicide, he took me off the desk and sent me up here to offer an assist if the county boys out here get in over their heads." He had sandy brown hair and the closely cropped haircut of a company man, unlike the gelled white-boy flattop he'd tried to rock in high school, which made him look like he'd stuck a wet finger in a light socket. His eyes were wide and the color of spring grass, and unlike Darren, he was clean-shaven today. He was, as Lisa had once told Darren, a handsome guy, and Darren certainly knew the effect Greg had on women. He'd been jealous of it as a teenager, the ease with which Greg could get a girl to do things she told other boys she wasn't ready for. Darren, not completely under-standing what Greg was doing at the press conference, opened the bathroom door as the two men headed out, Darren's boots clicking on the gray floor.

"There's nothing in Keith Dale's prison file that indicates he was running with the ABT on the inside." Greg said he'd checked with the Texas Department of Criminal Justice. He'd gotten a report from them just yesterday.

Darren said, "If the sheriff is alleging there's no ABT connection, why the need for the feds at all?"

"We don't know what this is. He hasn't been charged yet."

"And you don't find it odd that they're holding a press conference when he hasn't been charged with either crime?"

"My understanding is all the legwork has been done," Greg said, glancing at himself in the mirror above the sink. "I mean, you caught the guy, Darren. News of the arrest will just put folks at ease. And my presence will let folks feel like the sheriff and his men aren't trying any slippery shit with this."

"In other words, we're both props."

"We're doing our jobs, man," Greg said, appearing slightly put out that Darren didn't appreciate the opportunity he'd placed in his lap. "Someone's going to jail on this thing. Sheriff would still be talking about a robbery if you hadn't rolled into town. If I hadn't called you." He wanted that last bit clear.

"You talk to that guy out of Chicago? Wozniak?" Darren asked.

Greg nodded and said, "This is bigger than that now. There's a stringer out here for the *Times*. CNN sent a camera crew out of Houston. They're going to want to talk to you, too," he said as if he'd just remembered something, though it was clear from his excited demeanor, the way he kind of pitched forward on the balls of his feet, that in the last twenty-four hours this couldn't have left his mind for even a second. "I pitched a sit-down with the two of us for *Nightline,* you know, explaining—how I called you first." *There it is again,* Darren thought. It made him sad, the degree to which this kind of credit hogging mattered to Greg, that three years behind a desk had made him so desperate for the climb that a double homicide was seen as an opportunity first and a crime against nature second. But wasn't Darren a little guilty of this, too?

Keith Dale had likely killed his wife and had admitted to beating Michael Wright as near to death as a man could get. Randie was right: he was *not* innocent. Maybe justice was messier than Darren realized when he'd first pinned a badge to his chest; it was no better or worse than a sieve, a cheap net, a catch-as-catch-can system that gave the illusion of righteousness when really the need for tidy resolution trumped sloppy uncertainty any day. Keith Dale deserved to go to prison, sure he did, but Darren couldn't shake the feeling that what they were doing to Keith was no different from what had been done to black folks for centuries. Grab one, any one, and don't ask any more questions.

"Remember, you'd never even heard of Lark when I sent you the early details of the case," Greg said. "Well, it might make a good angle on the story."

"You know I can't speak to the media without running it by unit."

"After this, they're going to let you do whatever the hell you want."

They'd arrived outside the makeshift media room on the other side of the county courthouse. The plate on the door said LOUNGE, but the room had been made over for the press conference. Through the wire-glass window in the door, Darren could see at least a dozen reporters standing behind a cluster of video cameras, their lenses and microphones pointing toward a podium where Wilson, Van Horn, and one of his deputies were waiting on Greg and Darren.

He didn't speak through the entire thing, through the announcement of Keith Dale's arrest for the murders of Michael Wright and Missy Dale, the explanation of the Texas Rangers' involvement, even the questions directed at Ranger Mathews specifically, deferring with his silence to Wilson and Van Horn. This was their story to sell. He stood with his hands clasped in front of him, his spine as stiff as the trunk of a poplar tree, boots planted firmly on the ground.

Greg spoke. Of course he did.

He waxed philosophical about the role of the federal government in maintaining law and order for its citizens, adept as it was in investigating crimes of a sensitive nature—all without ever saying the words *hate crime* or being in any way clear about when or *if* anyone would be prosecuted for the death of Michael Wright, either by the state of Texas or the Justice Department. He talked of Missy only as a way to complete the narrative; he spoke of the need for the community to not jump to conclusions about the motive for the murder of a black man in Texas. Listening to all of it, Darren felt an odd sense of dislocation, like being in a dream state in which he both did and didn't recognize the world around him or the words spoken in his mother tongue. Wasn't this whole press conference a leap toward a conclusion, a desperate reach for a rope that could swing Van Horn and Wilson safely to the other side of this bubbling mess, bypassing the murky waters of history, the race swamp that would take you whole if you let it?

It was over quickly, before reporters even knew which questions to ask. Many, like Darren just four days ago, had never heard of Lark. Mystery and resolution were presented together in the span of a twelve-minute press conference. And the neatness of it was satisfying, like laying the last piece in the center of a puzzle, the soft snap of a picture becoming whole, a truth sealed.

After, Wilson patted Darren on the back and said he now had something real to take back to headquarters to get Darren's suspension lifted. He couldn't make a move before the grand jury made a decision about Rutherford McMillan, but he had hope for the first time that Darren could return to work.

"Especially if nothing comes out of the search of your place in Camilla."

"They did that search weeks ago."

Wilson, who had an olive complexion and salt-and-pepper hair, leaned in to Darren so he could lower his voice and still be heard. "Look, I would have said something if I could, but that would have been my tail. The DA just wanted another look around. It wasn't on me, Mathews. It wasn't my call."

They'd done a second search of the house, he realized.

"Jesus."

"They went in this morning."

"When they knew I was out of the county," Darren said. He couldn't shake the feeling that Wilson had provided the San Jacinto County DA with that information, and he didn't bother to hide the accusation in his tone.

"If there's nothing there, there's nothing there," Wilson said. "No reason to fear."

"There's nothing in that house."

But why were they searching his place when the grand jury had heard all the supposed evidence against Mack—when they were already deliberating?

Were new charges being considered?

Charges against Darren?

The thought of it shot panic through every part of his body.

"I wouldn't worry none on it," Wilson said. "You're a fine young man. And your uncle William was a man I respected like hell. Let's see what the grand jury comes back with on the other deal, and let me see if I can't get you back in the field, where you belong, Ranger." Darren had, Wilson said, shown a willingness to put the facts before his feelings, and his uncle would be proud. Darren resented the mention of his uncle and might have said something about William Mathews being a man who would never have swallowed this degree of uncertainty and unease about an investigation into the murder of a black man in order to make white folks feel better about the state of things in Texas. He might have said he was sure he was failing in his duty to pursue the truth, inconvenient and complicated though it may be—a duty passed down to him by the Mathews men who had raised him. But he held his tongue and pulled out his cell phone instead. As the last reporter and her cameraman were filing out, Darren found a quiet spot in the hallway and left a message on the answering machine in his mother's trailer, telling Bell that there was a few hundred dollars in it if she went out to the Mathews place in Camilla and cleaned up whatever mess the sheriff's deputies may have left in their wake—more if she could keep her mouth shut about it. He especially didn't want to worry Clayton with news that this thing with Mack might be taking a perilous turn in Darren's direction. *There's nothing in that house.* Besides, news of the sheriff's department tearing through his family's homestead for a second time would only deepen Clayton's resentment of law enforcement, and Darren didn't want to hear it right now.

As he ended his call, Van Horn approached him in the hallway and said with little fanfare or concern, "Geneva Sweet is free to go home now."

She refused a ride the first time he offered, insisting she would rather wait for her granddaughter. But after Darren called Faith in Lark—and she said she could use the extra help, having kept the cafe open against her grandmother's wishes—Geneva finally relented. Outside the courthouse, there were news vans still lined up along San Augustine Street, a few cameramen looking for a last shot of the courthouse, something to make the squat, boxlike brick building look more majestic than it was. Because the name Geneva Sweet had slid off no tongue during the short press conference, there was no interest in the nearly seventy-year-old black woman being led by Darren, who, having removed his hat, looked for all the world like her son or nephew, escorting her gently to the parking lot.

He tried to help her into the truck, but she swatted away his hand, and with a grunt and a muttered prayer managed to lift herself into the high-rise cab. By the time Darren made it around to the driver's side and slid in behind the steering wheel, Geneva had her seat belt on and her hands resting in her lap. He set his Stetson on the bench seat between them and kicked on the engine.

The climb into the Chevy had winded her slightly, and Darren, looking over, caught the play of light off the sheen on her forehead, a few of her tight gray curls sticking to her skin like gnats on flypaper. She adjusted the direction of the air-conditioning vent in front of her but otherwise didn't move or speak.

They set out on State Highway 87.

Darren debated whether to cut through the meat of the county and travel by scenic local roads to get back to Lark. This part of East Texas was near enough to Louisiana to put a dampness in the air, a kiss of moss blowing from Texas live oaks; it was a breathtaking country vista. But he figured Geneva wanted the quickest way home, so he turned toward Timpson, where he jumped on 59, heading south to Lark. He honored her silence for the first few miles. But in the end, he knew something had to be said. "I didn't have anything to do with you being arrested," he told her. He wanted to get that out of the way. But if he thought this would soften the stonelike set of her jaw, he was mistaken. He wondered how much she knew, either about Keith's arrest or the fact that Sheriff Van Horn was willing to let her go last night—that it was Darren who had pushed for more time, even if it meant a cold night in jail for Geneva. "I didn't mean you any harm in this thing," he said, glancing from the highway to the passenger seat. She didn't nod, speak, or smile, didn't offer him the least of her attention, so that Darren actually felt a flare of anger in his chest. Elderly or not, she was behaving like a recalcitrant child, stubborn and willful.

"You don't like me much," he said.

"Don't know you." The words came up out of nowhere, like a burp of bad air that caught her unawares. "Got no reason to trust you, that's all."

"I came out here to help."

"And look how that worked out for me," she said, smoothing the front of her skirt, a pale cotton blend that had been sullied during her night in lockup.

"You'd have been arrested for Missy whether I set foot in Lark or not. You made sure of that by not coming clean about seeing Missy the night she died, when you knew the sheriff was hunting for someone to put that on," Darren said, gripping the steering wheel till his nails met the palms of his hands, digging in. "If it wasn't for me shining a light on Keith, you'd likely still be in that jail cell, with the DA enjoining a grand jury to keep you there."

"Well, you got what you wanted, so now you can go on back to wherever you come from and leave well enough alone," she said, crossing her arms and staring out at the road. "Rest of us got to live in these parts long after you gone."

"What is that supposed to mean?" he said. Her words had lit up some part of his brain, warning his conscious mind to pay attention. He heard fear in her voice where he never had before, felt it vibrating between them in the truck's narrow cab. He turned to look at her across the seat, trying to read her expression.

"There's no proof Keith did it."

"Aw, he murdered that girl, no question. That son of a bitch robbed my grandson of a mother to look out for him in this world." She was sitting stiff and straight but was thrumming with rage, like a live wire. "And you're a fool if you think he didn't kill that black fellow, too. I just don't like folks coming down here, a town we been living in since before you could pee straight, a place you don't understand, and think you know every damn thing. You and the girl."

"I was born in San Jacinto County," he said. "And the girl has a name."

Randie.

"I wouldn't know it, since she never walked in my place and paid me any kind of respect."

"She lost her husband, Geneva."

"She not the only one."

Joe.

He was afraid to say the name out loud, afraid to break the spell.

"I loved the one God gave me," she said. "I knew what I had."

Geneva said nothing after that, and Darren tried to keep his mouth shut. But he felt protective of Randie and couldn't make sense of the affront Geneva felt at the mention of the young widow. "You don't know anything about her marriage to Michael." He was thinking of Missy and the whispers, Randie's stories of the other women that had populated their troubled marriage.

Geneva gave a tiny shrug of indifference.

"I know what he told me," she said. "What Missy said, too."

"Missy?"

She turned and looked through the glass at the countryside blurring green and honey-colored gold, the sky a constant and steady
blue. "You know what she told me they talked about that night,
her and Michael, what started this whole thing?" She turned, and
their eyes met across the bench seat. Darren felt his heart lift and
press against his breastbone. He felt a longing to understand.

"Love lost," she said. "My son; his wife. They'd both had something wrenched away from them, in different ways and for different
reasons. Missy saw something in Michael same way I did, time he
walked into my cafe."

23.

HE REMINDED her of her son.

Wasn't nothing you could put a finger on, just the age was right, if not the look or the life itself. It was just that a black man of a certain age and carriage—a learned restraint in his swagger, a cautious grace in his countenance—would always pinch at Geneva's heart, on sight. Even Darren, when he'd first walked into her place, had made her think of her son, she said. Last Wednesday, she was soaking red beans in the kitchen and brining a turkey for Dennis to smoke.

Around five o'clock that afternoon, she came in through the swinging door, wiping her hands on the tail of her apron. She heard the bell on the door just as a Lightnin' Hopkins song lit up the music box. *Have you ever loved a woman, man, better than you did yourself?* One of Joe's favorites, she thought as she smiled and looked up and saw Michael Wright. He was wearing a black T-shirt and dungarees, and the glint off the fancy car he'd rode in on shot through the windows and lit the air around him with an amber warmth. It was the last day of his life, she now knew, and the moment was forever frozen in time.

He had that guitar on him, in a battered case, the cheap leather
fraying after nearly fifty years. Huxley was down by Isaac's chair,
talking to Tim, who was getting a trim before he set out again on
the road. They may have even been running a card game off the
armrest of the green barber's chair. Michael took Huxley's stool at
the counter, then laid the guitar across the other two.

"You play?" Geneva asked as she handed him a paper menu,
which doubled as a place mat. Without asking, she poured him a
tall glass of water.

"No," Michael said, looking up at her as if he were deciding
something.

"He was about your color," she said to Darren now. But his eyes
were black, and he wore round wire-rimmed glasses made of a bur-
nished metal.

"No, ma'am," Michael said. "Never played."

"What can I get you?"

"Catfish plate."

"What sides?"

He glanced back down at the menu. "Uh...peas and tomato
okra."

"You want anything 'sides water?"

"I sure would take a beer if you had it."

Geneva turned to the refrigerated case that held glass bottles of
soda and beer. She grabbed a Coors and peeled off the top with the
bottle opener hanging from a string on the cooler door. She handed
the bottle to Michael, then hollered to Dennis in the kitchen. "I
need a fish plate with peas and okra."

Michael lifted the beer bottle to his lips, and Geneva saw the
wedding ring.

She couldn't place him. The plates out front said Illinois, but there was something familiar about him to Geneva, some aura about him that made him seem right at home in this one-room cafe in rural East Texas. Or, as she thought back on it, maybe it was the guitar that felt like it fit. She asked him about it again. "You ain't play, what you lugging that in here for?"

He set down the Coors, missing the original ring of beer sweat on the menu by a few inches. He looked up, studying her face, letting the seconds tick by, as Lightnin' continued to sing. *Have you ever tried to give 'em a good home same time she act a fool and left?* He tapped his hand on top of the guitar case.

"This belonged to Joe Sweet," he said, watching her face for a reaction to the name. "Joe 'Petey Pie' Sweet." He watched Geneva come around from behind the counter and open the case. It was a '55 Les Paul, a beauty. She ran her fingers over the wood, especially the places where the varnish was worn, the parts that told time. Michael stared at her and bit back a smile, a whisper of relief in his voice, that he hadn't come all this way for nothing. "You his wife?"

"This Joe's guitar?"

"Yes, ma'am. I was hoping to return it to him," he said, his voice halting a little. "I mean, I meant to, but I understand he passed. So this is yours now."

"How you know Joe? You not fixing to tell me you his long-lost son or some shit like that, are you?" She took a good long look at his nose and mouth.

"No, ma'am," he said, chuckling a little. "He and my uncle used to play together. Booker Wright. My people come out of Tyler." He nodded toward the front windows, as if Tyler was just right over the trees on the other side of the highway. "Booker was the first to leave Texas. Then my mama married my daddy, and they followed his brother north, settling in Chicago and never looking back. For better or worse, I put it in my rearview mirror, too. I'm sorry it took me so long to honor my uncle's last request. He wanted you to have this."

"Booker." She hadn't said the name in years. She remembered him well, remembered his silhouette in the doorway to the old Geneva's, how he lingered long enough to give Joe a chance to change his mind, to hop in the Impala with him and the rest of the band. There was a bitterness between the men that lasted decades. Joe sent a postcard or two over the years. But the only ones available in Shelby County, Texas, showed pictures of Lone Stars or live oaks, bluebonnets and scenes of prairie and cattle, and that likely did nothing to douse the hot embers of resentment Booker felt about losing the best guitar player he ever knew— a man he considered a brother and a friend—to rural Texas. "Joe loved him," she said.

"I know."

She smiled at Michael, enjoying the parts of her life that came alive again with the mention of Joe Sweet. "You sure you ain't know Joe?" she said.

"Just heard stories," he said. "Would have liked to, though. That was some love story Booker told about you and Joe back in the day."

"Joe always said a man can't be on the road forever."

The kitchen door swung out from the back room, and Dennis came out with a plate of fish fillets breaded in cornmeal, Lawry's seasoned salt, plus a spice blend that Geneva had done up on her own and kept to herself. Dennis set down the plate and slid a bottle of hot sauce across the counter in Michael's direction. For a while, Geneva let him eat in peace. She carried the guitar and its case over to an empty booth and set them on top of the table. It was the same booth above which the guitar now hung. Michael ate heartily, ordering a slice of white bread when he saw the opportunity to sop up the soup of hot sauce, grease, and tomato juice left on his plate. He followed the first beer with another and seemed in a good mood, satisfied with a meal unlike any he'd had since he was a child. He swung around on the vinyl stool and watched Geneva with that guitar.

"I'm sorry this took me so long," he said.

She waved away the thought, never taking her eyes off the instrument.

"You got a wife, got your own life to live." She nodded at his wedding ring. At this, Michael stiffened. He looked away from her and spun slowly around on the stool, sipping on the second beer. Geneva felt the change more than she saw it, as if a cloud had swallowed the sun. She left the case in the booth, then returned to her station. She bought some time by clearing Michael's plate and wiping down the counter. "I got some fried pies."

"No, thank you, ma'am."

He glanced at his watch, a spell broken.

"You got kids?" she asked.

"No."

"How long you been married?"

"Six years."

"Six years a long time with no little ones at your feet."

"My wife travels a lot," he said. He lifted the beer bottle to gesture for another, but then changed his mind. He set the empty in front of him and picked at the label with his thumbnail. "For work." He felt the need to explain. "She's incredibly successful, and I don't begrudge her that. And you don't see me quitting my job and following her from gig to gig around the world. It's not fair to ask her to give it up for me, I know that. But tell me, ma'am. Maybe I've had it all wrong. I thought men were the ones supposed to be the rolling stones."

"People do what they want—man, woman, whatever."

There was an indictment in there somewhere, and Michael got defensive.

"She's a good woman, and I ain't been perfect my damn self," he said. "Truth is, I don't know if I messed around 'cause she wasn't home or she wasn't home because I messed around. I just know we fouled it up some kind of way I don't even really understand. We loved each other once. I still do."

Darren, listening, felt an ache inside his own chest. Michael and Randie sounded like him and Lisa with the sexes reversed. Darren was the one who wanted to roam, who didn't know how to make a home. *People do what they want—man, woman, whatever.* Did Randie and Darren actually know more about what they really wanted than either of them was willing to admit?

At Geneva's, Michael left his beer bottle alone and asked if there was a place he could get something *real* to drink. She'd made him uncomfortable, and he was looking for a way out. She told him the only place around was an icehouse up the road, and he'd do well to leave that place alone. Her words had an ugly bite to them that he didn't recognize. "You don't want nothing to do with Wally's place," Huxley said as he came from Isaac's barbershop to refill his cup of coffee. Huxley drifted back to his card game, and Michael edged away from his own emotion, asking Geneva about her life. "You and Joe have kids?"

"Just one boy," she said. "We tried for another. But none of 'em would hold. So we just loved the family God gave us."

"Joe died in a robbery?"

Geneva nodded. "First night I'd ever left him alone. Me and my son, Lil' Joe, his wife, Mary, and my grandbaby had gone up to Dallas to get her a dress for her junior prom, and three men came in after midnight. Stole a week's worth of sales and shot my husband in cold blood." She folded up the rag she'd been using to wipe the countertop and stored it nearby. The muscles across her shoulders and back were taut with grief and the anxiety of a trauma recounted.

"Terrible what happened," Huxley said, and Geneva and Michael realized they were all listening. Isaac stopped his clippers an inch from Tim's head.

"Isaac saw the whole thing," Tim said.

Isaac cleared his throat and clicked off the clippers. "I was taking the trash out back when they come through the front door." Geneva had her head down, and Isaac, unwilling or unable to concern himself with the woman's feelings, kept talking. He was hopped up on the memory, really selling the danger of the moment and the heroics of his involvement. "I heard one gunshot. *Blam!* Like thunder, like a shotgun, and by the time I made it from the kitchen, I could just see them making off in they car." He pointed through the front windows, past Michael's black BMW to the gas pump and the highway beyond.

Michael turned to follow his gaze.

"It was three white men. Mr. Joe was lying here bleeding," Isaac said, pointing to a spot just behind the counter and near the cash register, not far from where Michael was sitting. "I was the one called the police."

Michael looked from the spot on the floor to the windows and then to Isaac. "How did you know the killers were white?"

"Pardon?" Isaac said as he fired up the clippers again and told

Tim to lean his head all the way down so he could clean up the back.

"It was night, you said." Michael looked at Geneva for confirmation. "And you saw them driving off. How, then, did you know they were white?"

It was the same question Darren had asked. He had tripped over the same bump in the story, which Geneva repeated again now, brushing away both Michael's and Darren's inquiries by saying the sheriff had come and looked into everything, and what did any of it matter with both her men in the ground now?

Soon as they pulled up into the parking lot at Geneva's, Darren saw two familiar cars: Randie's blue rental and Wally's enormous Ford truck, its chrome bumpers gleaming in the sun, creating a white-hot halo effect that burned his eyes. Darren insisted on helping Geneva from the cab, refusing to heed her protestations. He took gentle hold of her elbow as he walked her toward the cafe's front door. As they passed the blue Ford Randie had been driving for days, Darren took a tentative peek inside, not sure what he wanted to find but knowing it wasn't this: her leather duffel packed and waiting on the front seat, the black camera bag resting on top. The time had come. She was leaving. Darren was, too—today, probably. The mystery of what happened to Michael Wright—a man Darren felt he'd come to know and understand, a man who shared his East Texas upbringing—had slipped through his fingers. He'd failed the man in a way he couldn't quite name, save for the nagging feeling that they'd gotten this one wrong.

Inside Geneva's, Wally was behind the counter, helping himself to a beer from the refrigerated case. He popped the top with the plastic opener hanging from the cooler door, took a sip, and nodded hello as Geneva and Darren entered, as if they'd just come in out of the sun and into his front parlor, where he was waiting with cold drinks and conversation. He gestured with his beer to the stained cardboard covering the front door, against which the tiny brass bell was dully thudding. "I got a man coming out first thing in the morning to fix that door," he said to Geneva. It was hardly lunch hour, and Wally was deep in his cups, drunk and pink about the nose, a drinker's high blossoming across his face.

"That door will be fixed when I say it will," Geneva said.

Her manner was matter-of-fact, without shame or scolding. She simply waited for him to come to his better sense and get the hell away from her cash register. She didn't have to say it but once. Wally walked around to the front of the counter, passing Geneva as she attempted to take her rightful place at the helm of her world, on the kitchen side of the counter, looking out on Highway 59. As they came within a few inches of each other, Wally reached for her arm. There was a laying of claim in the gesture as well as a desperate plea in Wally's eyes, some unspoken thing he wanted from her. A look passed between them that boiled the air in the room. Darren caught it as well as the warning shot that flashed across Geneva's face as she yanked her arm from Wally's grip and pushed past him. Wally stood in place, staring after her a clean minute before moving on, perching himself on one of the red stools, two down from Huxley, who was sitting in his usual spot, a mug of coffee and a newspaper before him. Wendy was in one of the booths by the window, sitting beneath Joe's Les Paul. She was playing a complicated and made-up game of solitaire that involved checkers pieces as well as two decks of cards. She started to slide her aged body out of the booth to properly greet Geneva, who told her not to bother. She wasn't touching anyone or anything until she spent a good fifteen minutes standing under hot running water. She had her hand on the door to the kitchen when Wally spoke up again. "Lark ought to sleep good tonight, a cold-blooded killer behind bars."

"We closed, Wally," Geneva said, shutting down further conversation.

And when Wally looked around him at the food on display, folks eating, bustling commerce in nearly every corner, she added flatly, "I just decided."

He smiled, as if this woman never failed to entertain him.

He took another swig of beer as a tonic against whatever weakness had befallen him earlier, had laid bare a longing, something he needed from Geneva. He fiddled with the diamond on his wedding ring, swinging out his legs so he could cross them beneath the countertop, a pair of horned gators shooting from the legs of his black Wranglers. "I hope it ain't no hard feelings between us."

Geneva paused at the doorway to the kitchen, a wary look on her face.

Wally shrugged, as if it wasn't much of nothing. "I owed the sheriff the truth about what I saw, Missy coming up to your place the night she was killed."

Darren stepped forward. "You told Van Horn?"

"I might have mentioned something in the early stages of this thing, when it was wide open as to who done it, and Parker was just asking questions."

Huxley came off his stool fast, as if treachery were catching. He put a few feet between him and Wally, taking the seat opposite Wendy in her booth.

Darren took up the space he'd vacated, looking directly at Wally. He shook his head slightly, as if trying to loosen a thought, the pebble of doubt about these murders that remained lodged in a dark corner of his mind.

"No," he said. "It was the autopsy—"

"That confirmed it, yes," Wally said. "The food and all that."

He looked across the counter at Geneva, a prickly indignation set up as a shield against what she might do to him for talking. "But look, Van Horn knows I've been living across the highway from this place for near fifty years, that I can see every goddamn thing going on in here right from my front window."

"Said I was closed," Geneva said. Then, in a huff of anger, she slammed through the swinging door, hollering, "Where is Faith?" The door swung back, carrying the echo of her words on a gust of warm air scented by bay leaves and garlic. Wally seemed pleased by the exchange. That she had not hauled off and hit him or banned him from the premises put a smile on his face. He sucked down the last of the beer, belching before turning his attention to Darren.

"But hell if it didn't all work out," he said to him. "You put up Keith on two killings, and now you can leave this little town just like you found it."

He stood to his full six feet two inches, a decent haircut shy of Darren. He rapped his knuckles on the Formica countertop, then turned and walked out.

Darren watched him go.

He swung around on the stool and followed his every move, watching as he climbed into the Ford's cab, as he backed up the oversize truck and steered it back onto 59, crossing the highway to drive the short distance that separated Geneva's cafe from his front door. What had Wally said? That he'd been living across the highway from Geneva's for fifty years, that he could see everything that went on in here right from his front window. Darren looked at Geneva's regulars, Huxley and Wendy. "They ever find who did it?" he said.

"You talking about Keith?" Wendy asked, her brow knotted in confusion.

"No. The men who killed Joe Sweet."

Huxley met Wendy's eye, and the two pointedly remained silent a moment; an unspoken sense of propriety required it. Wendy broke the silence first, not with words but with a soft whistle, a blue note that hung in the air, a call that demanded a response. "What?" Darren said, looking between the two of them.

Wendy shook her head. "Naw. They ain't ever caught nobody."

"See, that's what always ain't sat right," Huxley said, a breathlessness creeping on him as the words came, an eagerness to speak of something taboo.

"The whole thing ain't sat right," Wendy said. "But we got but one sheriff, and he closed the book on that one 'fore Geneva got Joe in the ground."

"The story doesn't make sense," Darren said.

"No, it don't," Huxley followed.

Darren glanced toward the barber's chair, which sat empty, as did the stall where Isaac cut hair. He realized again he hadn't seen the man since the night of the shooting, when Geneva's door was shot to hell. "You think Isaac was lying?"

"Aw, Isaac don't know shit from shinola," Huxley said. "He only said three white men *after* the sheriff did."

"Whatever Isaac really saw that night must have spooked him good," Wendy said. "It's like the whole thing got buried along with Joe."

"Ain't nobody dare bring it up . . . until that black fellow come in here."

"Michael?" Darren said.

He felt a thrum in his chest, a vibration picking up speed, like a train coming, a locomotive of a feeling that he was getting close to something.

Huxley nodded.

Wendy said, "Geneva never wanted to talk about it."

"Still don't," they heard as the kitchen door swung open.

Geneva entered, still in the clothes she'd worn to jail. "That gal was out back looking for you," she said flatly. "Guess y'all be going soon." She said it as if she had all the time in the world to stand right there and watch him go.

"What did Van Horn tell you happened to Joe?" Darren said.

"What you bringing that up for?"

"Something's wrong, isn't it? With Isaac's story."

"We been living with this for six years now," she said. "It was a robbery."

The same thing they'd told Randie about her husband when she arrived in Shelby County.

"And you don't think it's odd," Darren said, "that it happened on the one night you left Joe in the cafe alone?"

"Don't know what that matters, unless you trying to say this is somehow my fault," Geneva said. "And if you think I ain't already been carrying that around for years, then you're not only mean as the devil but stupid, too."

"I'm saying that it's almost like somebody knew when to strike, somebody who's got a view of everything that goes on in here, right from his living-room window."

It flashed across Geneva's face, the realization of what he was implying, and she wasn't having it. "Leave it be, hear?" She'd grown increasingly angry, but Darren felt the pinch of something else beneath it, a hard and festering fear.

"What are you so scared of?"

"I'm not scared," Geneva said, and maybe she wasn't, at least not in the way he'd understood. Maybe the whiff of unease she gave off was more akin to acute caution, a fear of bumping up against the barbed fencing that time had put around her heart, keeping hope penned in. "I've just been living in this state a lot longer than you have, and I know how the law works for people like me."

She'd given up on the truth, just as Randie had.

It both saddened and infuriated him that he wore a badge that meant nothing to either woman, that justice and despondency were so inextricably intertwined that the former was often not worth the trouble of the latter.

"Show him the card the man gave you," Huxley said suddenly.

Geneva waved away the thought.

Huxley looked at Geneva, knew he was pushing nearer to where the ice ran thin, but he kept going anyway. "The lawyer fellow, Michael. He left Geneva a card, a place that looks into old cases, some folks he knew out of Chicago."

Darren said, "You still have it?"

Geneva shrugged, but Huxley came around the counter himself and plucked out a business card that had been tucked under a bottom corner of the cash register. He handed it to Darren, who studied the embossed letters: LENNON & PELKIN INVESTIGATIVE SERVICES. He looked at Geneva, who let out a heavy sigh.

24.

It was a private investigation firm run by two ex-cops who had over the years been hired numerous times by a local offshoot of the Innocence Project, run by a former University of Chicago law professor. A few phone calls and a thorough Google search by Darren explained why Michael Wright thought to suggest their help. While looking into the cases of men and women, mostly black and Latino, who had been wrongfully accused and often incarcerated for decades, the two investigators discovered a pattern: for every story about a black mother, sister, or wife crying over a man who was locked up for something he didn't do, there was a black mother, sister, wife, husband, father, or brother crying over the murder of a loved one for which *no one* was locked up. For black folks, injustice came from both sides of the law, a double-edged sword of heartache and pain. Lennon and Pelkin had carved out a whole division of their agency to work on unsolved murders in which race played a part—as in the race of the victim had put lead in the shoes of local law enforcement, slowing their pace and ultimately dulling their curiosity to the point of inertia. The *New York Times* had written a profile of the agency and its founders and the few unsolved murders they'd resurrected and solved. Michael had been offering Geneva a way to find Joe Sweet's killer.

Standing outside the cafe, Darren wondered if Wally knew that Michael had been asking questions about the death of Joe Sweet in the hours right before he died, wondered in fact where Wally had spent the hours leading up to Michael's death. The question felt urgent, and he was already reaching for his car keys when he looked up from his phone and saw Randie coming around the side of the cafe. She reached out and touched his forearm as she told him she'd been waiting to say good-bye.

"They've released the body," she said. "I'm taking Michael home."

"Don't go." He said it before he thought it through. He felt himself reaching for her permission or approval when his duty was ultimately to Michael, not her; justice didn't require the consent of those left behind.

"It's done, Darren," she said. "Look, I wanted to—"

"Randie."

"Thank you, Darren. I appreciate everything you tried to do for me, for Michael. I don't understand this place, this state, but Michael did. He would have respected what you're trying to do down here. He would have liked you."

"Randie, wait."

"I can't," she said. "There's nothing else for me to do here." She started for the driver's side of her blue hatchback. He grabbed her left arm to stop her.

"I think Keith is telling the truth about Michael," he said.

Randie's face hardened as she yanked her arm free. "Stop this."

"I don't think he killed him."

"I can't do this, Darren," she said, opening the door to her rental car.

"What if Michael's death didn't have anything to do with Missy Dale?"

"Then why?" she said, her voice rising to the edge of a scream, her brown eyes flashing red with rage. "Then why is my husband dead, Darren?"

"Joe Sweet."

She looked at him blankly. For a second, it seemed she'd forgotten the name, the guitar, and the love story, the whole reason Michael had driven Highway 59 into East Texas. And when the name finally landed, it exhausted her, the realization of what Darren was asking her to endure, more questions with no promise of an answer, when she could just get in the car now and drive.

"Michael was asking questions about the night Joe Sweet was killed."

"So?" She opened the car door wider, so that it put a wall between them.

"So somebody in this town might have had reason to put a stop to it."

Darren glanced back behind him, across the highway toward Wally's Monticello, musing on an approach, how he wanted to come at his hunch.

"Go or stay," he told her. "But I'm seeing this through."

He wanted to know one thing: had Wally and Michael crossed paths the night he died? Wally's icehouse was the last place Michael had been seen before he took a beating on the farm road. Darren wanted to track all Wally's movements that night. He crossed 59 and drove through the gate to Wally's mansion. No one answered the front door, though Darren saw Wally's enormous truck in the circular drive. Darren had in fact parked behind it. He was pressing the doorbell a third time when he heard sounds from around the back side of the house, footsteps through fallen leaves, then a door opening and closing. The sound echoed through the oak trees that were rising like specters and surrounding the house, their thick limbs casting black shadows over the roof. "Wally," Darren called. Hearing no response, he started around to the back of the house, coming within inches of the black Lab on its chain. It lurched toward Darren, barking and snarling. The dog came so close that Darren could feel its hot, moist breath through his pants leg. He slid by the dog, pressing his body against the side of the house, the rough edges of the red brick wall stabbing him down the center of his back.

"Wally," he called again, thinking he must be in the backyard.

But only silence answered Darren. There wasn't a sound out here but the rustle of leaves blowing across the expanse of Wally's backyard and the flutter of birds fleeing nearby trees, as if they knew something he didn't, could sense trouble coming. Darren felt it, too, a stillness around him he didn't trust.

The land behind the house was more raw woodland than landscaped garden. It was choked with the gnarled roots of a family of live oaks. Traditional East Texas pines stood sentry to the north and south, along the property line. There were a few buildings back here, small structures that were covered in fallen leaves and skeletal pinecones: a narrow greenhouse, as much a hut for storing tools as a hothouse, and a larger shed, the wood feathered with time, the color faded to a dull gray. Its doors were cracked open an inch or two, and the padlock meant to secure the shed was open, hanging like an ornament from its latch, a useless decoration. Darren saw something on the ground in front of the shed, and it stopped him cold. There were twin tire tracks that disappeared into the blackness on the other side of the wooden doors.

Where is the car?

He'd been asking the question for days. It was the missing piece that convinced him that Keith Dale might be telling the truth. Darren couldn't read tire treads any better than tea leaves, but he had a sinking feeling about what he would find on the other side of those doors. He pulled one of them open, cringing at the awful screech of the rusty hinge. This, he realized, was the sound he'd heard when he was standing at the front door on the other side of the house.

Before his eyes could adjust to the dark, he heard the sound of a gun cock, and he knew he wasn't alone. Through the thin shafts of light shooting through holes in the roof and the swirl of dust that hung in the air, he saw Isaac pressed against the back wall, pointing a tiny pistol at Darren's head. Darren went for his Colt, but before he could get it out of the holster, Isaac got off a shot. It went over Darren's shoulder, missing him by inches. Darren held a hand in front of his body and reached for his .45 with the other. "Isaac, put the gun down."

Isaac shot again, splintering a slat in the shed's door.

From inside the house, Darren heard a woman scream.

"Wally, somebody's shooting out there!"

So they *were* home, Darren thought.

He pictured the toddler in there and felt his stomach drop.

"Wally ain't gon' like this," Isaac mumbled.

Darren put his hands up. "Just tell me what you saw, Isaac."

He could see now that Isaac was terrified, eyes wide and red-veined. He may have been crying. He was inching closer to the door while Darren kept a safe distance, so that the two were in a strange, slow dance, arcing around each other, a pirouette that ended with Darren deep inside the shed, which was empty except for cans of old paint, and Isaac right at the shed's door. The BMW, if it had been here once, was gone now. Isaac backed into the daylight outside the shed, then slipped through the doors and ran.

Darren reached for his gun as he took off after him.

"Isaac, I don't want to hurt you, man."

But Isaac was swift and had the benefit of knowing the landscape better than Darren did. Within moments Darren lost sight of him in the surrounding woods. He was starting for the back door of the house when he came upon Wally. The older man wore a crooked smile as he held his hands up, eyeing Darren's gun.

"Where's the car, Wally?"

"I didn't kill that Chicago fella."

"Where is the fucking car?"

Darren heard a car peeling into the driveway on the other side of the house. A door opened, then slammed shut, and Darren heard clunky footsteps as a sheriff's deputy came huffing and puffing around the side of the house. Wally's smile spread, and Darren realized he'd walked into a scene Wally had staged. "Put the gun down, sir," the deputy said, his own pistol shaking.

"He was trying to kill me," Wally said.

"I said put the gun down!"

"You're talking to a Texas Ranger," Darren said. He was afraid to angle his body in a way that would show off his badge. He was afraid to make any sudden movement. "Call Van Horn and tell him I got the killer right here."

"He's on his way," the deputy said. "Laura called about a shooting, an intruder or somebody. Sheriff's got deputies looking up and down 59 for him now."

"Can you tell this man to get this gun off me?" Wally said.

"This man is under arrest," Darren shot back.

The deputy looked between Darren and Wally. He still had the gun pointed in Darren's direction, not sure whom to trust. The walkie-talkie on his belt squawked at him. He lifted it, and they all heard a voice on the other end say, "Sheriff, this is Redding. We still got an APB on that late-model BMW, black?"

Van Horn's voice came over the open channel. "Copy."

Darren felt a chill as he heard Redding say, "We caught it heading for the county line just a piece from Lark. Daniels and Armstrong picked up the driver. The wife is still over to that cafe out there. They bringing the car there now."

In a county full of police scanners, word had already spread. And when Darren pulled into the parking lot at Geneva's, there was an audience standing watch out front. Geneva and Dennis, Huxley and Faith, and a few of Geneva's other customers. Wendy, too. And Randie. In the end, she *had* waited for him. She had her arms folded against a late afternoon breeze that was lifting stray leaves and red dust from neighboring fields. She shuddered and looked across the cafe's parking lot. Her eyes met Darren's, and he thought to walk to her, to reach for her hand. But he stayed near his truck and Wally and the deputy who'd been in back of his house. Mr. Jefferson, as the young deputy called him, had consented to ride shotgun in the deputy's squad car. There were questions the cop had about what he'd seen, and the plan was to meet Van Horn here. It was a deputy's vehicle that rolled up first, driven by the one called Daniels. Darren saw the outline of Isaac behind the cage in back.

He was holding his head down low, looking at no one. Then, less than a minute later, the black BMW pulled up in front of the cafe. At the sight of it, Randie went weak in the knees. It was Geneva who reached out to hold her up, to keep her from hitting the pavement. The one called Armstrong had driven it here. The young man, thick-necked, with a lineman's shoulders, got out of the vehicle and walked to Van Horn, who'd arrived only shortly before Darren and Wally. "This that man's car, ain't it?" Armstrong said. "The one we pulled out the bayou?"

Randie tore from Geneva's clutch and ran to the squad car that held Isaac, beating her fists against the windows of the backseat and screaming, "What did you do?" Wally watched stone-faced as she ran from one side of the car to the other, and Isaac tried to sink from sight. Her voice was like piano wire stretched to its breaking point, so that it hardly made a sound, just a ragged whisper. "What did you do?" Darren went to her side, and only then did she take her eyes off Isaac, pressing her face into Darren's chest and weeping in a way that felt like grief being born, newly alive and raw. Van Horn looked from Randie to the small, freckled black man in the back of the squad car. "Get him out of here."

25.

HE'D SEEN the whole thing go down. Keith Dale dragging Michael from his car, the first punches thrown, and Missy screaming like the devil was at her back, hollering at Keith to quit it this instant. He saw the blood, the way Michael staggered on his feet, saw the moment Keith crossed to his truck and pulled out the two-by-four, which changed everything. Isaac watched it all through the trees between the farm road and the back of the icehouse, under cover of darkness and the fact that no one from Lark who looked like him would be caught dead around the cracker den that was Jeff's Juice House. It wasn't always that way. Used to be, when he was a little pup, you could go in there and buy a Coke if you felt like it. They had grape Nehi even when Geneva's ran out. It wasn't real friendly or anything, but you also didn't think you'd get skinned just for being there. It was them tattoo-looking whites in there now, heads shaved, some of them, who scared Isaac down to his toes. But he knew Wally would want to hear about the man who'd been at Geneva's, the questions about Joe Sweet. That's why he'd come around by the back door of the icehouse: to give Wally the news that trouble could be put down if they moved fast.

That he stumbled on the problem itself, already beaten half to death and down on his knees, was a fluke, an opportunity that rolled like a stone right up to his feet. He watched from the side of the road, buried in the brush and trees, as Keith Dale raised that stick of wood over Michael's head, and he heard Missy yelling, "He was just taking me home!" And when Keith still didn't drop the weapon, she said, "Do it and you'll have to kill me, too. You might could explain one dead, but I know you ain't smart enough to get out of two." Keith dropped the two-by-four and stormed to his truck, dragging Missy behind him. He nearly slammed her into the front seat before walking around to the driver's side, grumbling the whole time. Within minutes they were gone.

"What did you do?" Darren asked.

He was back in the tiny interrogation room at the sheriff's department in Center. Isaac had initially refused a seat, as if he thought he didn't deserve one, as if he could mete out his own punishment. But the interview, plus the weight of what he had to confess, had worn him down. He'd sunk into a corner of the room, back scrunched up between two dingy walls. Darren had squatted down before him so he could meet the man's eye.

"He was already down when I found him," Isaac said, slow-walking Darren through his muddled thinking that night. He wasn't sure if he had time, he said, to get down the highway to Wally's place, to let him know about the questions Michael had been asking, how he seemed to know what they'd done, the secret he and Wally had been keeping for years. What if, in the time it would take Isaac to run up the highway to fetch Wally, Michael came to and got back in his car and drove straight to the sheriff in

Center? Wally would for sure lay the blame on Isaac for fouling up, and who knows what all might happen then? He was as concerned about Geneva finding out as he was about going to jail. Geneva was like family to him; the job at her place was all he had.

So he acted quickly.

He picked up the two-by-four Keith had left in the dirt and grass. Michael wasn't completely out. He'd apparently heard Isaac's footsteps and was trying to rise to his feet when Isaac brought down the wooden board with all the strength he had. Michael went limp as a rag doll. Isaac hit him again. Panicked by what he'd done, he dragged the man off the farm road all the way to the edge of the Attoyac Bayou and kicked him into his final resting place. Surely someone would think Keith had done it. But when Isaac got back to the farm road, he realized the mistake he'd made, where his smarts had abandoned him, as they had so many times before. He knew folks called him slow, muttered *bless his heart* behind his back. And he grew angry with himself. He'd forgotten about the car. It was still sitting alone on the farm road, its engine breathing low and slow, idling among the trees, its headlights catching night moths in their glow. Isaac had no choice but to move it. He drove it straight to Wally, who, once he understood its significance, told Isaac, "I'll take it from here."

They'd been there before, the two of them, twinned inside a lie.

Isaac was scared to death of Wally, ashamed of what he'd done all those years ago, his terrible weakness. But he needed him, too. It was only together that he and Wally could ensure that Geneva never found out the truth.

26.

It was after hours, past midnight, that night six years ago.

Isaac had finished his sweeping and was having a little sliver of pound cake soaked in Dr Pepper, the way he liked it. Joe had a whiskey balanced on the edge of the cash register as he counted out the day's take. He'd been in a good mood. A Bobby Bland record he'd played on had come on the jukebox, and Joe was high on it and the whiskey, the memories of his life as a bluesman, the road he'd left behind for love. He was telling the story for maybe the fiftieth time, about the moment he laid eyes on Geneva, how the earth tilted, rolling him toward her like a pinball. "Wasn't nothing gon' stop what we had."

They both heard the bell on the door ring.

Joe said, "We closed," before he even looked to see who it was.

Isaac turned and saw Wally first. He looked strange, glassy-eyed and loose-limbed, and it took a moment for Isaac to understand that he was drunk.

Wally took a seat at the counter and laid a pistol on the Formica.

Joe saw it, then looked up and saw Wally.

Neither made any sudden moves. Isaac froze in his seat at the counter, so close to Wally he could smell the liquor on him, and something else, sweat and rage, which gave off a sour funk. Wally was red about his neck and face.

"When you gon' sell me this place, Joe?" Wally said. "'Neva not here, maybe I can talk some sense into you about it."

It was the pet name that set Joe off, the entitlement in it.

"Get out," he said.

"Course I could just take it," Wally said, a cockeyed grin on his face. He was in a wrinkled button-down shirt, the waist of his Wranglers sitting below a small belly that had come on Isaac couldn't remember when. He looked sloppy and almost childish in his petulant stance. Oh, he wasn't going nowhere, he said. "I could just take what's rightfully mine. The restaurant, the land, all of it."

"Isaac, get the sheriff on the phone," Joe said.

Isaac started to slide off his stool, but Wally slapped his palm on the countertop, near that gun, and ordered Isaac to "Stay your ass right there."

"I don't want no trouble with you," Joe said. "So I'm gon' say this real plain. This is my place, me and Geneva's. Bought fair and square from your daddy, and you know it. Seems you wrestling with a man who ain't here no more."

"Daddy had no right. This place, this land, is my birthright. You stealing from me. Every dollar that come out of this place is mine, far as I'm concerned. And I'll be damned if my half-nigger brother gon' get his hands on this one day."

He'd said it out loud.

He'd looked Joe in the face and said his son wasn't his.

There were things you just didn't do in Lark, Texas.

And picking apart bloodlines was one of them.

"You gon' have to get out of here, talking like that," Joe said.

"I'll be damned, hear? This is mine, all of it. Daddy should have let me have it, goddamn it. You hear me? Daddy should have let me have *her.*"

The last word caught both men by surprise.

Isaac, who had worked around the Jefferson house as a kid, just as Geneva had, remembered mornings Wally wouldn't take his eyes off Geneva, remembered the way he kind of doted on her, went doe-eyed when she was around, and how it all changed around the time his father built the cafe for her.

"What did you just say?" Joe asked.

Wally's face hardened, and he turned on Geneva, turned years of pining into pure acid rage. "Daddy was a fool. If it wasn't for her opening her legs—"

Joe lunged across the counter for Wally's neck, but Wally was quicker.

He had the pistol in hand and pointed it right at Joe's head as he finished his thought. "Wasn't for that, none of y'all niggers would have nothing."

Joe raised his hands. "Isaac," he said, begging the man for help.

Isaac stood and went for the pay phone.

He was dialing when he heard the shot. He spun around and saw Wally had laid out Joe with a shot to the head. Joe had crumpled behind the counter and was bleeding on the floor. Wally turned the gun on Isaac next. He held him there in place while they worked on the lie, Wally pocketing the money from the register to sell the story. It was Isaac who called it in. Wally waited to make sure he said the words right, then he took off when he heard sirens coming down the highway about fifteen minutes later. When the deputies came in, Isaac told the story about the white robbers, repeated it two more times—to the sheriff, then to Geneva when she and her family returned from Dallas. Now, years later, Isaac, lips moist with his own tears, mumbled softly, "Tell Geneva I'm sorry."

Darren drove from the sheriff's station in a daze, the lines on the highway blurring before his eyes as he considered all the ways he'd missed what was right in front of him, the tangle of family ties that made up the town's history and how it had all led to murder. He tried rehearsing what he wanted to say to Geneva when he saw her, but by the time he made it back to the cafe in Lark, the words had blown out of the cab of his truck, had been lost to the October wind.

The bell jingled as he walked into Geneva's.

Randie, in one of the booths, stood at once. Geneva, behind the counter, turned to stare at Darren, who was lit by a halo of light from the setting sun pouring through the windows. She knew what was coming, and when he asked to speak to her alone, she nodded to Randie, and said, "This is her story, too."

He walked both women to the trailer out back, sat them side by side on the living-room sofa, and ran through the story, top to bottom, going all the way back to the spring night six years ago when Wally had killed Joe Sweet, then arriving at the night Isaac had delivered the final blow to Michael Wright. Geneva cried. It was one of the most heartbreaking things Darren had ever seen. The mask fell completely, and she crumpled, her face and body twisted in agony over the madness that had taken her husband's life. She toppled like a totem, her head landing in Randie's lap. The younger woman started and then relaxed as Geneva trembled like a wounded bird, desperate for someone to hold her. They were safe now. But Darren stayed with the women for hours, standing watch.

27.

HE STAYED for two more days to see it through, long enough for Wally to be arrested for first-degree homicide in the death of Joe Sweet, just one of the heap of charges Shelby County rained down on him once anyone bothered to look closely. The prints Darren had lifted from his truck the night he found the bloody fox in the truck's cab belonged to Wallace Jefferson III. No one could put the drive-by shooting at Geneva's on him, but Van Horn—who himself had a lot to answer for, considering that all this shit had played out under his nose—arrested Wally for that, too. But the thing that made the Texas Rangers offer Darren his job back were the charges brought against Wally for drug possession with the intent to sell, based on evidence seized during a search of the icehouse: a small meth lab working out of the kitchen, bags of product and scales galore. Isaac might have been arraigned and already sitting in a cell in the county jail. But Wally's name was about to be added to the federal task force's suspect list. Darren had been right about the drugs and the Aryan Brotherhood running free in Lark, Texas, but he'd been wrong about everything else. Michael's and Missy's murders were race crimes, yes, but that was mainly because of the ways race defined so much about Lark, Texas, especially in terms of love, unexpected, and the family ties it created. He had forgotten that the most elemental instinct in human nature is not hate but love, the former inextricably linked to the latter. Isaac had killed Michael to keep Geneva's love, to have a seat at her hearth. Wally had killed Joe because he couldn't accept, or even understand, what he felt for Geneva, just as he couldn't stand the fact that they were, all of them, related. Geneva, Lil' Joe, Keith Jr., and Wally.

They were one big family.

It was the same with Keith, a man who, despite himself, loved a son who shared the blood of a black man. It was an eternal connection that shamed him, a fact he couldn't erase no matter how many Brotherhood tattoos he got when he ended up back at the Walls in Huntsville for killing Missy—no matter how much distance he tried to put between his white skin and Geneva's brown. Wally's and Keith's lives revolved around the black folks they claimed to hate but couldn't leave alone. It was, as his uncle Clayton would say, an obsession that weakened them, that enraged and eventually enslaved them within their own hearts, Darren thought.

The morning of Missy Dale's funeral, his mother called twice. Both times Darren let it go to voice mail: *We need to talk, son.* A term that felt like neither endearment nor fact but an angle, a naked play for his attention and affection. As he finally packed up his truck to leave Lark for good, he had a terrible sense of foreboding that there would be trouble waiting for him at home.

Geneva had twice asked if he was hungry, and then, unbidden, she made him a plate for the road. It was as close to expressed gratitude as she would ever get. That and the way she'd hugged him a bit longer than she needed to. She'd been in a bright mood for such a dark day because Laura had brought the baby by.

"I don't think he knows what's going on today," Mrs. Jefferson said as she handed Keith Jr. to his grandmother. "Missy's people left him in my care, and I don't think he really needs to be there." She was wearing a black dress with a ruffled collar, which she fussed with. "Why don't you take him?"

Geneva had the toddler on her hip, his chunky legs swinging at her waist as she stood at the door to her cafe seeing them off, Darren and Randie. As he backed out of the cafe's parking lot, he watched Geneva in his rearview mirror, and the sight of her put a lump in his throat, made him think of his own mother—long for her, even—in a way he knew would only cause him pain. He'd arranged for Randie's car to be picked up by the rental company so he could drive her to Dallas himself. He wanted a long good-bye with her and a chance to say the same to Michael—to in some small way pay his respects to a man whose wife he'd come to have tender feelings for, a man he'd tried to do right by, whose death was a reminder of the meaning of the oath he'd taken as Ranger. Along the ride, they talked about what was next for her. She wanted to stop working for a while, she said, maybe sit still somewhere. There was a town outside Vancouver she'd fallen in love with a few years back. Maybe this was her chance to start over. She wasn't sure about Chicago, wasn't sure she wanted any part of this country after it was all said and done and Michael was laid to rest—services she'd have to put together on her own. "You going to bury him up there?" Darren asked. "In Chicago?"

"Where else?"

He looked out across at the Texas landscape, the low hills and pines.

They were about forty miles outside of Tyler.

Randie grew silent. "Just think about it," he said.

They rolled into Dallas in silence, and as he parked the car outside the medical examiner's office, she reached across the leather seat for his hand. "I was wrong," Randie said. "About a lot of things." It mattered that Darren wore the badge. Those were the last words she told him as they stood in the hallway outside the room that held her husband's body, just after she said *thank you.*

Camilla

HE WAS just pulling off I-45 past Huntsville, turning onto the smaller state roads that cut into San Jacinto County, heading for home, when he got word that the grand jury had come back with "no bill of indictment" for Rutherford McMillan. It was official: Mack would not be charged with the murder of Ronnie Malvo. Darren wondered if Wilson had been given a heads-up that the district attorney was declining to prosecute, and if that, more than the drug arrest in Lark, was the real reason Darren got his job back. It didn't matter, he supposed. What mattered was that Mack's life had been saved. Darren's relief felt like a two-hundred-pound beast had been pulled off of him midattack. Clayton was ecstatic, calling from Austin to say that he wanted to host a celebratory dinner for Mack and his granddaughter, Breanna, at the house in Camilla tonight, and could Darren pick up seven pounds of brisket at Brookshire Brothers and a couple of chickens, too? Darren promised to clean the smoker and make sure they had enough hickory to keep a pit fire going for several hours. Clayton said he would pick up Naomi after his final lecture, and together they'd drive down from Austin.

"I invited Lisa."

296 • ATTICA LOCKE

"Oh," Darren said, feeling a strange flutter in his rib cage. He was actually excited by the prospect of seeing his wife, of touching her again. It was telling her there would be no law school that he wasn't looking forward to. He hadn't said the words to his uncle, either, but by tonight they would all know.

He was keeping his badge.

He was turning into the parking lot of the grocery store in Coldspring when he finally called his mother back. He wanted to know how bad the house looked after the search by county deputies, which he still didn't want his uncle to know about. He had only a few hours to get the house ready for a dinner party. Bell answered on the second ring, asking first and foremost about the three hundred dollars Darren had promised her.

"Did they break anything?"

"Wasn't no broken glass or anything that I could see," she said.

She was rolling a hard candy around her mouth, and Darren could hear it clicking against her teeth until with a loud suck she pulled it out with her fingers. "What's this all about anyway, that mess down to the courthouse with Mack? They saying he killed somebody, you know."

Darren parked in a spot near the front, staring at a kid rocking back and forth on an electric horse, his mother standing by with another quarter in hand. He felt himself growing irritated by his mother's small-town gossip, the half-truths and partial stories he'd heard over the years. She'd once tried to convince him that a county judge was once a week renting one of the cabins she cleaned for a tryst with a woman who wasn't his wife—when it turned out that the man's last name was Judge, and whoever the other woman was, it wasn't none of it any business of Bell Callis anyway. "That's not what happened," he said.

"You don't know for sure."

"I gotta go, Mama. We got people coming to the house."

"Oh, okay, I see. You big-time now."

Darren thought he heard her mumble *we'll see* before she hung up.

Inside, he roamed the narrow aisles of the grocery store, maneuvering his cart so as not to get the wheels stuck in one of the many cracks in the linoleum tiles. He knew each and every one, had been shopping at this Brookshire Brothers for years anytime he was home. He threw peppers and onions in the cart, corn to roast, and bags of salad, because collards would take too long. A vague sense of dread flooded his chest all the while. He lingered in the liquor aisle but ultimately decided against buying anything. Lisa was coming, he remembered.

Mack was the first to arrive, his granddaughter in tow, along with a fat bottle of Texas bourbon, his thank you to Darren. That was all it took. Darren was two drinks in by the time Clayton and Naomi arrived. "Pop," he said, smiling. Clayton, who'd never met a glass of bourbon he didn't welcome, caught up within the hour, so that the night felt as honeyed and warm as the setting sun lighting up the back porch. Clayton opened both the front and back doors so that the sweetness of hickory smoke swirled around them as they gathered in the front room, Mack in Wranglers, his long legs reaching from the couch all the way under the coffee table, boot heels resting on the Indian rug that had been there for as long as Darren could remember. The walls were whitewashed and filled with framed photos of the Mathews clan. Clayton, William, and little Duke, their baby brother, plus grands and great-grands going back generations, all of whom Darren didn't think he could name.

Naomi's wedding to his uncle William was documented here as well. She'd been a stunning bride at nineteen, hair in a chignon, her caramel-colored skin lit with joy. Darren made a point of leaving the photograph on display. It didn't seem to bother the new couple a bit. Clayton had what he'd always wanted and didn't begrudge his nephew the memory of something long gone. "Let's talk about school, son."

"Let's not, Pop."

"We had a deal, Darren," Clayton was saying.

He didn't answer because he heard his wife's footsteps.

There was a certain way her high heels hammered the wooden porch slats that both excited and terrified him. As she stood in the open doorway at the front of the house, Darren rose to meet her. Without being asked, Clayton, Naomi—her long coral-colored sundress skating across the floor—Mack, and Breanna stepped out onto the back porch, leaving Darren alone with his wife.

She'd come from work, her hair pinned, her waist cinched by a pale gray suit jacket, and he watched in mute wonder as she peeled away the armor, unbuttoning the jacket and removing a heavy cuff bracelet from her wrist. She hugged and kissed him, her lips plump and sweet, her breath bringing him back to life. He was close to pulling her into one of the house's three bedrooms to have weeks' worth of sex with her, every thrust and bite they'd missed in all that time, when she pulled back, brown eyes searching his, and said, "You're staying, aren't you?"

"I was hoping to come home," he said.

"I meant you're staying with the Rangers."

She'd known it the minute she looked at him.

"Yes."

There was a sigh of resignation, and then she said, "Okay."

Her words, that kiss, they made him bold. "That means wherever the job takes me," he said.

"Okay."

"Okay, I can come home?"

She paused for a very long time. "I don't like the drinking," she said.

This is because of you, he wanted to say.

This is what abandonment does to a man.

Good Lord, he was angry with her. He hadn't realized how much until now, until he was standing right in front of her, until he could see her face. She was so damn beautiful, so damn poised and smart, and so utterly in control of their lives that he felt a resentment he didn't realize had maybe always been there. It was only when he looked back on the night later that he realized he'd never actually said *yes.* He'd never said he was going back to Houston with her.

They sat next to each other at the dinner table, Lisa with a hand on Darren's thigh through half the meal. Mack talked about starting a little business of his own, felt he'd been given a new lease on things, he said. He maintained the Mathewses' property and a few others in the county, but he wanted to get into the more lucrative business of managing timber tracts for private or corporate owners. Clayton, before dessert was served, promised to write a recommendation for him.

After dinner, Naomi brought out a lemon cake, licking her fingers as she laid six pieces on blue-and-white china plates, the soft feathered lines around her eyes crinkling as Clayton complimented the cake's look and taste. Darren was pouring his fourth drink when he heard his mother's voice.

"Darren."

His hand froze over his glass.

Bell Callis was standing in the open doorway, a defiant look on her face as she squared off with her nemesis, his uncle Clayton. Darren felt a swift panic. He knew the joy his mother would take, if given the chance, in mentioning the police search of the Mathews home, an insult and injury that the Callis family had endured for years. *Your mama's people ain't shit,* Clayton used to say. To hear Clayton tell it, his mother's brothers spent so much time in the county jail that each of them had his own preferred cell and blanket he left behind for the next time. They were a bayou-fed clan of scavengers for whom hard work was a last resort. Bell had blamed Clayton for the fact that Duke Mathews never married her. *Over my dead body,* he'd said more than once when Duke was still alive.

Darren was afraid to let her speak freely.

He stood from the table quickly, blocking Bell from stepping too far over the threshold. Clayton didn't want her in the house and said so, whispering to his nephew, "Don't let her near the silver," of which they had exactly two items, a teapot and a single serving spoon, both tarnished to hell. Bell didn't want to be there any more than Clayton wanted her in his home. In fact she wouldn't talk to Darren in the house and asked him to step out with her onto the front porch.

Lisa reached for his hand solicitously. "Darren?"

"It's okay," he told her.

But he felt vaguely ill as he stepped onto the porch with Bell, closing the front door behind them, as if any minute the floor might rise to meet his face.

The stars were out by now, pinpoints of light against a blue-black sky.

There was a long unpaved drive that led up to the country house.

Darren couldn't see past the second parked car, the light from the front porch not strong enough to tell him where his mother had come from, whether she'd driven or been dropped off. Her black ballet shoes were coated in red dust.

"We need to talk, Darren."

"I don't have three hundred in cash, not on me," he said. "Tomorrow I'll stop at the bank in town, then I'll swing by the trailer before noon, okay?"

She stopped him to say, "I found it, Darren."

"What?"

"That little thirty-eight you didn't want the deputies to find."

Mack's gun.

The one the cops had been looking for.

"Why else would you have put it in the ground?"

"Mama, listen, I didn't—"

"Clayton likes to make a point that I wasn't ever welcome at this house, but me and Duke hung around here all the time when his brothers weren't home. I still know the place pretty well," she said. In the dark, her eyes looked coal black, and the lines around them were filled in by shadows. It gave her face a witchy quality, and Darren felt breathless and anxious around a woman he realized in this moment was a stranger to him; he didn't know her well enough to know what she might do in this situation, how much trouble he was in. "After I cleaned up the trash like you told me and took it out to the bins," she said, pointing to where they stood alongside the house now, "I looked at that tree right there and knew it hadn't been there before." She pointed to a burr oak that was indeed recently planted.

Darren had noticed it about a week after Ronnie Malvo was killed.

It had never occurred to him that Bell would notice it, too, otherwise he would never have let her anywhere near the old farmhouse.

Bell, talk of searches by the sheriff's department and Mack under suspicion ringing in her ears, had dug at the soft earth around the newly planted tree, finding the snub-nosed .38 just hours after the sheriff's deputies had left the house. She didn't know whose it was, but she knew it was significant and that in her hands it was a power over her son that she craved. She could make him do anything now. She could make him love her, even, maybe invite her to live with him; she could make him take care of her as she grew old.

She didn't say anything like that, not yet.

But Darren saw it all coming.

She held his gaze in the dark, pinned him in place. "What'd you do?"

Nothing.

He'd done nothing.

He'd known Ronnie Malvo was killed with a .38, but he hadn't asked Mack where his gun was. He'd noticed the new oak on his property, but he hadn't asked Mack when and why he'd planted it. He'd done nothing because Malvo was a bad guy, a cancer, a lump of hate that would spread untold destruction if left unchecked. He'd done nothing because, if he was telling the truth about it, Darren didn't care that the man was dead. He'd done nothing because Mack was a good man who'd never had any cross with the county sheriff, had never, in his nearly seventy years, done a thing wrong. He'd had all the facts right in front of him if he'd bothered to look. But he'd done nothing. He'd asked Mack no questions, behaving like a defense attorney when he'd taken an oath to be a cop. He got it confused sometimes, on which side of the law he belonged, couldn't always remember when it was safe for a black man to follow the rules.

He'd done nothing.

Did that make him no better than Mack and Mack no better than the killers in Lark? No, that couldn't be right. But Darren wasn't sure of anything anymore, his righteous clarity clouding in his bourbon-soaked brain. He looked across the dark porch at his mother. A pack of mosquitoes buzzed around her head, but she stood perfectly still, a faint smirk on her painted lips. In her dry and calloused hands, he saw she was clutching a sequined handbag. She'd dressed up for this, he thought. He sank into a metal lawn chair as he realized that of course she'd pocketed the gun when she found it, that she had it in her purse right now, that she held his entire career as a Texas Ranger in her hands.

Acknowledgments

I would like to thank Reagan Arthur, Joshua Kendall, Sabrina Callahan, and my new family at Mulholland and Little, Brown for the care and enthusiasm with which they've greeted me and my book.

As always, I'd like to express my gratitude to Richard Abate, whom I'm lucky to count as a manager and a friend.

Thanks to Lieutenant Kip Westmoreland of the Texas Rangers, who is not to blame for liberties I took or facts I bent for the sake of a good story. He was kind to share some of his time with me.

Thank you to my parents, Sherra Aguirre and Gene Locke, for instilling in me a deep love for East Texas.

Thanks also to Dr. Cheryl Arutt for every Thursday session along this journey.

Finally, this book would not exist without the love and understanding of my family, specifically my daughter, Clara, who missed her mother at many a soccer game while I was writing, and my husband, Karl, who often did the work of two parents. You two are answered prayers, dreams come true, and grace on earth.

About the Author

Attica Locke is the author of *Pleasantville,* which won the 2016 Harper Lee Prize for Legal Fiction and was long-listed for the Baileys Women's Prize for Fiction; *Black Water Rising,* which was nominated for an Edgar Award; and *The Cutting Season,* a national bestseller and winner of the Ernest Gaines Award for Literary Excellence. *Bluebird, Bluebird* won the 2018 Edgar Award for Best Novel. Locke was a writer and producer on the Fox drama *Empire.* A native of Houston, Texas, she lives in Los Angeles, California, with her husband and daughter.